FOREST AND OTHER GLEANINGS

FOREST AND OTHER GLEANINGS

The Fugitive Writings of Catharine Parr Traill

CANADIAN
SHORT
STORY
LIBRARY
No. 18

Edited by Michael A. Peterman
and Carl Ballstadt

University of Ottawa Press

Canadian Short Story Library, Series 2
John Moss, General Editor

© University of Ottawa Press, 1994
Printed and bound in Canada
ISBN 0-7766-0391-4

Canadian Cataloguing in Publication Data
Main entry under title:
Traill, Catherine Parr, 1802–1899
   Forest and Other Gleanings: The Fugitive Writings
of Catharine Parr Traill

(The Canadian short story library; no. 18)
Collection of short writing previously published in
   annuals, newspapers and magazines.
Includes bibliographical references.
ISBN 0-7766-0391-4

   I. Ballstadt, Carl, 1931–   . II. Peterman, Michael
A., 1942–   . III. Title. IV. Series.

PS8439.T7F67 1994   C813'.3   C94-900867-2
PR9199.2.T73F67 1994

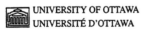 UNIVERSITY OF OTTAWA
UNIVERSITÉ D'OTTAWA

Series design concept: Miriam Bloom
Book design: Marie Tappin
Photo credit: Ms. Kathleen McMurrich, courtesy of
National Archives

DEDICATION

The editors respectfully dedicate this volume to Mr. T. R. McCloy of Calgary and the other descendants of Catharine Parr Traill who have worked over the years to preserve Traill's letters, journals, notes, and memorabilia. The Traill Family Collection at the National Archives (from which several pieces in this collection are drawn) stands as a growing record of that effort.

CONTENTS

Floral Sketches and Essays

ACKNOWLEDGMENTS

We would like to thank the following friends and colleagues for their help in preparing this book. Sandy Campbell, Jean Cole, Martin Dowding, Carole Gerson, Elizabeth Hopkins, Norma Martin, Donna McGillis, Lorraine McMullen, Catherine Milne, Sherry Lee Powsey, and Gordon Roper have all provided helpful information and encouragement. Our editorial colleague Elizabeth Hopkins has provided many insights and much encouragement despite her exacting administrative duties at York University. John Moss, editor of the Canadian Short Story Library, and the anonymous readers of the manuscript for the University of Ottawa Press also provided useful suggestions. Anne Goddard of the National Archives of Canada has helped us over the years in working with the Traill Family Collection, while the librarians at the American Antiquarian Society Library were instrumental in tracking down "The Autobiography of an Unlucky Wit." For their help in typing the manuscript we are grateful to Betty Curle and Shirley Hill of Trent University and Rita Maxwell of McMaster. Our deepest gratitude is reserved for Janet Friskney, a recent graduate of Trent's Frost Centre, who has helped us in so many ways to prepare the final manuscript; her skills in typing, research, and proofreading have been invaluable. Finally, we are pleased to acknowledge the support of the Social Sciences and Humanities Research Council for a grant that has allowed us to pursue this project.

INTRODUCTION

In the critical literature of the past several decades, the prevailing tendency has been to diminish Catharine Parr Traill, to make her seem a matter of lesser, indeed at best of minor, concern to those seriously interested in Canadian literature.[1] Even the current preoccupation with the post-colonial has helped to legitimize that agenda. Implicitly, Canada's colonial past has too often been categorized reductively and treated dismissively, as if it were only a matter of time until sufficiently intelligent observers set to rights the skewed and myopic priorities of earlier generations. But, as Brian McKillop has forcefully argued, to do justice to the past we should, when we consider a phrase like "the colonial mind" or "the colonial imagination," place the emphasis where it belongs, on the noun, not the adjective.[2] For mind and imagination there were, though they were often formally dressed in the language of gentility, moral responsibility, and religious propriety. It is worthwhile to attend more closely to those voices.

At the same time, in the case of Traill, there has been little fresh information on which to base a reconsideration. The old record of published works—*The Backwoods of Canada* (1836), *Canadian Crusoes* (1852), *The Female Emigrant's Guide* (1854), *Lady Mary and Her Nurse* (1856), *Canadian Wild Flowers* (1868), *Studies of Plant Life in Canada* (1885), *Pearls and Pebbles* (1894), and *Cot and Cradle Stories* (1895)—stands as a solid but seldom examined confirmation of unpretentious and modest achievement. Yet a writer who has been variously labelled as Little Miss Muffet and Mrs. Happy Homemaker is diminished by definition. And if such labels have cultural power, that writer would seem to have little hope of being revitalized.[3]

This collection is an attempt to arrest that diminishment. Drawing upon material published in nineteenth-century magazines in Canada, Britain, and the United States, or filed away in archival holdings, *Forest and Other Gleanings: The Fugitive Writings of Catharine Parr Traill* presents a fuller picture of Traill as a dedicated writer than has previously been available. In Robert Kroetsch's memorable phrase, it seeks to "unhide the hidden"—moreover, it seeks to do so in interrelated ways. In the first instance, it provides glimpses of a more complex writer than has heretofore been assumed. The variety of forms and voices in these pieces suggest a writer particularly conscious of self-presentation and keenly aware of literature as an agency of social, moral, and spiritual education. We see evidence of her evolution as a writer and the choices that lay behind her authorial personae. We see both the close links between personal experience and narrative and the comfortable discursiveness that characterize her writing. Secondly, it recovers for perusal and analysis a number of Traill's neglected texts. In this regard it makes clear that the work of assessing the Canadian—specifically the Upper Canadian—literary past is in part a matter of digging up what has been temporarily lost, ignored, or forgotten. Too much Canadian literary criticism in the past has been based upon a shockingly incomplete knowledge of its subject. If we are to get beyond the clichés of Victorian response, it is important to find out more about what a writer like Traill actually wrote and the conditions under which she had to work.

To that end, this introduction comprises two parts. The first is a biographical sketch of Traill's life designed to familiarize the reader not with the self-image that she sought to project in her major works, but with the known facts of her long, often impoverished life and the extent to which writing, to her, was often the only means of survival available. It was not easy to be a professional writer, especially as a woman, in early Canada, even if one had some claim to being well-published upon arrival. Traill's often numbing struggles to find publishing outlets and reliable, venturesome publishers give weight both to the complaints of so many of her literary contemporaries and to her own unyielding determination to do what she could with her life and her pen. The second section comments upon some of the qualities and ideas that stand out in these selections, qualities, and ideas that broaden our awareness of the ways in which Traill allowed herself to respond to her experiences in Upper Canada (later in her lifetime Canada West, and still later Ontario). To read this volume is to begin to know her better.

～

Traill was born Catharine Parr Strickland in Kent near London, England, on January 9, 1802, the fifth daughter of Elizabeth and Thomas Strickland. Shortly thereafter, her father left his importing and docks management position in London to seek a less stressful and healthier rural venue. Settling on Norwich, which became the focal point for his business interests, he meanwhile looked about for an affordable manor house where he could continue to raise and educate his children. When he bought Reydon Hall near the Suffolk town of Southwold in 1808 he was likely at the peak of his financial powers. By then his offspring numbered eight, six daughters and two sons.

Reydon Hall (and Stowe House, which the Stricklands rented from 1803 to 1808) did much to define Catharine Traill's predilection for the rural life. It was there that she benefited from the education and training supplied by her parents and on occasion by her older sisters, particularly Eliza. It was in that large old house amidst desolate garrets, closed staircases, and secret recesses that her imagination was nourished. It was on its grounds that her affection for and interest in the natural world were nurtured. Above all, as she recounts in the autobiographical sections of works like *Sketch Book of a Young Naturalist* (1831), the Strickland children learned the importance of taking responsibility for what they had and the value of self-reliance in their personal activities.

Only the boys attended school. The girls were given some instruction by their father when he was available and they had the run of his library, one based on his eighteenth-century tastes. Perhaps what they learned best was how to amuse themselves in the relative social and spatial isolation of Reydon Hall. Making up stories and plays and experimenting in writing were among the pastimes most favoured by the sisters. Though five of the six would become professional writers, Catharine herself was, despite her age, the first to be published. That surprising turn of events occurred shortly after the rather sudden death of her father in 1818, when she was sixteen. A friend of her father's picked up one of her manuscripts while visiting Reydon and took it with him to London, returning some time later with a published book and a modest fee for her.

Thomas Strickland's death left his wife and eight children property-rich and cash-poor.[4] While the practical and business-like Eliza soon left for London to begin what would be a successful literary-editorial career, the rest of the sisterhood continued to live modestly at Reydon. Catharine's accidental blueprint for pin-money soon blossomed into a "cottage industry" as four of the remaining sisters (Agnes, Jane Margaret, Susanna, and herself) actively pursued the growing London market for children's instructional literature, bent upon making some needed financial return for their labours. Their many small books of the 1820s for publishers like A. K. Newman, Dean and Munday, Harris, and Harvey and Darton are still a source of considerable confusion; in the British Library catalogue, for instance, problems regarding the dating of texts and the accurate identification of author continue to mar that record. Nevertheless, it is clear from a close reading of those works that Catharine specialized in two sorts of narratives— sketches and stories which were often autobiographical and linked to the natural world near Reydon (her most successful book, *Little Downy; or, The History of a Field Mouse: A Moral Tale* [1822], which she wrote on Reydon's lawn and which was published without her name, was reportedly still popular in the 1860s), and cautionary tales concerning proper behaviour with titles like *Disobedience; or, Mind What Mama Says* (1819) and *Prejudice Reproved; or, The History of the Negro Toy-seller* (1826). The known record includes some thirteen children's books written by her and published between 1818 and 1831. Other outlets she courted included the then-popular and very competitive Christmas and New Year's annuals that published both stories and poems. Though she managed to place several stories in these annuals, she was far less successful in this market than her more poetically inclined sisters, the older Agnes, who launched her remarkable writing career with several books of poetry in the 1820s, and the younger Susanna, who would become Susanna Moodie in 1831.

Beyond her writing, occasional visits to family in London, and her local friendships, Catharine's life was quiet and family-bound. She did, however, become engaged in the late 1820s to a young man of poor prospects, Francis Harral, whose father was a family friend and an influential editor and literary man. That engagement came to an end late in 1831, about the time that she met Thomas Traill, a fellow officer of her sister's husband John Moodie and, like him, an Orcadian of notable lineage. Heir to a large but heavily encumbered Orkney estate named Westove, Traill was a widower with two teenage sons.[5] With some haste, he and Catharine decided to marry in the spring of 1832 and to follow the Moodies' plan to emigrate to Canada. Despite considerable resistance to the marriage from her family, Catharine persevered in her new commitment and the couple set out via Scotland for their new life in the backwoods of Upper Canada.

Of the newlyweds Catharine was the better prepared, both emotionally and practically, for the trials that lay ahead. Thomas was something of a dilettante and had seldom had much to do with physical labour. Oxford-educated, conversant in five languages, and familiar with cultural life on the Continent, he was far more adept at friendship and talk than at building fences and clearing stumps. His aim, no doubt wisely, was to make his way in real-estate transactions rather than in farming, and to encourage his sons to lend their energies to his building of a new fortune in Canada. Conditions, however, conspired against his plans. The debts he had accumulated in moving to the New World proved very difficult to pay off. The family estate in the Orkneys was too encumbered to pay him a yearly stipend, the farm on Lake Katchewanook in Douro Township took years to clear, and he had only his half-pay pension and money from personal loans to rely on.[6] Moreover, he did not succeed in currying favour by way of government patronage and his sons opted to continue their educations in Scotland. As well, he suffered increasingly from debilitating periods of depression that, as Catharine soon learned, could best be dealt with by patience and solicitude on her part.

Nevertheless, the vision she described in *The Backwoods of Canada* was not a cosmetic creation; rather, it was a hasty and overly optimistic "take" on the life and prospects she found north of Peterborough in 1833–34. Written on the basis of but two years in the backwoods, it presents a salutary picture that accords at once with her own personality, her genuine interest in her new home place, her lack of knowledge of the details of her husband's financial situation, and the optimistic prospects for growth and development that pertained at that time in the Peterborough area. What she was not willing to entertain in 1834 was a recognition of how bad things might quickly become. She was happily married, she had become a mother for the first time in June 1833, and she shared with her husband the double hope that the Orkney estate would soon advantage them and that their investments in their Canadian property would yield a happy result. Farming problems, insistent debts, a fast-growing family, and a major economic depression (the effects of which were severe from 1836 to 1839) soon altered those glowing prospects.

Susanna Moodie provides a vivid glimpse of her sister's altered conditions in a letter to Sir George Arthur dated December 18, 1838. Despite the publishing success in Britain of *The Backwoods of Canada*, wrote Moodie, its "poor Author . . . is struggling in the Backwoods on a limited income, with four infant children and contending with difficulties which would scarcely be credited by Your

Excellency. The dark clouds that for the last three years have overshadowed the land, [have] dispell[ed] those pleasing anticipations of future independence, which pervade her cheerful volume. Mrs. Traill, would have written herself to your Excellency, in behalf of her husband; but, she is lying on a sick bed with a young infant of a few hours old, by her side, to remind her of her depressed circumstances." That child was her fourth. Moodie saw Catharine and herself during that dark winter of 1838–39 as "truly . . . sisters in misfortune."[7]

If *Roughing It in the Bush* is Moodie's complex reappraisal of the "pleasing anticipations" of *The Backwoods of Canada*, Traill herself wanted to clarify the picture she had given the world. Desperately in need of money (the 125 pounds she received for the copyright to *The Backwoods* went immediately to pay off a part of the debts her husband had undertaken in emigrating), she wrote a sequel comprising sketches and "letters" that her sister Agnes tried to sell as a book to publishers in London and Edinburgh. However, the manuscript she called "Forest Gleanings" did not meet the good fortune that had befallen "The Backwoods of Canada" when it found its way to a rather desperate Charles Knight in London.[8] Rather, it was broken up and parts of it were sold piecemeal by Agnes to various magazine editors. While no record of its full table of contents or its organization has survived, many of the pieces included here appear to have been parts of that doomed project. As such they often reflect not the more personalized and acerbic views of her sister, but her own more rigorous sense of the demands and perils of backwoods life. "Female Trials in the Bush," "Generosity of the Poor," "The Old Doctor. A Backwoods Sketch," and "My Irish Maid Isabella—A Night of Peril" convey the sense of vulnerability Traill had come to know and they help to foreground the importance of resilience, fortitude, and helpful (female) neighbours in struggling to survive in so isolated a situation.

When the Traills at last managed to sell their backwoods property in February 1839 and move to Peterborough, their circumstances did not greatly improve.

Catharine's plans to start a school foundered because of her uncertain health, her lack of appropriate supplies, and the deaths of two of her infant children in the early 1840s. Nor did Thomas Traill's ventures in land-trading succeed. In fact, the death of a young Scotsman for whom he had backed a loan left him virtually without resources and forced the Traills to give up a farm in Otonabee Township (about three miles from Peterborough) where they had lived for three years and which they had hoped to buy. In 1846, however, they were rescued for the moment when an old friend, the Reverend George Bridges, gave them rent-free for the year the use of his octagonal home near Rice Lake, which he called "Wolf Tower." The move proved to be a godsend, launching the Traills on a new set of connections and providing Catharine with a second distinctive locale to explore and write about.

The Rice Lake area would be their home until 1857–58. They moved from the Tower to Mount Ararat (a farm on the edge of a ravine above Gore's Landing), then to Oaklands, which they managed to purchase by means of the sale of Thomas's military pension and the help of the Moodies and her brother Sam Strickland. It was here that Catharine, now beyond her child-bearing years and relieved of much domestic labour by her daughters, wrote most prolifically and out of necessity. *Canadian Crusoes*, *The Female Emigrant's Guide*, *Lady Mary and Her Nurse*, and the sketches comprising another text she called "Forest Gleanings," which appeared in the *Anglo-American Magazine* (Toronto, 1852–53), were among the products of her years at Oaklands. At the same time there was little relief from the anxieties of looming poverty during this period. The demands of a large family, difficulties in farming for a profit, numerous health problems among virtually all members of the family, and persistent debts made the Traills' life at Rice Lake relentlessly grim. Catharine's writing in fact was often the difference between mere subsistence and the daunting possibility of losing their farm to creditors. It is characteristic of her persona as a writer that the sketches included here speak very fondly of the area, overlooking the difficulties that so often affected the author's daily life.

It was in August 1857 that an early-morning fire destroyed Oaklands and most of the Traills' belongings, once again setting back any gains they as a family had managed to make. Homeless, they were forced to rely on the generosity of friends and family. Thomas Traill died in the summer of 1859, and in the aftermath it became clear that nothing could be expected from the heavily mortgaged Westove property in the Orkneys. Needing a centre for her large family, Catharine returned to the Lakefield area north of Peterborough, aided in large part by her brother Sam, who had settled there in 1831 and had paved the way for the Traills' original settlement in Douro. He helped her to arrange the financing and building of a cottage, which she named Westove in honour of her husband. Thereafter Lakefield was her home, though, as her health allowed, she travelled more than she had previously been able to do, pursuing publishing opportunities and visiting her children, other relatives, and friends. Through the 1860s she was unlucky in her writing schemes, misled or disappointed by publishers who were in the final analysis unwilling to take a chance in publishing her work. It was a pattern she had come to know only too well; indeed, no literary connection misused her as badly as did the Reverend Henry Hope in his profitable exploitation of her *Female Emigrant's Guide*; Hope, who first published the text in his Toronto-based newspaper *The Old Countryman*, took it through at least ten editions and never, according to Traill, paid her for its publication as a book, despite his many promises. Indeed, it should be emphasized that, despite her occasional successes, Traill was, during her nearly seven decades in Canada, a writer in a colonial vacuum. Few beyond her own family were willing to help her make headway among the relatively scarce publishing opportunities and outlets then available.

It was the initiative of Agnes Fitzgibbon, Traill's niece and the daughter of Susanna Moodie, that led to her major publishing opportunities in the years after Confed-eration. *Canadian Wild Flowers*, which went through four editions, grew out of Agnes's determination to learn lithography, to orchestrate the hand painting of the individual plates, and to arrange sufficient subscribers to assure the publisher, John Lovell of Montreal, that production costs would be met. Agnes's efforts were also largely responsible for the publication of *Studies of Plant Life in Canada*, a major undertaking that she arranged from her new home in Ottawa. In both cases the aging author stood in awe of her niece's initiative and perseverence, well aware that she herself was no longer capable of such strenuous effort. Still, the important literary record of plant life, mosses, grasses, and trees was Traill's own, the work of a loving amateur botanist accumulated and documented over some forty difficult years; her working text was one of the few things she had managed to rescue from the Oaklands fire. Only recently has that record begun to receive attention for the singular achievement it is.[9]

In the 1890s, Traill, herself in her nineties, continued to pursue literary schemes, despite failing health, increasing deafness, and much-reduced mobility. Again it was through the help of a relative that her work reached the public. The friendship of her grand-niece Mary Agnes Fitzgibbon with Edward S. Caswell, manager of the Book Publishing Department of the Methodist Book and Publishing House, led to his active interest in Traill's work, the result of which was the publication of *Pearls and Pebbles* in 1894 and *Cot and Cradle Stories* a year later. The weak sales of the latter, however, curtailed plans for further publications with the House, despite Caswell's continuing interest.

As had been the case since the early 1860s, Traill lived modestly in Lakefield until her death. A "poor country mouse" as she once characterized herself, she lived remote from an active literary milieu and the energies of the age.[10] Only occasionally did she find herself a celebrity as when, in 1884, she spent several months in Ottawa working on the final text of the *Plant Life* manuscript. Though she was conscious of having left a respectable literary legacy, she was seldom recognized in public ways prior to the 1890s, when her great age itself became a claim to fame. Still, while newspapers took to labelling her as the oldest living author in the British Empire, she continued to live quietly and to work away, as her health allowed, on other literary projects, among them a history of her family that was a response to her sister's *Life of Agnes Strickland* (1887) and a reworking of *The Backwoods of Canada* to address her sense of the great changes she had witnessed during her sixty years in Canada.[11] A grant from the Royal Literary Fund in England and a financial present organized by subscription by her old friend Sir Sandford Fleming did, however, provide welcome relief from the continuing financial problems of her final years. For the most part as was her wont she deliberately kept to "the even tenor of [her] ways"; hers was a retiring life by choice, one in which she carefully kept watch over the spiritual and physical health of those closest to her. When she died on August 29, 1899, she had outlived all of her own family in England and Canada, as well as five of her nine children.

∽

The stories, sketches, and essays found here are but a selection of Traill's literary output over more than eighty years. Each is accompanied by a brief introduction designed to provide information on its evolution and publication history. In choosing individual pieces the editors have sought to provide a broad range of material of a largely Canadian emphasis. Even the pieces in "Reflections of the English Past" were written (insofar as the record shows) after Traill came to Canada. While "A Slight Sketch of the Early Life of Mrs. Moodie" provides an important addition to the published record concerning her sister, the other sketches reveal in particular that, as a young woman addressing an adult audience, Traill was a writer of wit and spirit who enjoyed such propensities in herself even as she recognized the need to discipline them. Indeed, one senses that Traill's self-discipline gradually suppressed this attractive penchant;

in time she seems to have adopted as her characteristic
Canadian self-image a more sober and reverent voice
appropriate to her roles, first as wife and mother, then as
grandmother, and always as citizen. She projected these
roles outward toward the fledgling colonial culture, seeking
to document and account for its features on the one hand
and to reconcile its contradictions on the other.

The book's longest section, "Backwoods Revisited,"
provides more detailed responses to pioneering and settlement than one finds, for instance, in *The Backwoods of Canada*.
In these sketches one encounters a much wider range of
experiences and points of view than were available in the
earlier book. The fear of losing a child in the labyrinthine
forests of the backwoods, a fear that haunted Traill as a
mother and transmuted itself into a group version of
Robinson Crusoe improvisation and triumph in *Canadian
Crusoes*, is here represented in two of its early versions.
Other subsections include both her personal journal of
the activities surrounding the Mackenzie Rebellion and a
fictionalized treatment of that event, her accounts of what
we have collectively called the "Customs and Ceremonies"
that characterized backwoods life, and her dramatizations
of some of the difficulties and fears faced by women in their
struggles to survive in the bush. As she later conceptualized
it, her aim was to write an authoritative cultural history of
colonial experience, emphasizing not "the public events"
nor matters of government, politics, and commerce; what
most interested her and what she felt should not be ignored
were "the domestic life habits, tastes, customs, language
[and] lives of the early colonists." Much would be lost, she
argued, if such a record were not written down and preserved for the future. What she wanted was veracity, not
"shadowy legends" or "scanty memorials."[12]

The final two sections comprise selections from
Traill's gleanings about the Rice Lake area and her essay-
length treatments and celebrations of the natural world.
Evident are a number of themes and ideas. What might be
called her ecological conservatism is everywhere present;

as a British pioneer and colonist she was of necessity committed to the project of colonial development; however, as a naturalist and a believer in an ordered but inscrutable universe, she wished above all to celebrate and preserve the fragile and precious elements of the natural world she encountered in Upper Canada. She clearly reflects the ambivalence of the sensitive settler whose existence is inherently tied to the dream of progress and imaginatively conceptualized in terms of the will of a beneficent but unknowable God. Never pretentious, never pretending to know more than she had experienced or read about, she tried to document what she saw and to leave an accurate record of the vanishing world she had once found unfamiliar, knowing from the experience of aging just how quickly what once abounded could pass from view. That sense of nature's fragility she linked to the fate of the Native peoples, who, as the years went by, she saw less and less frequently. Still, her journals and notes reveal that she kept an active interest throughout her life in the ideas, language, teachings, and personal lives of the "Indians," particularly those Native women she had come to know both in Douro and at Rice Lake.

Through all her experiences and despite all her losses and sufferings, what is perhaps most remarkable about Traill is the utter firmness by which she held to her Christian faith. She seems seldom (if at all) to have questioned God's wisdom and fairness, regardless of the ill winds that all too frequently assailed her and those she loved. Indeed, in her letters she proved time and again a genius in offering sincere consolatory advice to friends and family. She knew death's sting all too well, but she did not allow such losses to undermine her vision of an order and providence beyond human ken.

But if faith anchored Traill, her sense of her family, class, and racial stock were also keystones to the remarkable strength that characterized her life and her writing career. Poverty could not diminish her sense of who she was. She was a gentlewoman who had married well, who belonged to the officer class, and whose children could claim both an English and a Scottish heritage. An absence of means could not undermine what Traill described in *The Backwoods of Canada* as "that incontestable proof of our gentility." Neither could it diminish her curiosity, generosity, good will, sense of humour, and love of nature. She wished to be the record-keeper, the gleaner, of the domestic life and natural world she had known in Canada. This collection attempts to recover some salient parts of what proved to be a remarkably long, often difficult project.

Note on the text

Where the editors have had the choice of two printed versions of the same piece, the one used here is marked in its preface with an asterisk. For the most part those pieces are printed as they then appeared. Inconsistencies in spelling have been retained and intervention has occurred only where the editors were able to correct obvious typographical errors in names, places, the presentation of quoted material, etc. In the cases of "The Mackenzie Rebellion" and "My Irish Maid Isabella—A Night of Peril," which are drawn from the Traill Family Collection, the editors have worked with Traill's own manuscripts. Readers will note some differences between the Rebellion sketch as printed here and as edited by Edward S. Caswell in the appendix to the 1929 edition of *The Backwoods of Canada*. Some parts of "Isabella" have been moved within the text to provide greater coherence and less digression. "The Old Doctor" is printed here as it appeared in the 1985 "first edition," published by the Hutchison House Museum of Peterborough, Ontario, and edited by Jean Cole.

༄

1   Susanna Moodie has received far more attention than Traill in recent criticism. However, the case for Traill's importance is made in David Jackel, "Mrs. Moodie and Mrs. Traill, and the Fabrication of a Canadian Tradition," *The Compass*, 6 (1979), 1–22; Carl Ballstadt's monograph "Catharine Parr Traill" in *Canadian Writers and Their Works*, Fiction series, vol. 1, ed. Robert Lecker et al. (Toronto: ECW Press, 1983), 149–93; Michael Peterman, "Strickland, Catharine Parr (Traill)," *Dictionary of Canadian Biography*, vol. 12 (Toronto: University of Toronto Press, 1990), 995–999; and Elizabeth Thompson, *The Pioneer Woman* (Montreal: McGill-Queen's University Press, 1991).

2   A. B. McKillop, *Contours of Canadian Thought* (Toronto: University of Toronto Press, 1987), 5.

3   See Northrop Frye, "Conclusion" to the *Literary History of Canada: Canadian Literature in English*, ed. Carl Klinck (Toronto: University of Toronto Press, 1965), 844–45, and Marian Fowler, *The Embroidered Tent: Five Gentlewomen in Upper Canada* (Toronto: Anansi, 1982), 78.

4   Thomas Strickland died of complications from severe gout, an illness that had plagued him for years. Business reversals in 1817–18 may have worsened his condition.

5   Thomas Traill was the eldest son of the Reverend Walter Traill of the parish of Sanday. His first wife, Anne Fotheringham, had died in Vevay, Switzerland, in 1828 after a prolonged illness; the Fotheringham family oversaw the education of the two Traill boys thereafter.

6   Thomas's fond hope that the Westove estate would prove a bounty to him was never to be realized.

7   National Archives of Canada, Civil Secretary's Correspondence, Upper Canada Sundries, December 16–31, 1838 (R.G. 5, A 1, vol. 212), 116421–116999.

8   In his supervisory role for the Society for the Diffusion of Useful Knowledge, Charles Knight had fallen behind in the production of numbers for "The Library of Entertaining

Knowledge" and needed a book he could produce quickly for that series.

9   See Michael A. Peterman, "'Splendid Anachronism': The Record of Catharine Parr Traill's Struggles as an Amateur Botanist in Nineteenth-Century Canada" in *Re(Dis)covering Our Foremothers: Nineteenth-Century Canadian Women Writers*, ed. Lorraine McMullen (Ottawa: University of Ottawa Press, 1990), 173–85.

10   Traill to Frances Stewart, May 5, 1862, Baldwin Room, Metropolitan Toronto Library.

11   Traill was disturbed by the omissions in Jane Margaret's biography of Agnes and set out in a manuscript she entitled "The Stricklands. A Family Chronicle" to do justice to the offspring of the Strickland family, their upbringing, and their achievements. "A Slight Sketch of the Early Life of Mrs. Moodie" belongs to this undertaking. Her annotations to the original text of *The Backwoods of Canada* were included in the first Canadian publication of that book, edited by Edward S. Caswell for McClelland and Stewart in 1929.

12   See Traill Family Collection, National Archives of Canada, MG29 D81, no. 8764.

REFLECTIONS OF THE ENGLISH PAST

THE AUTOBIOGRAPHY OF AN UNLUCKY WIT

"The Autobiography of an Unlucky Wit" shows Traill as a comic writer with an agreeable "love of the ridiculous" and a gift for satiric caricature. The story was published in an American annual, *The Gift: A Christmas and New Year's Gift, for 1839*, 220–32, edited by Miss Leslie.[1] It was dated Westover [sic], U[pper] C[anada], suggesting that it was sent from, if not written in, Douro at the Traills' first backwoods home. While not ostensibly autobiographical, it carries interesting personal reverberations. Casting her narrator, Deborah Anne ———, as "a poor country curate's daughter," Traill tells of the perils of finding a suitable marriage partner within a society that offers but a small window of opportunity to young women without property or dowry. Its narrative juxtaposes a hard-earned wisdom that cautions against too indulgent a use of one's wit and satiric propensities with a still stronger force, a spirited temperament that values personal liberty too much to accept bondage of various types. In effect, the story never quite delivers on its moral of caution. Instead, it seems to promote Traill's own commitment to "pleasing myself in choice of husband." She herself did just that, accepting the proposal of the widowed Thomas Traill and opting for a life in Canada rather than playing a waiting game in Suffolk that might have ended in spinsterhood. In letters to Susanna Moodie, Agnes Strickland often lamented Catharine's choice of Traill, arguing that she would have been better to wait for an old, eligible suitor and to have stayed in England.

woman had better be born with no more brains than a goose, than be heiress to that dangerous possession—wit.—In the former case she is sure, soon or late, to find some honest gander for her mate, and, perhaps, some good uncle or aunt to make his or her will in her favour; but in the latter she is destined to die an old maid, and cut herself out of the good graces of all her friends and relations, by the sharpness of her tongue.

Having suffered all my life from the ill effects of this mischievous propensity, I would, from motives of pure philanthropy to the rising generation, entreat—advise—admonish and implore all guardians of the young of my own sex, mothers, aunts and governesses to check, crush and exterminate all tendency to mimicry, satire, repartee, sauciness, smartness, quickness; in short, all lively sallies that may grow up to form what is usually termed a *witty woman*. Let their young charges be dunces—the veriest pieces of affectation that ever minced steps at a dancing-master's ball. Let them be pedants—stuff their poor brains with astronomy, geology, conchology, entomology,—but let them not be wits—and, above all, do not let them imagine themselves possessed, in any way, of this most offensive weapon, for, ten to one, they will make fools of themselves through life.

While I was yet in my cradle, my mother discovered an unusual precocity about me, and a love of the ridiculous, which made me laugh ten times more than any of her other children had done at the same age; nay, she even attributed a certain comical cast that was perceptible in one eye during my childhood, to the droll way in which I used to squint up at nurse's high-crowned cap, which was at least half-a-foot higher than that of any old dame's in the village. I always thought it was turning that eye in an oblique direction to watch the movements of the pap-spoon, which, I shrewdly suspect, oftener visited the old woman's lips than the open mouth of her hungry, squalling nursling.

By the time I was three years old I was the veriest imp of mischief that ever lived; unfortunately, my freaks were laughed at, all my smart speeches duly repeated by a fond and foolish mother, and when I deserved to be whipped, I was forgiven on the score that I was so clever and such a *wit*. Now I verily believe half what is called wit in a child is folly, and if timely discouraged, the world would be spared much trouble in chastising, mortifying and disinheriting grown up culprits of this description.

At four or five I could mimic the voice, tone, gait and manner of every one I saw—even a comical face in a picture-book was a study for me, and once I amused myself at a lady's house, where my mother had left me to spend the day, by moulding my little face into an exact resemblance of the brass lion's head on the handle of the bell-pull, to the great amusement of all the company. For one frolic I got a sound box on the ear from my father—(it is a source of regret to me I have so few of those valuable salutations to record.)

Our landlord was a stiff old major, who wore a single-breasted coat, flapped waistcoat, a three-cocked hat and a big curled wig. At his quarterly visitations not a syllable must be spoken, but, ranged on our four-legged mahogany stools, my sisters and myself must sit as mute as mice, not a giggle must be heard, not a whisper, while politics (I remember it was Pitt and Fox time,) were discussed between my father and the old major.[2]

Oh, it was dulness of the most refined order to keep our tongues still, our hands in our lap, and our ears open.

I had somehow managed to secrete the clean-picked drum-stick of a goose from the dinner-table one Michaelmas-day, to make what we called an apple-scoop. Well, I looked at my dry bone, and I glanced at the wig. The major was in the act of describing a chevaux-de-frise[3]— I thought what an admirable one I could make of his wig. Unseen, unheard, I cracked my bone into a hundred splinters, and, favoured in my retreat from the circle by my quietly mischievous companions, I succeeded in sticking the wig as full of the white shivers of the goose-bone as I have since seen a sponge-cake soaked in wine and custard, (called a hedgehog,) stuck full of blanched almonds.

Imagine the grave, withered, crab-apple face of the major, and then think of the wig and its adornments—he wore, besides, a pigtail coming from beneath the wig. I was just putting the coup de grace to his appearance, by fastening a long bit of rag to the end of this appendage—it was too much for the risible organs of my sisters—a universal burst of laughter took place—it was like the bursting of a long pent-up volcano—it rolled on in spite of the awful frown of my father and the agitated look of the poor major, who was only partly unconscious of the ridiculous figure he cut. I shall never forget the scene, or the suppressed expression of mirth that gleamed and twinkled in my poor father's eyes, as he assisted to recompose the ruffled wig, (no easy matter,) and, in a thundering voice, demanded who had played the trick.

"I was only making a chevaux-de-frise," I said, trying not to laugh.

A thundering box on the ear sent me reeling to the further end of the room; given, I verily believe, more out of respect to the feelings of the offended major, than from genuine displeasure against the culprit—but it would not do—the dignity of the old soldier was mortally wounded; he never entered the house again, to the great mortification of my mother, who counted his few formal visits a great honour, and was wont to boast of the major as one of her grand acquaintance.

My next freak was a more fatal one to my own interests, as, by an unlucky speech, I made an implacable enemy of a maiden aunt who occasionally visited our house; sometimes in company with a younger sister. Aunt Martha seldom inflicted her society on us for less than a month at a time, to the infinite regret of every member of the household, from the tom-cat up to my honoured father.

Aunt Martha was a tall, lean, sour-faced woman of thirty-two; her nose had a sort of pinch at the top, which was very red, and her cheeks were somewhat of the colour of a red cabbage, only wrinkled a little more after the manner of a savoy-leaf; moreover, to complete the pleasantness of her physiognomy, she wore what was then in fashion, a cropped head, called a "Brutus"; no wonder that I should draw an unfavourable comparison between her young, pretty, good-natured, lively sister and herself—the latter I called my pretty aunt, by way of distinction.

One day a coach stopped at the door—one of my aunts was expected—I eagerly ran to peep through the banisters of the hall-stairs, half-dressed as I was, and in no very low tone asked if it were my "pretty aunt or my ugly aunt that had come?"—A withering glance from Aunt Martha, as she hastily brushed past me on the staircase, proved she had heard the question; she curled up her little red nose, and looked ten times uglier than ever. She never forgot nor forgave the insult—nay, she carried it to her grave, for in her last will and testament the unlucky speech was recorded against me, as a sufficient reason for cutting me out of her will. Younger sisters and brothers, tom-cats, parrots, and cousins to the eight remove, being sharers of her wealth, to the exclusion of poor me, though I had been scolded, starved, whipped and lectured into obedience to her auntly authority, till she had not outwardly a more dutiful niece in the whole list of brother's and sister's brats than myself.

Experience should have taught me wisdom, but a very small portion of that valuable acquirement fell to my share.

It was my misfortune to be the goddaughter of a proud, mean, vain old woman, some very, very distant relation of my father's, who graciously condescended to bestow upon me her own *beautiful* name, "Deborah Anne,"—horrible compound!—and when I had attained the mature age of sixteen, she benevolently signified her intention of taking me by the hand, and introducing me into company. In other words, I was to be her companion, *alias*, *white slave*, and if, on the supposition that I might in time become her heiress, I had the good fortune to marry some wretched old bachelor, ancient widower, or sickly dandy of family, I was to bless for ever the goodness and generosity of Mrs. Deborah Anne Pike.

In the meantime, till such eligible connexion could be formed, I must favour, flatter, and attend to the whims and caprices of my patroness and worthy godmamma; fill the important place of the ladies' maid and milliner, butler and housekeeper, amuse morning visitors, play the amiable to evening ones, play backgammon till my head was bewildered by the rattling of the dice-box, or pursue the monotonous draughtsmen across the board, till the white chickens looked black and the black white; and, of a rainy day, play billiards or bagatelle.

Our mornings were passed in solitary dulness, till the carriage was at the door to take us our daily round of calls on people as dull as ourselves; from five till six the business of the toilet occupied our time, and I was expected to attend to admire a face that even rouge could not improve, and a figure that resembled two boards bound together.

"Hum—ha—how do you like me now, Miss, that I have beautified a little?" was generally the closing speech, as she cast a satisfied glance at her withered charms in the old japanned dressing-glass.

Once I gave mortal offence by carelessly replying to "How do I look now?" "Much as you generally do, madam."

She was wont to make four things her boast: that she had never threaded a needle or set a stitch since she married the dear old general that was departed; never read any other newspaper than the John Bull, nor any books but the old Bath Guide and her prayer-book; never omitted taking an advantage at whist, nor gave more than a penny to a beggar at a time.

The first month was intolerable. In it I had given offence to one old beau and two danglers, and expressed my intention of pleasing myself in the choice of a husband— a glaring piece of folly and ridiculous assertion of my independence that could not be tolerated. The next—but happily my tongue for once did me a worthy service, and set me free from my worse than Egyptian bondage before the second month was out.

The old lady used to pester me to admire the beauty of a faded green stuffed parrot that stood in an old-fashioned hideous case, among Chinese mandarins, cups and saucers of old Dresden china, and other odd knick-knacks that filled up an ancient Dutch cabinet.

One day I unluckily was tempted to say, "I suppose, madam, you *starved* the parrot whilst it was alive, and *stuffed* it after it was dead." I said it playfully and in joke, but an awful cloud gathered on the offended lady's brow—silence ensued for a moment; then came a torrent of rebukes, and reproaches, and invectives. I apologized—it was only said in joke. Joke!—to joke with a person of her wealth—her dignity—and I a poor country curate's daughter, that she had taken from obscurity and beggary to make something of. This was too much—the pride of all my race rose up to my aid, and I retorted. The carriage was ordered to the door, and the old woman flung into it, commanding me to go to my room and pack my trunk. Next morning I was duly installed on an *outside* place on the mail—and—the right owners got me by six the same evening. The same mail brought a letter, the essence of spite, from my amiable relative, which, after dwelling on the heinousness of my enormities, concluded with these emphatic words:—

"Miss was too independent and too great a WIT for her station; humility had become the daughter of a poor curate better, and might have been rewarded with not less than £3000."

I lost the chance of this fine fortune, but I did not lose my detestable name, for the infliction of which I was never remunerated, but I gained what was inexpressibly dearer to me than ever it had been before—my liberty. Nay, even to this hour, though something old, and poor, and single withal, I cannot help congratulating myself on my miraculous escape, convinced, as I am, that had I remained the abject dependant of my rich relative, I should have been left, after a life of slavery, with no better recompense than a broken spirit and an empty purse; the too frequent reward of a rich old woman's *companion*.

I was a little tamed for a while after I came home, but by degrees all my old propensities returned, and I now became worse than ever. I quizzed all my acquaintance, laughed at the old beaux and bachelors of our village, teased the young ones, ridiculed my female friends, with the exception of one or two whom I made my companions, these aped my fashions and manners, and repeated all my sayings. In short, I considered myself as a star among them.

So sharp was my wit at last that few dared enter the lists to answer me, and if I happened to be in one of my *brilliant* humours no one was safe from my raillery. I could not endure to pass by an opportunity of displaying my talent— friend or foe, young or old, were alike exposed to my sarcasm.

I had nick-names for all my acquaintance, and prided myself on their significance, though now I am inclined to think the practice is vulgar, illiberal and foolish to a degree, besides being excessively ill-natured. In more than one instance I had the mortification of finding these names had reached the ears of the only persons they were not intended for, and that they gave much offence.

The surgeon and apothecary of our village, a huge bachelor with large unmeaning glassy eyes and whiskers of no common size, with an extensive practice, a new white stuccoed dwelling, with vinery and green-house at the end of the village, a stud of horses, and a kennel full of wretched cur dogs, was held in great esteem by the single ladies of the neighbourhood and their mammas, who did not fail to say the doctor would be a good *catch* for some one. One old maid, who had set her cap indefatigably at the good man during the space of eight whole weary years, was pleased to be very jealous of some attention he paid me at a race-ball, and in an audible whisper she said, stretching her scraggy neck across so as partially to eclipse the poor doctor:

"If Mr. L—— makes you an offer, I would advise you to *snap*!"

I coolly thanked her for her advice, but said—"I was not quite in so great a hurry to *snap* (as she elegantly expressed it,) as she might be." The doctor laughed, and the scraggy lady withdrew her crescent-shaped face in evident wrath.

For some time the doctor was looked upon almost as my declared lover, but I happened to hear that he should say, if I had come in for my share of Aunt Martha's legacy, or had been the *certain* heiress of Mrs. D.A. Pike, he might have been *induced* to offer his hand, his house, his vinery, his horses and dogs to me, for I was very clever and a dashing sort of a girl, though, 'pon honour, rather too sharp for him. I was incensed at his mercenary conduct, and resolved to revenge myself in some way. As to my mother, she excused his foible and hoped for the best, and my sisters still thought something might yet be done to bring him on, if I would but be a little meek, and not tease his dogs, and talk very affectionately of my rich godmother.

But the doctor's dogs were my aversion, a set of wretched living skeletons, that followed yelping at his heels, scratching and whining at his patients' doors like fiends of ill omen.

The oft-repeated proberb of "love me love my dog," which he never failed to repeat with a tender squeeze of my hand and a languishing stare from his gooseberry orbs, failed to win my admiration. One might have managed to tolerate one dog, but the doctor had six, though to be sure the whole half-dozen would not have made one respectable-sized lady's spaniel. I called these miserable beasts the doctor's patients—himself the *"man of pills,"* and the "gooseberry-eyed monster," while his assistant, the elegant, dandified Mr. C——, was the "stork"—he was six feet three inches, and slender to a degree—both were extravagantly proud of their perfections, and, though on the *fortified* side of thirty, the doctor was quite as vain as the youthful Adonis, his companion.

It was Valentine's day. I was resolved to revenge myself for the slighting manner in which of late the man of Pill had treated me, and I dashed off a caricature, in which my quondam admirer, with huge bear's whiskers, and eyes as big as saucers, was in the act of drawing an old woman's tooth; his huge frame ridiculously contrasted with a crowd of half-starved—not patients—but puppies of all sorts and sizes. Over the surgery door in legible characters was written TEETH DISTRACTED HERE. The centre figure was an admirable likeness of Mr. C. mounted on a stork's legs, and with a bird's head; on the *bill* were inscribed pills, draughts, powders, &c., with an enormous sum-total added up. The resemblances were excellent; in spite of the incongruous appearance of the unhappy doctor and his assistant, every one that saw the group, recognized the originals with shouts of laughter.

"Oh do let them have it," "Pray send it, they will never find out," "It is so clever they can't suspect," cried several of my *best* friends; and go it did, to be returned, not by the postman, but by the dignified, offended object of my satire, Mr. L——.

One of my treacherous bosom friends had betrayed me, for the sake of ingratiating herself in the doctor's favour. I was mortified, vexed, ashamed; forced to apologize; but all to no purpose. As I grew meek, the doctor grew more spiteful, and ended with telling me I should soon become an ill-natured, satirical, sour old maid. I lost my admirer, and had the mortification of seeing my treacherous acquaintance become mistress of the stuccoed house, vinery, &c., and flaunt past me at church, in a pink satin hat and feathers, with the six dogs prancing before and behind her.

After this adventure, I received an invitation to stay at —— Hall, with the aunt of Sir Charles S——. He was an elegant, sentimental young baronet; just recalled from his continental tour, by the death of his father. I had been ill, and was a little tamed by my misfortunes. Sir Charles was interested in me; was delighted with my singing, my drawing—I had been making sketches of the Hall, its old chapel, and the romantic scenes of his native village. I was proud, pleased, gratified at his praise. I began to indulge in visions of future bliss, to feel that I was not indifferent to the young baronet; I felt I could love him. Matters were in this train, when Sir Charles, one morning, announced his intention of taking his aunt and me to a race ball, at ———.

His good aunt presented me with a beautiful gauze and satin dress. I had never seen myself full-dressed, in such style. I was elated by my good looks. I should appear to advantage in the eyes of Sir Charles; my conquest would be complete; he had never seen me well-dressed, or in spirits. Sir Charles was a London-bred man. I must lay aside my country manners, and show him what I *could be*. I was all animation and gayety, full of repartee and lively sallies. I did not notice at first that as my spirits increased, so in proportion did Sir Charles become silent, abstracted, and grave. I rallied him at last, teased, quizzed; he looked displeased, and said little. I was blind to my danger, and when we reached the ball room, I flirted with the officer to whom I was introduced as a partner, with the hope of raising my lover's jealousy; but it would not do. I became reckless; pride would not allow me to notice Sir Charles's coldness and neglect. I exerted all my powers of wit to fascinate and charm. I heard my words repeated with admiration on all sides; but one voice alone was mute.

Sir Charles hated a spirited woman; a wit or female satirist was his detestation; he admired the soft, the gentle, the silent, the unaffected, simple country girl, more than the fashionable belle esprit.

As we entered the supper room, I heard him say to his aunt, "I am disappointed, disgusted by her conduct, much as I admired her. I would not now make her my wife, for all the world! I abhor a witty woman!" I heard no more; my head whirled; I turned sick, giddy and faint.

Sir Charles never renewed his attentions, but left the Hall soon after; I saw him no more. Disappointed and grieved at my folly, I left a spot where I had been only too happy to mourn over hopes that my unfortunate propensity had blighted.

And now on the verge of fifty, I find myself with a narrow income, shunned and feared by a limited circle of acquaintance, that unfortunate person, a poor satirical old maid. The only reparation I can make to society, is by publishing this short memoir, as a warning example to my sex, to shun that too common error, a sarcastic temper, and flee from the reputation of being thought a WIT.

Westover [sic], U.C.

∽

1   Eliza Leslie (1787–1858) was a Philadelphia author and editor who achieved great success in the magazine world of the United States in the 1830s and 1840s.

2   The period of the 1790s and early 1800s when England was at war against Napoleon's France. William Pitt (the younger) (1759–1806) was prime minister and Tory leader; Charles James Fox (1749–1806) led Whig resistance to Pitt and the costly war.

3   Chevaux-de-frise—any form of portable wire entanglement.

COUSIN KATE:
OR THE PROFESSOR OUTWITTED

"Cousin Kate: or the Professor Outwitted" was published in the *Anglo-American Magazine* 2 (1853), 510–14, in Toronto and was signed Oaklands, Rice Lake. Another of Traill's mischievous and mischief-loving stories, it celebrates a victory of feminine wit, cleverness, and *esprit* over male priorities and professional solemnity. The story is rooted in Strickland family experience, for Sarah Strickland, the beauty of the family who was four years older than Catharine, married Robert Childs in the late 1820s. A member of the famous Childs family of Bungay, Suffolk, who were involved in Methodism and publishing, Robert was by all reports an eccentric and scholarly type especially devoted to the new (pseudo) science of phrenology; indeed, he was famous locally for keeping a large hall in his house expressly for casts and skulls. The Strickland sisters dubbed the hall, which Childs himself punningly called his "Scullery," Golgotha. Another sister, Agnes, reportedly had a cast of her head taken by Childs. Her experiences may have been the basis of the description provided by the fictional Kate Lillestone of Dublin in the story. In her *Life of Agnes Strickland* (1887), Jane Margaret Strickland omitted any mention of Sarah's first marriage, focussing rather on her later marriage to an Anglican clergyman. Robert Childs apparently took his own life in 1839.

"Sarah, child, when am I to have a cast of that little head of thine?" said Professor Lindsay, as he leaned lovingly over the back of the chair, in which reclined a dark-haired girl, whose sparkling beauty formed a striking contrast to the plain, but sensible countenance—not quite devoid of a certain sly humor—of her philosophical lover. The girl shook a shower of silken ringlets over the arms of the Professor, and said, with a pretty, pouting air,

"Sir, I am eighteen years of age, and do not choose to be called a *child*, as if I were a baby. I do not choose to have a cast of my head taken."

"The plain why and because, Miss Sarah?"

"The why is because I don't choose, and the because— it will spoil my curls;" and the young lady gave a decidedly rebellious toss to the ringlets, to free them from the profane hands that had clutched hold of the beautiful head, and was admiring—not with the eye of an artist, but of a phrenologist—the fine contour it displayed.[1] The effort was not successful; the head was still imprisoned between the Professor's unholy paws, as Sarah disdainfully called the large, not very white, hands of her lover.

"I will not free the head till you promise me to grant what I ask."

"I promised you my heart, and some time or other, my hand, but I never said a word about my head," said the incorrigible coquette.

"Nonsense; the heart is nothing."

"My heart nothing! How dare you say so? I will give both it and my hand to some one that I know will not despise it."

"Sarah, this is downright flirtation. Give me the head and the hand, and I do not care a pin for the heart. It is nothing but a living timepiece that beats regularly when the rest of the machine is in order."

"The heart of man is deceitful and desperately wicked," said Sarah, very softly, as if speaking to herself.

"It is a mistake in the translation. That same doctrine about the heart being the seat of the affections and feelings is all a heathenish chimera."

"David was not a heathen?"

"He was not a phrenologist. You shall read the rough copy of my treatise, 'Heads *versus* Hearts.'"

"I couldn't read two pages, my dear Edward. I do not believe you could read it yourself."

The Professor looked enquiringly.

"You write such a hand that I cannot read it,—that little note you sent me last night. I have puzzled my poor brains over it, and all I can make out is that you are going to a dance next week."

"A dance! me! I going to a dance! Why, Sarah, you know my horror of dancing—and a man of my age and habits. I wrote to say that I was thinking of going to France. There is a celebrated chemist going to lecture in Paris on some subjects that I am greatly interested in just now."

"Well, Edward, I am concerned at my stupidity; but, indeed, I did try to make out the note; and now I suppose you will be greatly offended."

"No, indeed; for I am aware that I write a most abominable scrawl. What do you think Murray[2] said of it?—'It was like the vagaries of a mad spider, whose legs had been dipped in ink.' And so you will not look over my MS.?"

"I will wait till I read it in print, and then I will write an answer to it, and call it 'Hearts *versus* Heads.'"

"Well, let me have the cast of the pretty head, and I will forgive all your sauciness," said the lover gallantly, raising to his lips the small hand that he had taken in his, while he looked in her bright eyes with a glance of entreaty that would have softened the most obdurate heart; but the mischief-loving girl knew her power, and delighted in exercising it. She re-arranged the disordered ringlets at the mirror, and very demurely told the Professor that she was not going to yield to flattery. "There is Kate; why do you not ask her to let you have a cast of her head?"

"A pretty cast, indeed, my head would make!" replied her sister, almost indignant at the proposition. "It would be worthy to sit beside that of John Bull, the little savage that Edward showed us with such pride of heart yesterday in the—Scullery."

"My Studio, Miss Kate," said the Professor, by way of amendment.

"Or Golgotha!"[3] added Kate. The Professor looked grave, then almost savage.

"By the bye, Sarah," he said, suddenly looking up. "What do you think that little wretch did this very morning?"

"What, Kate?"

"Pooh, no: John Bull, the negro boy that I made the cast from—you know he sleeps on a matrass in the—"

"scullery,"[4] interposed Kate. The Professor shook his cane at her.

"After I had taken the cast I showed it to him, and he was highly delighted, grinned a thousand grins, and cut ever so many capers, saying 'White John Bull, nice boy, he no more nigger boy now.' However, a friend of mine hinted that it would be more effective if I varnished the cast with lamp-black. So to work I went, and in a few minutes the cast was finished and placed on a high stand beside Sir Walter Scott and Napoleon, where it stood forming a capital contrast to the intellectual developments of the two casts. I had made up my mind to lecture on that very cast at our next meeting. Well, when I came to unbar the door of the studio and rouse up my imp of darkness, judge of my mortification, when I saw the little black wretch sitting on the floor with the cast in his lap, diligently scraping away the lamp-black from the face with an oyster shell, and grinning with infinite satisfaction at every patch of white plaster that was reproduced by his energetic labors. I could have laughed, but for very rage at seeing the beautiful head that I was to have lectured upon so disfigured."

"What did you do?" asked Sarah.

"Do? I gave the little black rascal a crack over his woolly pate, and sent him spinning across the room, with the cast after him. As ill luck would have it, I missed my aim, and instead of knocking him down, tumbled over two superb idiots that were the pride of my whole collection, and smashed them to atoms. I would not have taken five guineas for these specimens, they cost me a set of china tea-things, a new gown, and a scarlet cloth cloak, as presents to the mother before I could prevail upon her to let me take the casts of those two darlings, and lots of sweetmeats to the young wretches themselves, though poor things they knew nothing of my design after all, and I had to give one of them a sleeping draught to make him be still."

"How shocking!" exclaimed Sarah, indignant at the philosophical coolness of her lover.

"I am delighted at John Bull's cleverness," said Kate. "I shall make a point of bestowing upon him some especial mark of favour, by way of a little encouragement. Sarah, we must give him bulls eyes and candy to console him for that barbarous treatment of his poor woolly pate."

The Professor looked rather sour, fretted, fumed, and at last bounced up, and declared he would not remain to be laughed at.

"The Professor has the organ of combativeness and destructiveness largely developed," whispered Sarah, glancing at her irate lover through her redundant curls.

"Why combativeness?"

"The assault and battery just confessed."

"And destructiveness?"

"Aiming at the poor little nigger boy's head, and the demolition of the casts of those precious idiots, to do it."

The Professor tried to look angry, but could not manage anything more formidable than a sarcastic grin. "Has your discernment made any other discovery?"

"Yes, the organ of Unreasonableness."

"There is no such organ," he replied triumphantly.

"I have heard you call woman an unreasonable animal twenty times."

"Pooh, child, you mistake parts of speech terribly; girls always do. I have explained the cerebral development fifty times."

"Yes, and always ended by calling me a giddy goose, or some such very complimentary epithet, because I could not remember all your hard names, and then I felt marvellously disposed to box your ears. That was being combative I suppose."

"Did you ever feel disposed to wield the poker or tongs," slily asked the Professor, then added in a coaxing tone, "Come Sarah, don't let us quarrel. Be a good girl and let me have the cast."

"What, to reward you for such savage conduct? I marvel at your audacity in asking for it."

"Well, here comes your Aunt Lillestone, Edward, let us hear what she has to say," exclaimed Kate.

"I am very glad of it, Aunt Lillestone is a very good friend of mine, and an enthusiastic disciple of phrenology. She has had two casts and a half taken," said the Professor, with great animation—"And cousin Kate too—that girl is a pattern for some other Kates that shall be nameless. Do you know, Sarah, she actually consented to have her beautiful hair shaved off, just to oblige me with a good cast."

"She must have been desperately in love with you to make such a sacrifice," said Sarah coldly.

"Well here she is, and now I will insist on a true and veracious statement of the process and all she endured."

"True and veracious—hum—synomimes," maliciously interposed the Professor, "girls always make use of two words where one would suffice."

"Organ of language," retorted Sarah. What polite rejoinder the phrenologist might have made I cannot say, for the door opened and in sailed the portly figure of Aunt Lillestone, with her lively fashionable daughter, whose petite height and delicate proportions, formed a very striking contrast to her own full and majestic person. The Professor hurried to meet them—"Glad to see you aunt, glad to see you cousin Kate, Kate of Kate Hall, the prettiest Kate in all the world."

"That is to say, the prettiest shrew, the nicest little vixen in all the world; thanks for the compliment my worthy coz," gaily replied the young lady taking the seat which the Professor pushed towards her. There was something eccentric and *outré* even in his most polite humours.

"Aunt Lillestone, you have come to decide a knotty point, a question of, to be, or not to be," he began, planting himself opposite the capacious form of the lady, and fixing his dark grey eyes on her face with intense earnestness, as if his happiness for life depended on her decision.

Mrs. Lillestone looked inquiringly from her nephew to the two girls, who stood with arms entwined beside the window, looking very pretty and very animated. Mrs. Lillestone thought that there could be only one very momentous question pending between Sarah Dalton and her nephew. This was the important decision respecting the wedding-day. The old lady drew herself up to her most majestic height, settled the flowing folds of her ample satin gown, and assuming an air of becoming gravity, turned to her nephew and said:—

"Edward, my dear, you know that in delicate matters of this kind, the lady or her friends are the parties to decide. Now, till Mr. Dalton returns home from the continent, you know that the wedding cannot take place; Sarah, of course, could not marry till her father's return."

"But, my dear aunt," interrupted the Professor, coloring to the very top of his head.

"I know quite well the arguments that you men always employ, my dear nephew. When I was engaged to your uncle, Captain Lillestone, he never ceased to importune me, poor dear man, till I named the happy day."

The poor Professor did not know which way to look, and the thought of the embarrassment that his lady-love would be thrown into by this *mal apropos* speech increased his confusion. The Professor was, with all his oddities, a modest man and especially delicate when such matters as courtship and marriage were being discussed. As to Sarah, she tried at first to look demure, but the two wicked Kates were convulsed with laughter. One stolen glance at her discomfitted lover was enough to overset her gravity. She was fain to bend her face down over the rose that she was looking at in the vase, to conceal the dimples that would make themselves visible in her round damask cheek.

"Really, young ladies," remonstrated Mrs. Lillestone, greatly shocked.

"Really, mamma, how can we help laughing?" said her daughter.

"It was not a question matrimonial, but phrenological, madam, that you were called upon to decide," said her nephew.

"The Professor wants Sarah to submit to the process of having a cast of her head taken," said Kate Dalton, "and Sarah is as hard-hearted as a flint, and she has been at loggerheads with Edward for the last hour on the subject."

"I must say, Sarah Dalton, that I am surprised after having heard the splendid arguments of Combe, and Crook, and De Ville, and Fowler,[5] and—" "Professor Lindsay," whispered Kate Lillestone—"that you should refuse your assent to the most magnificent soul-ennobling science that the wisdom of man ever conceived. For my part, I would have had a dozen casts of my head taken if I could have been convinced that its poor development could have added one more fact to the glorious system of Phrenology."

A very faint giggle from the recess in the bay window might have been heard by Mrs. Lillestone, if she had not been decidedly a little deaf.

"Now, Kate Lillestone, I appeal to your experience, and I rely upon your candor, to tell me about this same cast. Edward says you submitted to have one taken just to please him," said Sarah, turning to her friend.

"My dear, he (the Professor) was never more mistaken in his life; it was not to please him, but myself."

"O you naughty girl!" cried out the indignant Phrenologist, holding up his hands. "Did you not make a great merit about sacrificing your beautiful hair, and put me to the expense of false hair, and gauze caps, and flowers, and blonde trumpery, to cover your baldness, till you half ruined me."

Kate laughed, and said, "Confession is good for sinful souls, the priests say; so I will make a clean breast of it, and confess the truth. I quite forgot to tell you, my dearly respected coz, that I had had my hair shaved off a month before you came to Dublin; I had a bad fever. Dr. Macneil insisted upon it, and though I fought most tigerishly in behalf of my poor curls, I could not save them."

"Why, Kate, you deceitful puss, and were not those shining ringlets and glossy braids your own?"

"Of course they were, my good cousin. They cost me a deal of money at Rozier's; and if you had not been so liberal in providing me with fresh sets, I should have been half ruined."

The Professor looked absolutely confounded at the trick that had been played him; his eye instinctively wandered to the region of Secretiveness; but the envious head-dress guarded the organs from his penetrating glance. He had not a grain of deceit or intrigue in his disposition. The poor Professor was as honest as the day. He had been fairly outwitted; but while he was pondering over the matter, Sarah and Kate Dalton had enticed the pretty delinquent into giving them a faithful description of her experience in the cast-taking process.

"Now, my dear, pray lay aside your usual levity of tongue," said Mrs. Lillestone, "and make use of the fine sense that you are endowed with, in describing the operation to these young ladies. Lay aside all exaggeration, and let us have nothing but the unalloyed truth. You know the saying, my dears, that truth is stranger than fiction."

The girls exchanged glances, the Professor took a large pinch of snuff, seated himself by the table, and began sketching phrenological developments on the visiting cards from the card basket.

"Well, my dears, as I like to be very precise and particular, I shall begin at the beginning, and tell you that when my cousin Edward came to visit mamma and me in Dublin, he took it into his wise head to imagine that my wig covered a splendid set of organs. How he came to think so is more than I can say; but I believe he had not seen you, Sarah, at that time, so he might have fallen a *leetle, only a very leetle* in love with me. Well, he worried me day by day, till at last, in an evil hour, I was rather in love with a new *tête* that I had seen. I was, you see, tempted by the promises he voluntarily made of elegant head-dresses and point lace lappets, if I would only consent to have my head shaved. Moreover he vowed eternal gratitude, and that not an eyebrow nor an eyelash should be removed during the process.

"One morning, after a deal of fuss on my part, and vows," here she stole a glance at the Professor, "and protestations on his, I came down without my wig, and, to do the dear unsuspecting soul justice, he never questioned the trick I had played him, but fairly over-whelmed me with the excess of his gratitude." [A low deep growl from the Phrenologist.]

"Now, Kate Lillestone, how could you be so deceitful? I really am half angry with you myself for imposing on Edward's good nature," said Sarah, who felt a sort of natural indignation at her beloved having been so duped.

"My dear girl, do not open your black eyes so wide, and look so indignant at poor me. After all, you know it was only my cousin, and then is very rich, and could very well afford to pay handsomely for this precious pericranium of mine. Why, the very development of the organs of Acquisitiveness, Secretiveness, and Caution was worth a great deal."

"And the absence of Conscientiousness," growled out the Professor, in an under tone.

"Go on, if you please, Miss Lillestone," said her mother, "there is no end to your digressions. Your friends are all attention."

"Hear, hear, hear!" softly whispered Kate Dalton, clapping her hands under the flower-stand.

"The first thing," resumed the fair narrator, "that my cousin did, was to send for a pint bottle of the finest rose oil—I preferred it to Macassor—a fine damask towel was wrapped about my neck and shoulders, and then, Selwyn, mamma's maid, deluged my poor bare head and anointed my eye-brows and eye-lids, with the oil, with a camel's-hair pencil. I was then led with great state into the laundry, where stood the long ironing dresser, and whither my good cousin had preceded me with his factotum, John Allen, who was busily employed mixing a pailful of plaster-of-Paris with water—it looked marvellously like hasty pudding. The apparatus consisted of a pewter basin with a broad flat rim to it like a pie dish only there was a hollow place to admit the back of my neck, a whipcord, some small thin wooden wedges, a little mallet, a great iron spoon, like a dripping-ladle, and a white sheet.

"My curiosity became greatly excited. I began to regard myself as a living sacrifice to the sublime truths of science, as mamma consolingly told me. I was enveloped in the white sheet. I ascended the three-legged stool beside the ironing board, and giving my hand to my cousin, resigned myself unresistingly to my fate. My executioner, for as such at that minute I regarded him, lowered me gently down till my head gradually sunk into the pewter basin of cold—wet—plaster!"

"How did you feel, Kate?"

"An icy shudder ran through my blood. I felt as if suddenly transported to the polar regions. Another minute, and I was complete *fixed*, as the Yankees say. The plaster began to set, and in [an]other two minutes a genial warmth began to take place of the icy coldness I had at first experienced. Warmer and warmer became the plaster, and I now began to entertain some fear of being baked alive in my crust by some mysterious process."

"I would have started up and made my escape," said Kate Dalton.

"My dear child, the thing was impracticable; besides, my curiosity was now aroused, and I was heroically resolved to see the end of the Parisian plaster mysteries at all hazards. In about five minutes' time the back of the cast was set. I thought the worst was over, but I was mistaken. The divine part of the ceremony was yet to come. The Professor now came, and carefully arranged the little wedges along the rim of the pan, or mould, and then, having wetted the piece of string, laid it over my head, bringing it down over my forehead, along the bridge of my nose, mouth, and chin, till it rested on my breast. It felt like a cold worm creeping along my flesh. He then introduced two straws into my nostrils."

"What were the straws for?" asked Sarah in utter amazement.

"To breathe through, my dear. While Edward was arranging the wedges, Allen, his assistant, was mixing a fresh bowl of plaster, and in another minute came to the side of my bier, as I designated the table, whereon I lay like a shrouded corpse. 'Now, Kate, not a word: do not start or stir for your life.' I was as mute as a fish, wondering what was to come next. Presently, dab went a great spoonful of cold plaster on my head—another and another; then came a spoonful on my right ear, then over my left. I became deaf to all sounds, save the ringing and singing in my own head and a far off, faint, hollow murmur such as I once heard in St. Paul's, when I staid beneath the dome and listened to the distant sounds of the city bells coming to my ears like the beating of the ocean's waves upon the sea-shore. And now a sensation came—that of utter darkness, blindness that might be felt, so complete, so intense was the blackness that every particle of light was banished. Presently a brick wall seemed built against my teeth. I became dumb. An intolerable weight was on my throat. I felt suffocating."

"I would have screamed out when the plaster came on my face."

"So would I; but I remembered having seen the cast of a little fellow, Archy Bell (not the cat), who opened his mouth to cry, just as a spoonful of plaster came upon it, which he spat out, and caused an awful chasm in the face, like the rugged edges of the crater of a volcano; and having endured so far, I manfully resolved to bear all to the end."

"And how did you feel when hearing, and sight, and speech were all shut out?" asked Kate Dalton.

"I felt like a warrior taking his rest,
With his martial cloak around him."

"Nonsense, my dear; but how did you feel? Do tell me."

"Exactly like a person who had been buried alive, and has had the supreme felicity of awakening to life in his coffin."

"Horrible!" exclaimed Sarah, shuddering. "Well, go on; how did you get out of your tomb?"

"The warmth of the plaster, the weight, and want of breath made the few minutes that I lay seem an age. Presently I heard as though my tomb were invaded by resurrection men. I was sensible of hammering and a noise, as if of bricks and mortar being knocked about my head. This was the removing of the wedges, then some one took the end of the string and ripped up the cast, it cracked; then my cousin, taking each side of the mask, tore it from my face. I felt as if my skin were accompanying it. But oh! the delight of the deep-drawn breath of delicious air, the sight, the hearing restored! Of one thing I am sure, that I never felt so truly grateful for the use of those precious senses before, and so new and singular were the ideas that crowded in upon me as I lay there in the darkness and silence of the grave, that, now that it is past, I think I would not have foregone the experience of those few minutes—strange and disagreeable as in some respects they were—for a great deal. I would certainly rather have had my cast taken than have gone to a delightful party."

"Kate, Kate, this levity is very unbecoming a girl of your age."

"Dear mamma, do you know that I am nearly twenty-one, and if you talk so seriously about my age, people will begin to think that I must be very venerable. Now, Sarah, has my fascinating description decided you in favor of having your cast taken?"

"It has decided me [the Professor looked up] that nothing on earth shall tempt me to run such a fearful risk of my life." The head of the Professor sank on his breast again.

"And how did you look, my dear, after your resurrection?

"I looked a perfect wretch. I might have fancied myself transformed into a bricklayer's slave. My head was covered with mortar, as if I had been carrying a hod on it. When the inner cast was finished, and the outer mask was taken off, and the roughnesses all smoothed and polished, and Edward with great satisfaction introduced me to my second self, I had the mortification of finding that I had hollow cheeks, and a long chin and nose considerably off the line of beauty. My vanity received a severe shock. In fact, I felt a marvellous inclination to knock my double down and that ungrateful cousin of mine. Instead of rewarding me for the great sacrifice I had so disinterestedly made for the good of his pet science, he had the barbarity to assure me that I had a great many of the bad organs largely developed, and few of the good ones. So, of course, I voted Phrenology a—"

"Humbug! you were about to say," broke in the Professor.

"Exactly so, my dear cousin."

"Have you done, Miss Lillestone?" said her mother, reprovingly.

"Yes, mamma, for I am perfectly exhausted. I am sure I must have convinced my auditors that if I have nothing else, that I have the organ of—"

"Prate!" said the Professor, rising, and tossing into his cousin's lap a clever caricature sketch of the scene she had so ably described.

And did the Professor gain his point? Yes, my dear reader. Sarah's father returned from abroad, and in less than one month Sarah and the Professor were married, and very soon after the wedding a beautiful cast of the bride's head graced a marble pedestal in the Professor's studio; but cousin Kate was not one of the bridesmaids; the honest-hearted philosopher never quite forgot or forgave her outwitting him in the affair of the wig.

C.P.T.
Oaklands, Rice Lake.

1   Phrenology was a psychological theory and analytical method based on the idea that certain mental faculties and character traits are indicated by the configurations (and bumps and valleys) of an individual's skull. Phrenologists mapped the skull locating characteristics by name and number. A vast literature sprang up to articulate "the new science"; in the 1820s, according to Susanna Moodie, there was "a perfect mania" for information about it.

2   Likely the English publisher, John Murray (1778–1843).

3   Golgotha—Calvary, or the place of burial (from the Hebrew for skull).

4   Susanna Moodie offers her version of the story of young John Bull in "Washing the Black-a-moor White. A Page from Life," which appeared in the *Canadian Literary Magazine* 1 (1871): 163–65, and was reprinted in *Voyages: Short Narratives of Susanna Moodie*, ed. John Thurston (Ottawa: University of Ottawa Press, 1991), 253–56. In her account John Bull was a twelve-year-old African who was rescued from a sinking merchant ship of the same name and brought to England where he was placed in service to Robert Childs. The boy was the guardian of Childs' "scullery." In Moodie's narrative no violence is done to the boy for trying to remove the black polish from the white cast of his own head.

5   George Combe (1788–1858) and his brother, Dr. Andrew Combe (1797–1847), were both British phrenologists; the former wrote *Elements of Phrenology* (1824) and the latter "On the Effects of the Mind." British phrenologist James De Ville published *Outlines of Phrenology, as an Accompaniment to the Phrenological Bust* (1824). American brothers Orson Squire Fowler (1809–87) and Lorenzo Niles Fowler (1811–96) collaborated on *Fowler on Memory: or, Phrenology Applied to the Cultivation of Memory* (1842).

A Slight Sketch of the Early Life of Mrs. Moodie

During the 1880s Catharine Parr Traill began to draft a series of sketches of the members of the Strickland family and the conditions of her youth in Suffolk. The appearance of Jane Margaret's adulatory biography, *Life of Agnes Strickland* (Blackwood and Sons), in 1887 merely increased her desire to recall those early years, for it was this part of Agnes's life that Jane ignored, scarcely mentioning Stowe House, Reydon Hall, the sisterhood, their education, and their creative energies. "A Slight Sketch of the Early Life of Mrs. Moodie" is part of "this Family Record." It offers internal evidence of at least two stages of composition— one while Moodie was still alive and one after her death in 1885—and it provides a rich store of information about Susanna Moodie's early life, much of which is available nowhere else. Of perhaps most interest is the contrast Traill offers between Susanna's "genius" and "independence of character" and her own more modest sense of herself. Catharine herself fully believed that she had "no genius for invention" (Traill Family Collection, no. 8436) and little by way of poetic aptitude and skill. The picture she paints of Moodie reflects both her admiration for her sister's imaginative gifts and her knowledge of the temperamental excesses one came to expect of her on occasion.

This sketch is found in the Traill Family Collection (nos. 9878–9891) in the National Archives of Canada and is here published for the first time.

My sister Susanna was the youngest of the six sisters, and was by no means the least remarkable for talent among us. From her earliest childhood she shewed an originality of thought that developed itself apart from teaching or situation.

She early shewed a lively imagination. She lived in a sort of dream world of her own, clothing the fanciful images of her fertile brain in language that often partook of the poetical rather than the plain matter of fact words in which children usually express their ideas. The fact was Susie was an infant genius. When she was about four years old she would suddenly look up with her earnest grey eyes, and relate some wonderful romance of her own creation which usually began with, "When I was a little boy and lived in Souf America." And what the story of her childish dreams was I have now forgotten—only I recollect she used to talk of great rivers, and big trees, and white ants, and snakes and crocodiles. Sometimes it was told as a dream but more often as a fact that she had seen. Possibly some of these images were gathered up by the child from our father's conversation, or passages from books of travel read out by our parents.

One day Susie was found sitting on the doorstep hugging some little thing in her lap—caressing the little dolly-like bundle and saying, "Oh you. Pity dear, I do love oo so." To the horror of the nurse-maid it proved to be a lizard that she had found and wrapped up in her pinafore. The maid snatched the strange nurseling away. The child cried for her "beautiful darling" and it was hard to comfort her. She was a great admirer of frogs and toads of which she had no fear, they had beauty in her wondering eyes.

When Susanna was born, she was a tiny weakly baby, so much so that it was thought desirable that she should be baptised within a short time after her birth. Great was the excitement among my elder sisters about the name to be chosen for her. Elizabeth suggested Cassandra, for they were just then deep in Pope's Homer's *Iliad*. Agnes insisted on the grand sounding name of Andromache, her hero Hector's wife, while Sarah meekly suggested Hecuba.

Fortunately baby escaped the infliction of being given such remarkable names. I remember our Mother mentioning the circumstance one day in after years when Susie was rather lamenting that the Jewish name of Susanna had been given her. But she was reconciled to its homeliness and quite thankful when she heard of the escape she had had from such out-of-the-way names as Cassandra, Andromache, and Hecuba! The last especially roused her indignation. How could she have lived with such a heathenish name? She might have cried out "Hecuba Strickland! Phoebus what a name—."

Susie was one of those eccentric children that are little understood, and being a little wild and original in her ways was often in trouble. She was either full of spirits or easily depressed, often seeing things through an excited imagination. As a very young girl she was often unhappy. It is the common fate of genius to see things through an unreal medium, either too great or too small.

Like the rest of her sisters she was a great reader. As early as the age of nine or ten years she began to clothe her ideas and feelings in verse. Her facility for rhyme was great and her imagination vivid and romantic, tinged with gloom and grandeur more than wit and humour, though in later years this element was not wanting in her writings.

It were useless to recall all her more childish years. She and I were devoted to one another. I was not of so imaginative a disposition. Our tempers and abilities were unlike, and possibly it was the contrast between us in many ways that had the effect of binding us nearer to one another. Our faithful friendship was never broken, it is still dear to our hearts, as it was in our childish days. Now in our extreme old age we cling to each other with a love and trust that knows no change or coldness. We feel as we draw near to that hour when all that love must part, that we cannot long be severed. May God grant the reunion through our mutual faith in the Lord of life and light, in that land where partings are no more to divide those who love the Lord who bought and ransomed them by his precious blood.

The breaking up of the home circle (when my father retired from the Management of the Dock at ———, his health requiring the change, being afflicted by gout, so much so that he was always obliged as long as I can recollect to walk with a cane or crutches) or rather the division of it, threw us more closely in communion with one another, as my eldest sisters were more frequently with our father, at Stowe House near the historic town of Bungay. Sometimes my Mother too would be away leaving one of my sisters with the servants and such of the younger ones as did not go with her to stay at the city house with my father.[1]

Susanna was naturally of an impulsive temper, and as is often found in persons of genius, she was often elated and often depressed, easily excited by passing events, unable to control emotions caused by either pain or pleasure—morbidly sensitive to reproof, which if conscious of fault in herself created self-reproach and made her unhappy and for a time miserable, but if undeserved, roused in her a spirit of resistance against what she regarded from her point of view as tyranny and injustice, and having made her protest against it, she retired into herself and made no concessions to the higher powers. I think I must often have acted the part of the brake on the steep hill, for the safety of the inside passengers. The strong affection that this dear sister always felt for me had great power in toning down the troubled spirit. A few tender words had the effect that oil poured on water has—it smoothed the waves of irritated feelings, and calmed the rising storm, saying in the words of Him who spake as man never did, "Peace be still." Susie was controlled by love—it was the magnet that she ever obeyed. Opposition, stern remonstrance would only have produced the contrary effect. Our tempers were different, we did not always see things in the same light yet we never quarrelled. Once indeed, I remember being moved to anger and provoked by some unreasonable fit of obstinacy on my sister's part, I forget the exact circumstance of the case, but I was wrong no doubt. I struck her a sharp blow. I was the oldest of the two and I think about twelve years old—too old to give way to such a fit of passion. I shall never forget the feelings of anguish and remorse on my part that followed this unsisterly deed, nor the surprise and dismay of Susanna at this unusual display of temper coming from one who had never struck her before under any provocation. I think she cried more from grief than from pain of the blow—but such an outrage never again occurred to break the love and harmony of our long lives which was broken only by death which severed the <u>earthly</u> tie, but could not extinguish the love to be renewed in the presence of Him whose name and attribute is Love.

There existed in my sister from childhood, an inherent love of freedom of thought and action. This independence of character showed itself when she was older with respect to her religious views. She was suddenly awakened from a state of indifference, to one of doubtful questioning alternating with indifference, which again gave way through the energetic preaching of an enthusiastic clergyman of the English Church rousing her sensitive nature to a consideration of the importance of her spiritual state. A great conflict was going on in her mind at this time, "Within were fightings, without were fears." The strivings of the awakened soul can only be understood by the converted Christian beholding his reflected image in the mirror of Christ's Gospel when he cries out in despair, "Woe is me for I am of unclean lips." Among her religious friends was one tried and true, the wife of the Banker at Southwold, Aunt of a celebrated physician, Sir Henry Thompson, then only a babe. Mrs. Thompson was the last descendant of the martyred Anne Askew,[2] whose name she also bore when single. She was a beautiful example of every Christian virtue, beloved by every one who knew her, and revered by the young whom she drew around her by her gentle loving graciousness of manner. She might truly be called a Christ-like woman—making religion captivating to the youthful heart. Such was Susanna's Christian friend and in her house she met many very charming persons who remained faithfully attached to her during years long after she came out to Canada.[3]

When the clergyman whose words had produced the change in her left the neighbourhood, he commended her to the care of a worthy earnest Nonconformist Pastor, whose Christian teaching he had much confidence in, and to several religious friends whose influence he thought would be of great value in strengthening her faith in the truths of the Gospel, to which her eyes were now directed. Under the ministrations of the Revd. Mr. R[itchie] my sister received rest and comfort, but her secession from the established church was very distasteful to our Mother and sisters, and for a while, was the cause of disunion & a withdrawal of the old harmony & confidence which had hitherto existed in the family.[4] We were staunch adherents to the English Church, faithful in our Sunday attendance at the services; it was the church of our forefathers, and to enter that of a Nonconformist was regarded at that time as bordering on heresy. Yet at the time of which I write, the greatest state of deadness and supineness existed, not only in our Parish Church but in all the neighbouring ones. There was a state of spiritual destitution, against which no one lifted up their voice to remonstrate, so indifferent had people become. The Parishioners listened patiently to long-winded homilies. The poor labourers said, "No doubt our parson gave a bootiful sarmin but it was not for poor folk like us to understand such larnin." The sermon that had aroused my sister was the first truly Gospel sermon we had heard preached in Reydon church for years, but this state of things was not always to continue. This was more than sixty years ago. There are now no fox-hunting, horse-riding men in our Suffolk churches. The old race is now dead and gone, and better men now fill their pulpits. Those were the dark days under the reign of the Georges.

The R's were superior persons, the Pastor a worthy, learned and excellent man, and his wife an accomplished woman, and the children clever, sensible and intelligent. Mrs. R. was a beautiful flower artist, and my Mother allowed my sister to take lessons in drawing and water-color painting from her—and as Susanna possessed a decided talent in that line, she made good progress in a short time. In after years she became remarkable for her artistic talents, which seems like an heirloom to have descended both to her children and grandchildren.

When Susanna was about sixteen my Mother received an invitation from a married sister (whom she had not seen for a number of years) for one of her nieces to visit her. My Aunt had not seen any of us since we were babies. It was decided that Susanna should be the one chosen to go to London. This was the first time she had ever been from home. The unknown Aunt did not take kindly to her—the truth is she fell in love with a young man, who was not at all her equal; he was a Nonconformist and her Aunt was naturally very much displeased—and after a few weeks my sister did not find her sojourn a pleasant one. She went to visit my <u>father's</u> only sister—Aunt Sara Stone—who received her kindly, and with this Aunt and Uncle she remained some months very happily, returning home the following spring.

It was after Susanna's return home that she commenced writing some of her early productions, and we passed very pleasant times reading, writing and taking long walks, and I think it was that year or the following that she wrote her Historic tales of "Spartacus" and "Jugurtha".[5] They were among the first of her juvenile writings. During the following years she published several popular books which were much liked. Among these I may name "The Little Quaker", "Hugh Latimer", "Prejudice and Principle", "Roland Massingham". Also, she wrote many small poems that appeared in the Annuals of those years, which gained the friendly notice of some Authors and Authoresses of note—Miss Mitford and others. On being encouraged by some of her literary friends, she again visited the great City, while her volume of poems was passing through the Press, edited by a friend who took a sincere interest in her success. This book was published under the title of "Enthusiasm and other Poems" by Susanna Strickland. I am not aware if the book went into a second edition, though the first edition was soon exhausted and it was very favourably reviewed. But we had little knowledge in those days of the mysteries of the trade in pushing an unknown Author's works into notice and already the taste for poetry was beginning to decline. There were no new Scotts and Byrons. Campbell had written himself out. Southey, Coleridge, Wordsworth and Rogers held the field in poetry and there were a host of minor writers, but the public began to turn their attention more to prose than verse. Miss Landon, Miss Mitford and Mrs. Hemans were the only women of note in poetry at that time.

During my sister's visit to London she was the guest of the Poet Thomas Pringle, the Secretary of the Anti-Slavery Society, and in his house she met many writers of that day and was herself much noticed. Her lively manners and bright original turn of thought gained her many friends. She has in one of her novels given reminiscences of some of the characters she met during her stay with the Pringles. Nor was she entirely idle; her pen was employed by Mr. Pringle in writing in behalf of the great Anti-Slavery cause, in which she felt the greatest interest, entering into the subject of the emancipation of the Negro race with all her heart and soul.[6]

It was while at the house of the Poet Pringle on a visit to London that she met her future husband, Lieut. Moodie. A natural attachment took place, which ended in an engagement, and the following year my sister was married at St. Pancras Church. I was her bridesmaid and Mr. Pringle gave her away. The wedding was a very quiet one. The Moodies remained for a while in private lodgings, and then went down to Reydon, and after a visit to my Mother and sisters, the Moodies took a small cottage at Southwold, where their eldest child was born—a dear little girl, afterwards Mrs. Vickers, named after myself, and my godchild. The birth of this dear little child was a source of great rejoicing among her Aunts and the dear grandmother. I had remained in London for many months after the Moodies went down into Suffolk. When I joined the family again I found that my brother-in-law had determined upon emigrating to Canada. Not long after this resolution was taken he was joined by his friend Mr. Traill, a brother officer in the 21st Royal Scotch Fusilieers. They had been friends since boyhood, both Orkney men; they decided to try their fortunes in the Colony to which many families were about to emigrate. I became the wife of Thomas Traill. It is needless to dwell here on the subject as it occupies a place in my own autobiography, which will form the last part of this Family record.

I have confined myself in this homely and imperfect sketch of my beloved sister's life to the days of childhood and girlhood, when we two lived in childlike confidence and harmony, as we grew up side by side as loving friends, our lives running in parallel grooves, and this continued even after we married and left the old home at Reydon to share the untried fortunes of the new world in our forest homes in what is now Ontario.

The early account of our settlement and individual experiences [in Canada] each of us has given to the public; in my own Letters from "The Backwoods of Canada" which appeared in Knight's Library in 1835–6 [and] Mrs. Moodie's graphic and popular volume "Roughing It in the Bush" followed some years later.

These were interesting books furnishing information on the subject of domestic life in the Colony of which little, at that time, was known by the intending emigrant at home. The "Letters from the Backwoods," though badly edited and brought out, as to appearance and type and illustrations, was a success, became very popular, and must have paid the Publishers well, though it was not very remunerative to the writer. It must now be out of date, and out of print. Mrs. Moodie's is still much esteemed, especially in Ontario, and in the United States, and will no doubt re-appear in Canada in a newer form.

The most important of Mrs. Moodie's writings were in the form of novels. "Roughing It in the Bush" was followed by others—"Mark Hurdlestone" a book of much power in the delineation of character, "Flora Lindsay,"

"Dorothy Chance," "Life in the Clearings," and many other sketches of life in Canada, and other subjects.[7] I do not think a perfect collection of her works in verse, or prose, has ever been before the public. But it is possible such will one day be issued as an addition to Canadian literature.

But while I notice her literary and artistic talents, I must not omit to record that they were not her only ones. She was as remarkable in her skill in domestic life, in the regulation of her household & her bread, pastry, preserves, etc. were of the best. She excelled too in needlework, and all the many and various details that the life of a wife and mother involve were scrupulously attended to.

In this my sketch of my sister's life I have left [out] *much* that would be most interesting to the public, but it was not my intention to enter into her Colonial life—the trials, the joys, and the sorrows during a life of many long years. She has herself touched upon [it], and left the ravelled threads to be gathered up and woven into a perfect whole by other hands than mine, who now at an advanced age lay aside the pen with a saddened heart, for the sorrow of that which I dreaded has fallen upon me.

Out of the three that left England for a home in Canada, there remains but *One*, the oldest of the trio, *and I, only I, am left.*

"Ever so Lord for such is Thy Will"
C.P. Traill

∽

1   The Greenland docks at Rotherhythe. Once in the country Thomas Strickland kept two homes, one in Norwich, where he saw to his business interests, and the other near Bungay. Susanna Strickland was born near Bungay on December 6, 1803, and baptized in that town; from 1803 to 1808 the family lived at Stowe House, a manor house on the Flixton Road just outside of Bungay, a place that Traill fondly recalled in other parts of her memoir.

2   Anne Askew—a Lincolnshire woman who was burned as a heretic on July 16, 1546, at the age of twenty-five, for seeking the exact meaning of biblical texts and in the process defying her husband's authority. When she sought a divorce from him, she defended her action using the words of St. Paul.

3   A letter from Henry Thompson to Susanna Moodie— dated Framlingham [Suffolk] November 26, 1846—is part of the Patrick Hamilton Ewing Collection, Rare Books and Manuscripts, National Library of Canada. The letter, which is a fragment, discusses the Ritchie family in the present, reminiscences about shared experiences, and seeks to assess the state of religious belief in England in the 1840s.

4   The Congregationalist minister, Andrew Ritchie (1790–1848) of Wrentham (see Susanna Moodie, *Letters of a Lifetime*, ed. Carl Ballstadt, Elizabeth Hopkins, Michael Peterman [Toronto: University of Toronto Press, 1985], 16–17 and *Letters of Love and Duty: The Correspondence of Susanna and John Moodie*, ed. Ballstadt, Hopkins, Peterman [Toronto: University of Toronto Press, 1993], 6, 20, 33).

5   *Spartacus; A Roman Story* was published in 1822. No evidence has been found of a book (or story) by Susanna Strickland entitled "Jugurtha." For further details of Moodie's life and works see *Letters of a Lifetime* and *Letters of Love and Duty*.

6   *The History of Mary Prince. A West-Indian Slave* (1831) and *Ashton Warner* (1831).

7   "Dorothy Chance" was the title under which Moodie's last novel, *The World Before Them*, was serialized in the Montreal *Transcript* in 1867.

Backwoods Revisited

Lost Child

THE MILL OF THE RAPIDS.
A CANADIAN SKETCH

"The Mill of the Rapids. A Canadian Sketch" first appeared
in *Chambers's Edinburgh Journal* 7 (November 3, 1838),
322–23. Likely a part of Traill's proposed sequel to *The
Backwoods of Canada*, it was sold by Agnes Strickland to
the Chambers brothers as a separate entity. The events
described took place in the autumn of 1837. As a record of
an exciting canoe trip north to Young's mill (now Young's
Point) to have corn ground into grist, it bears comparison
with Susanna Moodie's sketch "A Trip to Stony Lake," in
Roughing It in the Bush. Both sisters give glowing accounts
of the hospitality and talents of the Young family and were
much taken by the scenery of Upper Katchewanook, the
falls at the Youngs' mill, the splendid openness of Clear
Lake, and in Moodie's case the rocky grandeur of Stony
Lake to the north of Clear. Of interest as well is the story
within the sketch of Betty and John Young being lost in the
"Smithtown" bush; this may be the first published account
by Traill of children lost in the backwoods, a subject that
would claim her attention for years.

One day last week I took a pleasant little trip up the lakes to Yorrit's mill;[1] the canoe was going with corn to be ground into grist, and as my husband was one of the party, and the weather very serene for the time of the year, I made up my mind to accompany him; so, leaving my little ones under the care of cousin Jane,[2] and well wrapped up in my Scotch plaid cloak, I took my seat among the sacks of grain, and determined to enjoy myself as much as I possibly could; my only business being to keep a watch-ful look-out for the blocks of granite and limestone-rock that lie so profusely scattered up and down the rapid waters by the islands in our lake, and give timely warning of "rocks ahead!" to the steersman—the water at this time being very low, so that it required great skill in the management of our frail craft to keep her from striking on the sunken rocks. In spite of all our care, and my vigilance, we were twice wedged between two blocks of granite, and it required all the united strength of the party to get the canoe afloat again. After these trifling delays, we got on delightfully; the rapids were soon overcome, and we found ourselves gently pursuing our calm and easy course in still deep water, with nothing to disturb the glassy mirror of the lake but the sudden plash of the wild ducks (flights of which passed us in abundance, winging their course towards warmer streams, where they might pass the coming winter), or the regular strokes of the oars, as they were plied with steady arm by our rowers. The deep shadows of the dark fringe of pines slept upon the waters, giving you the idea of perfect repose. The deciduous trees were leafless, and the long sea-green-tree moss hung in motionless but melancholy drapery from the cedars and soft maples that clothed the utmost verge of the low shores along which our little vessel was steered. Here and there I noticed little thickets of woody shrubs, leafless, but gay with bright scarlet berries, which are here called partridge-berries, from these birds making them their food at this season of the year. Of the nature of this shrub, or its fruits, I can at present give you no information, as I have never been able to examine either leaf, blossom, or berry, minutely: I only know that nothing could equal the beauty and brilliancy of its effect that morning, for the early sun had not yet melted away the icy crust that encased each separate berry, and they glittered resplendant in his beams, contrasted with the dark evergreens behind them.

After passing the Katchewanook—that, you know, is our lake—with its rapids and islands, and Bessaquaquan lake—on the shores of which is M——'s clearing, we entered a narrow channel, with a peninsulated shore on either side; the banks, from being low and somewhat swampy in parts, now became steeper and more rocky; large masses of bluish granite and limestone lying in heaps against the shores, as if a natural embankment cast up by the waters. Passing this narrow strait, we entered upon another expanse of water, which is called by the settlers "One-Tree Lake," from a small islet exhibiting on its barren surface a solitary stunted tree—oak, I think it looked like. The head of this lake presented more variety; the shores were prettily indented with little bays, though still nothing that you could call decidedly picturesque. The islands at the upper part were steeper, and I noticed some pretty trees. As to the shore on the left hand, it was dull and monotonous, presenting only that aspect of barrenness and desolation which the fire leaves behind in its track. Beyond this lake the waters flowed with great rapidity: the channel becoming narrower, and losing its lake-like character, it once more resumes the semblance of a wide, majestic, and swiftly flowing river. In short, I recognised once more my old friend the Otonabee here set free from beds of rice, and choking rushes and reeds, that curb its impetuous career, and deform the purity of its sparkling waters.[3] The higher up we proceeded in our voyage, the narrower and the wilder grew the stream—steep banks, and rapid current so strong, that the nervous strokes of the oars could barely impel our loaded vessel along the upward channel. An upset here might have been attended with fatal results, at least to one of the party: but I felt no fear; the little risk just served to excite and keep one's energies alive and watchful. During the spring floods, and after heavy autumnal rains, these rapids are very strong. One of the Miss Yorrits showed me a little bridge over a cut in the mill-race, above which the water had flowed that spring. The water in the race was then seven or eight feet below the high-water mark.

The mill, with the miller's large clearing, stands on the Smithtown shore, at the head of the rapids, and just below Clear lake, a fine expanse of water several miles in extent; from the transparency of its waters it takes its name.[4]

I was not sorry to step on shore and warm myself beside the open hearth of the hospitable miller and his kind industrious daughters, who gave me a most hearty, and I believe sincere welcome, to their dwelling. The family had been settled some years on this spot, and possessed in themselves many comforts and some luxuries, to which the later emigrant must long be a stranger. Yet these had had to struggle hard for some years with every disadvantage, for the soil they were located upon was in most parts an accumulation of limestone rocks, and they were many miles from a store, and few lots settled for miles round them, and these only by a few poor pensioners. They had one grand point in their favour: they possessed able-working hands in their own family, the largest part of whom were sons; and with the united strength and industry of the young men without, and the daughters within, the work of the farm went on well. But one of the great resources of the male part of the family was hunting and shooting. The skins of the game were the great object they kept in view. Pat and Francis not only kept the house well supplied with every kind of game, but they made something very considerable every year by the sale of the skins and furs of the animals they caught. These chiefly consisted of beavers, bears, deer, otters, martens, minx, racoons, squirrels, and muskrats, for which they found a ready market at Peterboro or Cobourg.

The house was never without the finest fish, which they all knew how to spear in the lakes—white fish, salmon, trouts, and bass, which were either dried after the Indian fashion, and exposed to a few hours' smoke in the chimney, or pickled if they could not dispose of them fresh; deer hams and bear hams were among their winter stores, and the flesh of the beaver, especially the beaver's tail, they reckoned among their dainty meats.

When I first came in, I found the two young women busy dyeing some silks and ribbons black, to make up into bonnets, and I was astonished at the nice fresh black they had produced. The art of dyeing, I must tell you, is among the common accomplishments of a Canadian settler's wife and daughters. All the homespun dresses and stockings, &c. are dyed in the yarn by them, and few of the older settlers' houses are without its indigo vat. Many of the native woods and barks are used in the various processes of dyeing. The butternut produces a fine brown in spring, and a good black can be made with it in the summer and fall. The white oak gives a beautiful purple. The leaves of the stramonium or thorn-apple give a delicate straw colour—with many others that I cannot now call to mind. With the uses of foreign dye-woods and drugs they are all well and practically acquainted. As a considerable portion of the emigrants of this province are mechanics, it is no difficult matter to get the yarn prepared by the farmer's household woven into cloth. "We make every thing we want, and every article we use for home consumption, with the exception of groceries, salt, spices, and tea, and the finer sorts of wearing apparel," said Miss Yorrit. "We spin, we card, and dye our own yarn; we make up the clothing, both gowns for ourselves, and coats and trousers for our brothers and father; we knit all the stockings, mits, nightcaps, and comforters, with under garments for ourselves, during the long winter evenings; we burn candles or lamps of the fat we prepare from the beasts that are brought in; we make abundance of sugar and molasses and spruce beer from the maples; we are never without plenty of preserved fruits, for we have sugar at command; we make quantities of soap, hard as well as soft; as to feather beds and pillows, we have more than enough from the common fowls, and the wild ducks that the boys shoot; we even make our own shoes, and our brothers make theirs." In short, I cannot describe to you all the useful things these two good industrious girls do.

After I was well warmed, I left my two hostesses to pursue their domestic occupations undisturbed, while I walked out on to the clearing, to see the operations of the grist-mill; but as I suppose you would not feel deeply interested in my remarks on the machinery, which I should be at a great loss to describe, I shall only take you with me in my out-of-door rambles over the rocky field that skirted the river. Here, indeed, I found abundant food for observation, fresh objects of interest starting up beneath my feet continually in the blocks of limestone that beset my path; these seemed one mass of fossil vegetable or animal substance, sometimes covering the surface of the stone like the rough coating of a rock melon; here were thousands of tiny cockleshells, some so minute that you could scarcely distinguish the form, others large and perfect, presenting the peculiar appearance as if a finger and thumb had compressed the valves. There was one fossil of such frequent recurrence, that it attracted my attention, and not a little excited my curiosity: this was the outline of a fish; the backbones, with the long bones attached on either side, and even the forked bones near the fins, in a perfect state. I consumed at least a couple of hours in my rambles amidst these interesting objects, after which I made the best of my way to the mill-house. And now behold us at dinner at the hospitable board of the worthy miller. Many were the apologies which were uttered by Betty and Nora for having no better fare to set before me than what were to us dainties, in the form of a fine, fat, tender, boiled saddle of venison, delicately corned, and cooked most excellently, and served up with greens of the most verdant hue, and white floury potatoes, besides a dish of the finest and most delightful fried fish that I had ever tasted, the preparation of which did infinite credit to Nora's culinary skill. For my part, my voyage up the lakes, and the walk I had taken afterwards, had given me an excellent appetite, and I greatly relished my dinner.

When the repast was over, as I had expressed my intention of walking as far as Clear lake, Miss Yorrit very kindly offered to show me the path which led to it, as she was fearful I should hardly be able to find it without a guide. The afternoon was so fine, and the air so clear and pure, and yet so mild withal, that I felt my spirits quite enlivened; and though the cares and sickness of five years had somewhat tamed the elasticity of my step, and sobered the vivacity of my temper, I found I could enjoy a scramble through the wild woods yet, and overcome the difficulties that beset our rugged path in the shape of huge moss-grown trunks and blocks of granite, with as light a heart as ever I had done. After a winding walk of about half a mile, the hardwood trees began to give place to the sombre hemlock, spruce, and cedar; the ground became more thickly interspersed with stones and huge roots twining and interlacing each other like a strange net-work; we knew from these signs that we were drawing near the object of our journey; and soon the bright gleam of the waters, quivering like a sheet of silver beneath the full rays of the afternoon sun, broke upon our view. Another minute, and we found ourselves on the rocky margin of Clear lake; and well did it deserve the name from its most transparent waters—so pure that it looked indeed like fluid crystal.

The eternal spirit of silence seemed to preside over this lonely but not unlovely spot; its broad still bosom reflecting on its waveless surface the deep azure of the sky, with its few scattered shining white clouds. The long lofty lines of pines that fringed the bays and promontories, were mirrored there; but not a sound broke the stillness of the scene, not a bough stirred. There was not even an insect on the wing: bird, beast, and fish, were all mute and moveless. The only living thing visible besides myself and my companion, was a solitary heron, on the dry bough of a stunted tree that overhung the lake on the opposite shore, watching with patient vigilant eye the still waters for its finny prey. The sober dark plumage of this lonely watcher, and his quiescent motionless form, rather added to the silent spirit of the landscape, than gave to it the least tone of animation.

At the head of Clear lake are two islands, which form the entrance into Stony lake. One, which I think I heard called Big island, was a majestic elevation of pines. The soft blue haze that rested on these islands had a charming effect, mellowing and softening the dark shade of the evergreens that crowned them with hearse-like gloom. This same Stony lake do I most ardently long to see. I am told that it contains a thousand wild and romantic scenes, and, in miniature, resembles the lake of the thousand islands in the St Lawrence. In many parts the rocky islands are more picturesque, some of them shooting up in bare pointed craggy pinnacles abruptly from the depth of the water, while others are fancifully grouped, and clothed with flowers and trees. The Indians frequent this lake greatly. As we stood on the margin of Clear lake, on a huge block of stone which I had mounted for the benefit of a more extensive view, I noticed a barrier of limestone rock opposite to us. The land above was cleared. This, I was told, was called the "Battery;" and, in good truth, it would have been a fine natural defence in any situation that had required such an embankment. Whilst I was admiring the Battery, and pitying the possessor of the barren-looking plain above it, my attention was called by my companion to another mass of rock not twenty paces from that we occupied. "I never look at that stone," said Miss Yorrit, "without its bringing back to my mind the time when my brother John and I were lost in the woods."

Now, I have almost as great a love for a story about being lost in the woods, as I had when a child on the knee for the pitiful story of the Babes in the Wood.[5] I eagerly besought Miss Betty to favour me with the history of her own and her brother's wanderings. It seems that some six weeks after the family first made their settlement in the bush, they had occasion to procure a supply of flour, but whether from some distant settler's farm, or from Peterboro, I cannot precisely remember; be it as it may, they had no road at that time cut, but only the uncertain path marked by a blaze cut on the trees. It is no difficult matter to suppose that two inexperienced bush travellers should lose their way, and that, once lost, they should be left without a clue to regain it. After wandering up and down, hither and thither, in every direction, the poor forlorn ones became completely bewildered, and night set in upon them, amid the pathless gloom of the forest. It was just about the beginning of the fall. The summer had been long, hot, and dry, no rain of any account having fallen for weeks, so that the creeks and springs were all dried up; not a drop of water was to be found; not a berry to relieve the thirst that oppressed them, and which increased to an intolerable degree. Luckily, the young man had a steel and flint in his pocket; but this would have availed them but little, had not his ingenuity supplied him with a substitute for tinder; he stripped the thin silvery bark from the birch, which is of a very inflammable nature, and having beaten it fine upon a smooth stone, and kept it in his bosom to dry it thoroughly, it was found to ignite very readily; and by this means they were soon able to raise a cheerful fire, which answered the double purpose of relieving their minds from the dread of wild beasts, and imparted a cheerful warmth to them during the chilly hours of night. Even as early as the last week in August, the nights and early mornings are frosty, and fire is not only acceptable, but necessary to the comfort of any one obliged to pass the night abroad.

After a long search the following day, they discovered a little water in the hollow of a decayed stump, which had probably been collected for many weeks, and most unpalatable it proved; but thirst like theirs knew no nicety, and they were glad to swallow plentiful draughts of a beverage they loathed; and then they mingled some of it with a portion of the flour they had with them, and baked a cake upon a flat stone by their fire; but they felt little hunger compared with the dreadful thirst that tormented them. The next day and part of the night were spent in unsuccessful wanderings; on the morning of the third, when despair had begun to take possession of their hearts, they found themselves among a dense thicket of hemlocks and cedars, and soon their eyes were gladdened by the gleam of water sparkling through the branches. Pushing hastily forwards, they emerged from the mass of evergreens to the rocky margin of a fine expansive sheet of water. "It was here, at the foot of this very block of stone, that we emerged from the forest, and never was the sight of water so precious or so beautiful as this appeared; we knelt down and drank, and bathed our faces, our hands, and our feet in it again and again; nor did it once enter into our minds that we were almost within sight of the smoke of our own cottage; on the contrary, we supposed ourselves to be on the shore of Mud lake,[6] or some of the higher waters, not being aware that our rambles had led us within half a mile of our own home." Under the impression that they were on the opposite side of the township, the question naturally arose to them, what course to pursue to ensure their safe return. This involved some difficulty, their future safety depending upon their decision. At last the young man came to the conclusion, at all events, to follow the downward course of the water, which must eventually lead to some civilized spot, while the contrary direction would as certainly lead them to the wild unsettled portions of the country. After a minute and attentive examination of the flow of the water, and the appearance of the shores, he at length determined which way the current flowed. "Judge of our surprise and delight, madam," said my companion, "when, after a few minutes' walk along the stony shore, we found ourselves beside the rapids in front of our own clearing, though at that time the ground was covered thickly with trees. We could scarcely credit our good fortune; and now we think that in all probability we were never farther than a mile from our own home, when we had supposed ourselves to be far away from it."

Tales of persons wandering in the woods, and being lost for days, when all the time they were within a short distance of their own habitations, are quite common in the uncleared parts of America.

When we returned from our walk, we found the house beautifully swept, and made as neat as Nora's busy hands could render it. As the grinding of the grist was not yet finished, and we had an hour's moonlight to depend upon, we were easily prevailed upon to take an early tea, which was quickly prepared, with that ready hospitality which is so truly valuable, as it studies the convenience as well as comfort of a guest, imposing neither restraint nor delay. And, truly, if I enjoyed my dinner, I was no less gratified after my walk in the woods by the nice light cakes, baked in a frying-pan before the glowing embers of a log fire, and the delicious cranberry jam, preserved with maple molasses, that accompanied them, to say nothing of the good fresh butter, and an enormous shanty loaf, hot from the bake-kettle on the hearth. But what I enjoyed yet more than the good cup of tea and the nice cakes, &c., was the conversation of our host, a respectable white-haired hale old man.[7] And many were the wild romantic tales he told of "ould Ireland" and the scenes of his infancy. The time, the season, the character of those about you, the peculiar circumstances attending such narrations, will give a charm to it which more sober realities have not the power to excite. The shadows of the evening were beginning to grow grey around us as we stood grouped round the red blazing logs of the wide stone chimney—the old silver-haired man, with animated face, speaking with all the energy that an Irishman could throw into his voice; the deep attention and fixed looks of his daughters, drinking in each word he uttered; while in a rude block of stone in the chimney corner, his hands resting on his knees, and his thin pale face upraised with wondering eyes, sat a little orphan boy, the child of a neighbour who had died, leaving three helpless babes to the protection and charity of the world. (I have more to tell you about these orphans, but not here.[8]) Ever and anon the pauses between the old man's voice were filled up by the hoarse dashing of the mill-stream, and the deep cadence of the wind among the heavy pine tops on the opposite shore. There was something in all this that harmonised with the subject in discussion, and I had entered so fully into the spirit of the scene, that I was grieved when the summons was sent from the boat to say all was ready for departure.

Bidding a hearty farewell to these hospitable people, we once more embarked on the swift-flowing waters. It was a lovely night; the rapid downward current bore us along with little effort or exertion on the part of the rowers; the moon and stars shone brightly on our watery way; no accident occurred; the canoe did not so much as once grate her sides against the treacherous rocks; and I enjoyed my calm voyage as much as I had done the rest of the day's adventure. The joyous voices of my little ones as we drew near the house told me all were well and safe, and you would have envied papa and mamma the endearing kisses from the sweet lips that were held up to greet them, and the shout of delight with which they received the bits of maple sugar which these good girls had given me for James and Kate.

∽

1   Young's mill. Yorrit is either a misreading of Young by the Chambers' compositors or a deliberate change of name on Traill's part.

2   Thomas Traill's cousin, Jane Alcock, came out to Canada from Scotland in 1836 to be a companion to Catharine and to help her with her two children, James (b. 1833) and Katherine (b. 1836). A third child, Thomas *Henry* Strickland, was not born until 1837.

3   Because of its narrowness in places, the early settlers thought of Lake Katchewanook, which is really little more than a widening of the Otonabee north of present-day Lakefield, as several distinct small lakes—Katchewanook and Bessaguaguan (Bessikskoon according to Moodie) to the north where the Moodies had their farm and clearing, and One-Tree Lake.

4   The Otonabee River is the dividing line between Douro Township on the east and Smith Township (Smithtown) on the west.

5   "Babes in the Wood" or "Children in the Wood" is a ballad in which a wicked man employs two ruffians to kill his young niece and nephew in order to acquire the property left to them by his brother. Unable to go through with the murder, one of the ruffians kills the other and then abandons the children in the wood; they subsequently perish.

6   Mud Lake is Chemong Lake to the west of Clear Lake but still in Smith Township.

7   Old Francis Young had brought his family of nine to the area in 1825 as part of the Peter Robinson settlement. His sons William and Patrick took the lead in developing the grist mill and adjacent properties.

8   A reference to the sketch "Generosity of the Poor."

A Canadian Scene

"A Canadian Scene" appeared in an American magazine, *The Ladies Garland* 4 (1841), 270–71, and later in *Chambers's Edinburgh Journal** 12 (1843), 79. No explanation exists for this American connection, though, given the fact that at least one other Traill sketch, "The Autobiography of an Unlucky Wit" (1839), found an American outlet about this time, Traill was likely doing her best to find American markets for her work. Certainly, her family's financial situation in the late 1830s called for such efforts on her part. "A Canadian Scene" is one of several sketches in which Traill dealt with the pioneer family's abiding fear of losing a child in the backwoods or bush. "The Mill on the Rapids," which is included in this collection, contains such a narrative. Both "The Lost Child" (*Chambers's Edinburgh Journal* [September 7, 1839]) and "The Two Widows of Hunter's Creek" (*The Home Journal* 1 [1849]), which are not included here, focus entirely on the subject. Rupert Schieder provides a careful examination of the ways in which such early sketches led to Traill's first and only Canadian novel, *Canadian Crusoes*, published in England in 1852 (see Catharine Parr Traill, *Canadian Crusoes: A Tale of the Rice Lake Plains*, ed. Rupert Schieder [Ottawa: Carleton University Press, 1986], xvii–xx).

On a raw Sabbath morning, after a night of heavy rain, in the month of August, we were assembled round the breakfast-table in our log-cabin, when the sound of a horse's hoofs, followed by a smart rap on the door, announced a visitor. It was Mr. Reid, who informed us that his child, which had been missing on the plains the night before, was not yet found, and begging of us, as we were near the ground, to turn out and assist in the search.[1]

What are called plains in Canada are ranges of high ground, which stretch through the country, usually parallel to some lake or river, and extend in breadth from two or three to twenty or thirty miles.[2] The soil is sandy, and except near a stream, thinly wooded; while the ground is covered with swarth, intermixed with the most brilliant wild flowers, and occasional beds of blaeberries and wild strawberries; thickets of brush, frequently interspersed, rendering it difficult for a stranger to keep his course.

It is usual to make pic-nics to these fruit-gardens, and several of our number had been there the day before. On their return, they mentioned Mr. Reid searching for his child, but we had no apprehensions for its safety. Some immediately started for the appointed rendezvous, while those who were left behind to look after the cattle were not slow in following. Scarcely had we reached the foot of the ridge, which was about a quarter of a mile from our house, when a severe thunder storm commenced, accompanied by heavy rain; and as we entered the forest, the roar of the storm, with the crash of falling trees, had a most awful effect. We thought of the terrors which must be felt by the poor lost one, and fervently wished it might be in some place of safety. Holding on our way, the smoke of a large fire soon brought us to head-quarters, where we found a number of people assembled, going about without any sort of organisation. The father had gone to seek some rest, after wandering the woods all night, calling on the name of his child, for they had got a notion that any noise or unknown voice would alarm the child, and cause her to hide.

Inquiry was now made for those who lived near and were best acquainted with the woods, and all of us were assigned different portions to search. My course lay through a dense cedar swamp, in the rear of our clearing. I wandered alone until towards evening, and never did I spend a Sabbath whose impressions were more solemn. My footsteps fell noiselessly on the deep moss, beneath which I could frequently hear the trickling streams, while the thunder roared above, and the hoary trunks of the gray cedars reflected the lightning's flash, or, shivered by its fury, fell crashing to the ground. After wandering for some time without success, I took shelter from the rain in a ruined log-house, which, by the remains of a rail fence, showed that a small clearing around had been once rescued from the forest; but the gloomy desolation of the scene seemed to have driven its possessor to seek a habitation nearer the society of men. We met at even without success, but, on comparing notes, were not disheartened, as we had yet searched only the out-skirts of the plains; the object of our search, we fancied, might have wandered deeper into the woods; but then came the awful reflection, that they abounded with wolves and bears, which often alarmed the settlers themselves; and stories were not wanting to render her situation more alarming. We were now, however, compelled to return, leaving a party to keep a look-out, and continue the fire. Next morning, the news having spread over the country, our number was increased to about two hundred. So great seemed the anxiety, that the store-keeper had left his store, as well as the farmer his hay unraked. All seemed to think only of the lost child. We first formed parties of ten or twelve, and ranged in different directions; then long lines were formed, each so near his neighbour, as to command the ground between. The Indians, belonging to a village eight or ten miles off, were sent for; every effort was used.[3] Stretching far into the heart of the forests, not a bush was left, not a log unexam-ined. But again we returned without success. Some of our number were again left, thinking that in the stillness of the night they might hear the cries of the child and, wandering about, might thus discover it.

This morning was fine, and our number seemed increased to three or four hundred. Twelve or fourteen Indians were also there, on whom much dependance was placed. They, however, and with reason, would not search where we came. We again entered the forest, and traversed some of the heavily wooded parts. The scene was in many parts magnificent; and advancing in a straight line, we were led into many spots where human feet but rarely trod. The deer and foxes rushed affrighted from their lairs, and the sporting propensities of many of our friends were hardly restrained by fear of alarming the child. We began now to get disheartened, and instead of a steady search often scattered ourselves over the beds of blaeberries, or feasted on strawberries, which were frequently scattered in rich clusters along the ground. The wild flowers, too, in the thinner woods, were most brilliant; many of them are bright scarlet, and from the calmness of the atmosphere, their colour attains to great perfection. The joyous news was now spread that the Indians had found tracks; but on examining the spot, I felt certain they were my own footsteps around the old log-house; the ground being soft, they had contracted, so as to appear like a child's. These Indians fell far short of the intelligence with which they are usually painted. They were sullen and taciturn, not, seemingly, from a want of desire to converse, but rather, as I imagine, from sheer stupidity. The Indians having failed in following out the tracks, we were again thrown on our own resources, and leaving a watch, returned home.

This morning a large number again assembled, many from a considerable distance. But the search seemed carried on with less energy as the prospect of success diminished; the day was spent in traversing the woods in long ranks, but many seemed careless; and though the finding of a saucer which the child had carried seemed to revive hope, we parted at night fully persuaded that we should never find her alive.

Mr. Reid had now been out with us every day, and looked fatigued both in body and mind. This morning, on meeting in an altogether new quarter, he told us he had now no hope of finding his child alive, but it would be some satisfaction to ascertain her fate; and if we would use our utmost endeavour this day, he dare hardly ask to trespass further on our time.

We now started with a determined energy, and beat round for some hours. At length we mustered the whole party to go back four or five miles to a burn, beyond which we imagined she would not wander; every thicket was examined, and many places seen which had been missed before. It was beautiful to see the deer bound harmless along our track, as the old hunters raised their sticks, wishing they had been rifles; yet we reached the hill overhanging the burn without success. Here we at once stretched ourselves on the sunny bank, and soon stripped the blaeberries of their black fruit. The younger part of us raked about the banks of the burn, while the elders lay down to rest, satisfied that our fruitless labour was now done. When the sun began to decline, we all started homewards, like the company breaking up from some country race-course. Many used praise-worthy endeavours to bring us to order, but in vain. Sometimes we formed line; again it was broken by a startled deer or a covey of pheasants; after which numbers bounded, shouting and yelling with unseasonable merriment. Some trudged along, deep in conversation; while others, in short sleeves, overcome by heat, seated themselves on a log, or, leaning on their companions, jogged lazily along. At length we descended into a hollow thicket, in whose cool shade we again recovered a sort of line. Scarcely had we begun to ascend the opposite hill, when a faint cheer was heard; immediately the woods re-echoed the response of our whole line, and we rushed onward, heedless of every impediment, until we reached a large clearing, amidst which stood an empty frame of a house; and approaching it, there was Mr. Reid, with his child in his arms. I will not attempt to describe his joy; we all crowded round to get one glimpse, and then returned to our homes, elated with our success. After being in the woods from Saturday morning until

Thursday evening, the child was found by a party of two or three who had straggled from the rest. They saw her standing on a log, and her first question to one of them who advanced was, "Do you know where Mr. Reid lives?" What had been the sufferings of the little creature for six days and five nights in the open forest, may be left to the imagination of the reader.[4]

          〜

1   Robert Reid (1773–1856), one of the founding settlers of Douro, was a large landholder and farmer who first came to the area in 1822. The Reids were related to the Stewarts, with whom they emigrated from Ireland, and the Stricklands, Sam Strickland having married Reid's eldest daughter Mary in 1827. All but one of the Reid children were born in Ireland; the lost girl may have been Catharine Charlotte Reid (b. 1821) though her age makes the case suspect in terms of Traill's own experience. Interestingly, Traill adopts the voice of a male settler of Scottish birth in telling this tale. It is one of only a few stories in which she employs such a narrative strategy.

2   Traill refers here to the higher land to the east of Lake Katchewanook and the Otonabee River, which includes Douro and parts of Dummer Township.

3   Likely the Native peoples from the Hiawartha reserve on the north shore of Rice Lake.

4   The text reads "three days and two nights" but this is clearly inconsistent with the details of the search as described.

FEMALE TRIALS IN THE BUSH

This sketch appeared first in England in *Sharpe's London Journal* 15 (1852), 22–26, and a year later in Toronto as sketch No. 7 in "Forest Gleanings" in the *Anglo-American Magazine* 2 (1853), 426–30. Its heroine is Louisa Herriot[t], born Francis Louise Irvine (the daughter of William Irvine, Staff Physician to the forces). She married Herriott in July 1834, emigrating with him to the little clearing on the Otonabee River north of Peterborough, which he called Selby (now Lakefield). Herriott, whom Traill identified enthusiastically in *The Backwoods of Canada* as "an enterprising young Scotchman, the founder of the village" (Letter XV, September 20, 1834), had leased the Douro river-front property from James Thomson and built a bridge and a mill there in 1833. He was, however, soon in trouble because of bad luck, unpaid debts, and limited available resources; in fact, by 1835, though he had invested more than 2,000 pounds, he had lost to Thomson both the property and what was by then a double saw mill and grist mill. In a petition to Sir John Colborne, Herriott asked to be protected from his immediate debts and to be granted a government lease to the property; letters from J. W. D. Moodie, Thomas Traill, Sam Strickland, and others supported the value of his efforts. The government refused to act, however, deeming it a private business matter between Herriott and Thomson.[1] Having lost all, the Herriotts apparently returned to Britain.

What Traill used in *The Backwoods* as a stellar example of initiative and progress thus became (even before her book went to press) the subject of a grim, cautionary tale in the spirit of Susanna Moodie's darker moods. Still, in attending to the realm of women's experience, Traill makes it clear that a reverse in fortunes can stimulate a positive reversal of attitude; hence, Louisa Herriott's initial disappointment with the backwoods gives way under duress to her discovery within herself of resources she hadn't recognized or drawn upon previously. Readers may be interested to note that Traill's story "The Bereavement" (see *Pioneering Women: Short Stories by Canadian Women*, ed. Lorraine McMullen and Sandra Campbell [Ottawa: University of Ottawa Press, 1993], 39–50) recounts the suffering of another woman associated with the Selby mills at this time, the wife of the mill's overseer who was not of the same social rank as Traill herself or Louisa Herriott. For all her interest in the range of human experience, social rank was never far from Traill's mind. "Female Trials in the Bush" is also reprinted in *The Prose of Life: Sketches from Victorian Canada*, ed. Carole Gerson and Kathy Mezei (Downsview: ECW Press, 1981) and *Canadian Short Fiction: From Myth to Modern*, ed. W. H. New (Scarborough: Prentice-Hall, 1986).

t has been remarked how much more prone to discontent, the wives of the emigrants are than their husbands; and it generally is the fact, but why is it so? A little reflection will show the cause. It is generally allowed that woman is by nature and habit more strongly attached to home and all those domestic ties and associations that form her sources of happiness, than man. She is accustomed to limit her enjoyments within a narrow circle; she scarcely receives the same pleasures that man does from travelling and exchange of place; her little world is *home*, it is or should be her sphere of action, her centre of enjoyment; the severing her at once forever from it makes it dearer in her eyes, and causes her the severest pangs.

It is long before she forms a home of comfort to herself like that she has left behind her, in a country that is rough, hard and strange; and though a sense of duty will, and does, operate upon the few to arm them with patience to bear, and power to act, the larger proportion of emigrant wives, sink into a state of hopeless apathy, or pining discontent, at least for a season, till time that softener of all human woes, has smoothed, in some measure, the roughness of the colonists' path and the spirit of conformity begins to dispose faithful wives to the endeavor to create a new home of comfort, within the forest solitudes.

There is another excuse for the unhappy despondency too frequently noticed among the families of the higher class of emigrants; and as according to an old saying, "prevention is better than cure," I shall not hesitate to plead the cause of my sex, and point out the origin of the domestic misery to which I allude.

There is nothing more common than for a young settler of the better class, when he has been a year or two in the colony, and made some little progress in clearing land and building, to go to England for a wife. He is not quite satisfied with the paucity of accomplishments and intellectual acquirements among the daughters of the Canadians, he is ambitious of bringing out a young lady, fit to be the companion of a man of sense and taste, and thoughtlessly induces some young person of delicate and refined habits to unite her fate to his. Misled by his sanguine description of his forest home and his hopes of future independence, she listens with infinite satisfaction to his account of a large number of acres, which may be valuable or nearly worthless, according to the local advantages they possess; of this, she of course knows nothing, excepting from the impressions she receives from her lover.

He may in a general way tell her that as a bush settler's wife, she must expect to put up with some privations at first, and the absence of a few of those elegant refinements of life which she has been accustomed to enjoy; but these evils are often represented as temporary, for he has rarely the candour to tell her the truth, the whole truth and nothing but the truth.

Deceived by her lover and deceiving herself into the fond belief that her love for him will smooth every difficulty, she marries, and is launched upon a life for which she is totally unfitted by habits, education and inclination, without due warning of the actual trials she is destined to encounter.

There is not only cruelty but even want of worldly wisdom in these marriages. The wife finds she has been deceived, and becomes fretful, listless and discontented; and the husband, when too late, discovers that he has transplanted a tender exotic, to perish beneath the withering influence of an ungenial atmosphere, without benefitting by its sweetness or beauty. I need hardly dwell on the domestic evils arising from this state of things, but I would hold such marriages up as a warning to both parties.

Some will say, but are these things so? and is the change really so striking between a life in England and one in the colonies? I speak that which I have seen, and testify that which I do know. Even under the fairest and most favorable circumstances, the difference must necessarily be great between a rich fertile country, full of resources, and one where all has to be created or supplied at the expense of time and money. But I speak more especially of those, who, living in the less cultivated and populous portions of the colony, are of course exposed to greater privations and disadvantages, as settlers in the bush must be. In towns and populous districts these hardships are less remarkable.

I remember among many instances that have fallen under my notice, one somewhat remarkable for the energetic trials of female fortitude that were called forth by a train of circumstances, most adverse and unexpected.

A young man residing in our neighbourhood, of sanguine disposition and slender property, had contrived by means of credit and a little money to start a large concern, a saw mill, a store, tavern, and other buildings, which were to form the germ of a large village. Full of hopes of the most extravagant kind, if he deceived others, I believe he also deceived himself into the vain belief that all his various castles, were destined to make his individual fortune, and confer a lasting benefit on the country where they were situated. Under this delusion, and finding moreover that it was absolutely necessary to raise resources for carrying on his schemes, he went home, and was not long in forming an acquaintance with an accomplished young lady of some fortune. She was an orphan, and charmed with the novelty of the life he described, she consented to marry him and become the queen of the village of which he gave her so glowing a picture. Perhaps at that period he was not fully aware of the fact, that the property of the young lady was under the control of trustees, and that the interest only was at her command, and fortunate it was for her that the guardians were inflexible in their principles, and resisted every solicitation to resign any part of the capital.

The young bride, accustomed to the domestic beauties and comforts of the mother country, beheld with dismay the long tract of gloomy pine wood through which she journeyed to her forest home, and the still more unseemly fields, blackened by charred pine and cedar stumps, in the midst of which rose the village, whose new and half finished buildings failed to excite any feeling in the breast but bitter disappointment and aversion; and she wept and sighed for all that was fair and beautiful in her own beloved country, rendered now ten times more lovely by the contrast with all she beheld around her; yet though she was miserable and discontented, she clung with passionate love to her husband, and, with womanly fondness, made every sort of excuse for him—even to herself, and always to others. It was this love which, as it increased, upheld her as the sad reality of ruin arrived. Misfortune, as an armed man, came fast upon the devoted pair—every fair and flattering prospect vanished. Unable to provide for the satisfaction of his importunate creditors as he had expected to do from his wife's property, they would no longer be put off and he became a perfect prisoner in his own house. The land, buildings, all, faded as it were from his grasp; even the yearly income arising from her money, had been forestalled, and all her costly clothing went by degrees, all her pretty ornaments and little house-hold business were disposed of piece-meal, to supply their daily wants. All, all were gone, and with fresh trials, fresh privations, came unwonted courage and energy to do and to bear. She was now a mother, and the trials of maternity were added to her other arduous duties. She often lamented her want of knowledge and ability in the management of her infant, for she had been totally unaccustomed to the trouble of young children. To add to her sorrows, sickness seized her husband, he who had been used to a life of activity and bustle, scarcely caring to rest within doors, unless at meal-times was sunk under the effects of confinement, chagrin and altered diet, and a long obstinate intermittent ensued.[2]

Though to some persons it might appear a trifling evil, there was nothing in all her sad reverse of condition that seemed so much to annoy my poor friend as the discolouring of her beautiful hands; she would often sigh as she looked down on them and say, "I used to be so vain of them, and never thought to employ them in menial offices, such as necessity has driven us to."

Poor thing! she had not been trained to such servile tasks as I have seen her occupied in, and I pitied her the more because I saw her bearing up so bravely under such overwhelming trials; she who had come out to our woods, not two years before, a bride, a proud fastidious woman, unable and unwilling to take part in the best household labour, who would sit on the side of her bed while a servant drew the silk stocking and satin slippers on her tiny white feet, and dressed her from head to foot—who despised the least fare that could be set before her by any of her neighbours—who must despatch a messenger almost daily to the distant town for fresh meat and biscuits—and new white bread, was now compelled to clothe herself and her babe, to eat the coarsest fare, black tea unsweetened and only softened with milk, instead of rich cream which she walked twice or thrice a week to fetch from my house or that of my sister-in-law,[3] bearing her stone pitcher in one hand, with the additional weight of her baby on her arm. So strange a thing is woman's love, that she, whom I had been wont to consider decidedly selfish, now showed a generous and heroic devotion towards the man whose thoughtlessness had reduced her to that state of poverty and privation that seemed to make her regardless of poverty. What personal sacrifices did she not make, what fatigues undergo? I have met her coming from a small field where oats had been sown, with a sheaf on her back, which she had cut with her own fair hands to feed an old ox—the only remnant of stock that escaped the creditors, and which was destined to supply the household with beef the ensuing fall. Yet she was quite cheerful and almost laughed at her unusual occupation. There was a poor Irish girl who staid with her to the last and never forsook her in her adverse fortune, but she had been kind and considerate to her when many mistresses would have turned her out of their house, and now she staid with her and helped her in her time of need.

One day I came to visit her, fearing from her unusual absence, that something was amiss with the child or herself. I found her lying on a rude sort of sofa, which she had very ingeniously made, by nailing some boards together, and covered with chintz, after having stuffed it with hay,—for she was full of contrivances; "they amused her, and kept her from thinking of her troubles," she said. She looked very pale, her fair hair being neglected, and there was an air of great languor and fatigue visible in her frame. But when I expressed my apprehension that she, too, had fallen a prey to ague or fever, she eagerly replied,—"Oh, no, I am only dreadfully tired. Do you know, I was wandering in the woods a great part of the night!"

"On what errand?" I inquired, in some surprise,—on which she related her adventures, in these words:—

"I had reason to suppose that English letters of some consequence had arrived by post, and as I had no one to send for them, to whom I dared trust them, I made up my mind, yesterday morning, to walk down for them myself. I left my little boy to the care of Jane and his father, for, carrying him a distance of so many miles, and through such roads, was quite beyond my strength. Well, I got my letters and a few necessary articles that I wanted, at the store; but what with my long walk, and the delay one always meets with in town, it was nearly sunset before I began to turn my steps homeward. I then found, to my great distress, that I had lost my faithful 'Nelson,'—[a great Newfoundland dog that accompanied her wherever she went.] I lingered a good while in the hope that my brave dog would find me out, but concluding, at last, that he had been shut up in one of the stores, I hurried on, afraid of the moon setting before I should be out of the dark wood. I thought, too, of my boy, and wondered if his father would waken and attend to him if he cried or wanted feeding. My mind was full of busy and anxious thoughts, as I pursued my solitary way through these lonely woods, where everything was so death-like in its solemn silence, that I could hear my own footsteps, or the fall of a withered leaf, as it parted from the little boughs above my head and dropped on the path before me. I was so deeply absorbed with my own perplexing thoughts that I did not at first notice that I had reached where two paths branched off in nearly parallel directions, so that I was greatly puzzled which of the two was my road. When I had walked a few yards down one, my mind misgave me that I was wrong, and I retraced my steps without being at all satisfied that the other was the right one. At last I decided upon the wrong, as it afterwards turned out, and I now hurried on, hoping to make up, by renewed speed, for the time I had lost by my indecision. The increasing gloom of the road thickly shaded with hemlocks and cedars, now convinced me I was drawing near swampy ground, which I did not remember to have traversed in my morning walk. My heart thrilled with terror, for I heard the long-drawn yell of wolves, as I imagined in the distance. My first impulse was to turn and flee for my life, but my strength suddenly failed, and I was compelled to sit down upon a pine log by the side of the path to recover myself. 'Alas! alas!' said I, half-aloud, 'alone, lost in these lonely woods, perhaps to perish miserably, to be torn by wild beasts, or starved with hunger and cold, as many have been in this savage country! Oh my God! forsake me not, but look upon the poor wanderer with the eyes of mercy!' Such was my prayer when I heard the rapid gallop of some animal fast approaching—the sudden crashing of dry boughs, as the creature forced his way through them, convinced me it was too near for escape to be possible. All I could do was to start to my feet, and I stood straining my eyes in the direction of the sound, while my heart beat so audibly that I seemed to hear nothing else. You may judge of the heartfelt relief I experienced when I beheld my dear old dog, my faithful Nelson, rush bounding to my side, almost as breathless as his poor terror-stricken mistress.

"You know that I don't often indulge in tears, even when overwhelmed with trouble, but this time I actually cried for joy, and lifted up my heart in fervent thankfulness to Him who had guided my dumb protector through the tangled bush to my side that night. 'Come, Nelson,' I said, aloud, 'you have made a man of me.' 'Richard is himself again, dear fellow, I shall fear neither wolf nor bear while you are with me.' I then fastened my bundle about his neck for my arm ached with carrying it, and on we trudged. At first I thought it would be best to retrace my steps, but I fancied I saw light like a clearing breaking through the trees, and conjectured that this bye-road led in all likelihood to some of the bush farms or lumberers' shanties. I resolved to pursue my way straight onwards; nor was I mistaken, for some minutes after brought me to the edge of a newly burnt fallow, and I heard the baying of dogs, which no doubt were the same sounds, I, in my fright, had taken for wolves.

"The moon was now nearly set, and I judged it must be between one and two o'clock. I peeped into the curtainless window of the shanty, the glimmering light from a few burning brands and the red embers of the huge back-log in the wide clay-built chimney showed the inmates were all asleep, and as the barking and growling of the dogs, who, frightened by Nelson's great size, had retreated to a respectful distance, had failed to rouse them, I took bush-leave, opened the door, and stepped in without further ceremony. On a rude bed of cedar sticks slept two females, the elder of whom was not undressed but lay sleeping on the outside of the coverlet, and it was with great difficulty that I managed to rouse her to a consciousness of my presence and my request for a guide to the mills. 'Och! och! och! my dear crayter' she said, raising herself at last upon her brawny arm and eyeing me from under her black and tangled locks with a cunning and curious look, 'what should a young thing like yourself be doing up and abroad at sich a time of night as this?'

"'Good mother,' I said, 'I have lost my way in the bush, and want a lad or some one to show me the way to the mills.'

"'Sure,' said the old woman, 'this is not a time to be asking the boys to leave their beds, but sit down there, and I will speak with the master.' She then pushed a rude seat in front of the fire, and roused up the logs with a huge hand-spike, which she wielded with strength of arm that proved she was no stranger to the work of closing in log-heaps, and even chopping, and then proceeded to wake her partner, who, with three or four big boys, occupied another bed at the farthest end of the shanty.

"After some parleying with the man it was agreed that at day-break one of the elder boys should be sent to guide me home, but not sooner. 'There Mistress' said the man, 'you may just lie down on my old woman's bed, the girl has the ague, but she is as quiet as a lamb, and will not disturb you.' I preferred sitting on my rude seat before the now blazing fire, to sharing the girl's couch, and as to a refreshment of fried pork and potatoes which my hostess offered to get ready for me, I had no appetite for it, and was glad when my host of the shanty and his partner retired to bed, and left me to my own cogitations and mute companionship of Nelson. One feeling was uppermost in my mind—gratitude to God for my present shelter, rude as it was; the novelty of my situation almost amused me, and then graver thoughts came over me as I cast my eyes curiously around upon smoke-stained walls and unbarked rafters from whence moss and grey lichens waved in a sort of fanciful drapery above my head. I thought of my former life of pride and luxury. What a singular contrast did it present to my situation at that moment. The red flashing glare of the now fiercely burning logs illumined every corner of the shanty, and showed the faces of the sleepers in their humble beds. There lay close beside me on her rude pallet, the poor sick girl, whose pale visage and labouring breath excited my commiseration, for what comfort could she have, either mental or bodily, I asked myself. The chinking in many parts, had been displaced, and the spaces stuffed with rags, straw, moss, wool and a mass of heterogeneous matter, that would have plainly told from what part of the world the inmates had come, if their strong South of Ireland brogue had not declared it past all disputing. Few and scanty were the articles of furniture and convenience. Two or three unplaned pinewood shelves, on which were arranged some tinware and a little coarse delf, a block of wood sawn from the butt end of a large timber tree, and a rude ricketty table, with a pork and flour barrel, some implements of husbandry, among which gleamed brightly the Irish spade, an instrument peculiar to the Irish laborers' cabin, and a gun which was supported against the log walls by two carved wooden hooks, or rests, such was the interior of the shanty. I amused myself with making a sort of mental inventory of its internal economy, till by degrees weariness overcame me, and leaning my back against the frame of the poor sick girl's bed, I fell sound asleep, and might have slept on till broad day, had not my slumbers been suddenly broken by the rolling of one of the big logs on the hearth, and looking over, I almost started at the sight of the small, sinister-looking eyes of my host, which were bent upon me with so penetrating a glance, that I shrunk from before them. In good truth more stout-hearted persons might have been justified in the indulgence of a cowardly feeling, if they had been placed in a similar situation, so utterly helpless and alone; but my courage quickly returned. I thought it wisest not to show distrust, and addressed the uncouth-looking personage before me with a cheerful air, laughing at his having caught me napping. Yet I remember the time, when I was a youthful romance reader, I should have fancied myself into a heroine, and my old Irishman into a brigand; but in my intercourse with the lower class of Irish emigrants, I have learnt that there is little cause for fear in reality. Their wild passions are often roused to a fearful degree of violence by insult, either against their religion or their nation, to acts of vengeance; but such a thing as murdering or robbing a helpless, unoffending stranger, seeking the hospitable shelter of their roofs, I never yet heard of, nor do I believe them capable of an act of covetousness or cruelty so unprovoked. While I thought on these things my confidence returned, so that I would not have hesitated to take the man for my guide through the lone woods I had to pass, trusting to this impression of the Irish character, which, with many defects, has many virtues, while that of hospitality is certainly one of the most prominent.

"The first streak of daylight saw the old woman stirring, to prepare their morning meal of pork and potatoes, of which I was glad to partake.

"One by one came stealing sleepily from their nests four ragged urchins, whose garments I verily believe were never removed for weeks, either by day or night. They all had the same peculiar smoke-dried complexion, a sort of dusky greyish tint, grey eyes, with thick black lashes, and broad black eyebrows, with a squareness of head and a length of chin which I have not unfrequently noticed as a characteristic feature in the less comely inhabitants of the Irish cabins. The boys stole looks of wonder and curiosity at me, but no one spoke or ventured to ask a question; however, they bestowed great marks of attention on Nelson, and many were the bits of meat and potatoes with which they strove to seduce him from my feet.

"When our meal was ended, I gave the old woman a small piece of silver, and, accompanied by Master Michael, the biggest boy, I left the shanty, and was glad enough to seek my own home, and find all as well as when I had left them, though some anxiety had been felt for my unusual absence."

Such were the midnight adventures of my poor friend. It was only one of many trials that she afterwards underwent before she once more regained her native land. She used often to say to me, "I think, if you ever write another book on the backwoods, some of my adventures might furnish you with matter for its pages."[4]

I would not have it inferred from these pages that, because some young men have erred in bringing out wives, unsuited by their former state of life, to endure the hardships of a bush-settling life, there are no exceptions. I would warn all who go home for British wives, to act openly, and use no deception, and to choose wisely such as are by habits and constitution able to struggle with the trials that may await them. It is not many who have the mental courage that was displayed by her whose adventures I have just narrated.

⌒

1   See Archives of Ontario, Upper Canada Land Petitions, "H" Bundle 19, 1835–36 (RG 1, L3, vol. 238).

2   Intermittent fever or ague.

3   Mary Strickland.

4   *The Backwoods of Canada* was sent as a manuscript to England in 1835 and appeared in print in January 1836.

GENEROSITY OF THE POOR

This sketch first appeared in *Chambers's Edinburgh Journal*, according to Traill (though it has not been found in a search of the magazine). This version appeared in the *Maple Leaf. A Juvenile Monthly Magazine* 2 (1853), 166–71. Traill clearly thought of it as a part of her sequel to *The Backwoods of Canada*, but here let it be used in the aid of the widowed Mrs. Robert Lay, who was struggling to carry on the magazine in the wake of her husband's sudden death a year earlier. Internal evidence suggests that it was originally written about 1838.

Of interest as a representation of female struggle and heroic activity, the sketch also provides evidence of Traill's self-positioning as author. Though clearly a woman of the middle class and proud of her position, she remained an optimist about human possibilities and the inherent "virtue" and "benevolence" to be located in members of the lower classes. "Generosity of the Poor" makes the case for pioneering—onerous and horrific as it could be—as the crucible in which character and fortune are made. The "hopeless and despondent" of the old world awaken to their inner possibilities and strengths when tested by "the wants and privations of a new colony." For Traill, the records of endurance and gain she could locate in the poor families of Douro and Smith townships stood for the strengths of character to be found in the hearts of human beings, regardless of class.

Having taken considerable interest in the trials and struggles of the emigrants on their first coming to Canada, I often converse with them, and listen with pleasure to the simple recital of their early sufferings, and manifold difficulties; some of which are sufficient to excite the sympathy of harder hearts than mine. In many instances they serve to awaken feelings of admiration for the noble energies that have been called forth in the hearts of the British peasant, feelings, and powers, that had lain dormant, because, unawakened, or been crushed, and kept down by the cheerless influence of poverty, and its soul-depressing consequences. I have seen the poor man who, while at home, sank hopeless and despondent, beneath the chilling blast of want and disease, here, brave with manly energy the wants and privations of a new colony, and battle, without shrinking, the storms of adversity. Cold, hunger, excessive toil, disease, all in their severest forms, were met, and by turns overcome, or endured without murmuring. In all probability, it is these very trials which the members of an infant colony endure in their first outset, that give them that strength and energy, for which they have ever been noted, and which is ultimately the foundation of the true greatness of their adopted country, and of their prosperity, and that of their families.

I have met with many persons among the rich, and the thoughtless votaries of luxury, and pride, who maintained that the virtues of the poor, were at best but negative qualities—that there were few who acted well, but from interested motives, or from fear of the law; and that genuine, exalted virtue was rarely, if at all, to be found in the abodes of want and poverty. How many opportunities have I had both in England, and since my sojourn in this colony, of proving the untruthfulness of these allegations. A bright and beautiful example of disinterested benevolence at this minute recurs to my mind, and, as I love to look upon the sunny side of the picture, I shall make no apology for introducing to your notice, one of our poor neighbours, a young woman, who lives three miles up the river, in the opposite township,[1] whose conduct is a lovely illustration of the widow, who was seen by our Lord, casting two mites into the treasury,[2] for she, of her penury, hath done that for the fatherless and motherless children of her poor neighbour, which many persons better circumstanced than herself, would have hesitated to do. It is now between three and four years since, a poor settler named Bulger, was accidentally killed by the fall of a tree, while chopping in the bush, (a casualty that sometimes happens,) his widow had three small children, the eldest boy not quite seven, the youngest child just able to run alone. Under these sad circumstances, the neighbours, who are not very well off, owing to the sterility of their lots of land, did for her all they could. They helped to put in her spring crops, sow a little patch of potatoes, and corn, drew in firewood, logged her summer fallow, and showed by a thousand little kind acts, their genuine sympathy for her desolate situation. The summer passed, and the fall brought with it a sore and deadly sickness, a malignant intermittent, which bore close resemblance to the typhus fever. Among many fatal cases which occurred in the neighbourhood, was that of the widow Bulger. The fever attacked her with great violence. Destitute of those little comforts, so necessary to the restoration of the sick, with only occasional attendance, such as her poor neighbours were able to afford, distressed in mind by the wants and wailings of her little ones, and possibly weighed down by her melancholy state, no wonder that she fell a victim to the disease, crushed beneath an accumulation of evils. Still in her dying hours she wanted not the consolation of one kind tender friend to close her eyes, and assure her that she would be a mother to her orphan children. For ten days did this good young woman, Mrs. Jones, tend her on her sick bed, though within a few weeks of her own confinement, and with the tie of three small children at home. She devoted as much time as duty to her family would admit, and it was in her friendly arms that the poor widow breathed her last. When all was over her sorrowful nurse took her [children] away through the woods, to her own humble dwelling, bearing in her arms the youngest child, while the two elder ones clung to her gown weeping—"and sad enough it made me to hear the poor creatures ask me day after day, to take them back to see poor mammy," said the kind creature, when telling me, with eyes filled with tears, of the sad death of the widow. After a little time two of the neighbours, who could better afford their maintenance, took the two elder children, who would soon become useful to them, though none seemed disposed to burden themselves with the helpless little one. But it became dearer each day to the heart of its adopted mother, and precious in her eyes. It ate of the scanty portion of her children's bread, and drank of her own cup, shared the cradle-bed of her own babe, and was to her as a daughter.

"Indeed Madam," she said, "I have had little Bridget now two years, and she is as dear to me, every bit as any of my own, for the little thing seems to know that I have been good to her, and clings to me with more than a daughter's love. If I am away for a few hours, she is the first to run smiling to me, and say, 'Mammy Jones come back.' She is as gentle as a lamb, and seems to have thought beyond her years; for she is sure to tell me if any thing has gone wrong during my absence. I do not think I could bear to part with the child, unless I were well assured she would be taken good care of; and she shall never want the bit or the sup, while I have a potato, or a drop of milk to give her." At this very time, want and sickness had visited her log-hut, and potatoes and milk were all she had to support her family. The harvest had proved a failure, and her own babe was languishing at her breast from want of nourishment. I saw her not many weeks ago, she was in ill-health, and her baby was dead, but she told me with tears of joy shining in her soft hazel eyes, that a kind good lady had taken her little adopted one, and had promised to bring it up, and do well by it, "better indeed than I could do for her; and she was dressed so beautifully, just like a lady's child, but she says she will never forget her mammy Jones." Indeed it were a pity she should ever forget the kind hearted friend, who had cherished her in her desolate infancy.

This poor woman has had her own share of trials since she came into the bush. You would have been interested in the account she gave of the first year of settlement; "we were" said she, "too poor to make any stay at a town, when we came up the country, after paying the first instalment on our lot, (which is unfortunately of the worst description, almost one block of stone,) we had but a few dollars remaining; so I agreed with my husband, as it was then early in the spring, to go directly to the land, and try what we could do in putting up a bit of a hut, which people told us, a man with a little help from his wife could do in one day; but it was nightfall before we reached the place, and much ado we had to make it out; I had two little children, one at the breast, and another not much more than a babe. These I had to carry, one on my back, the other in my arms, while my husband bore what bedding and utensils he could carry on his back. As ill-luck would have it, before we could get even a few boughs cut down to shelter us, one of the most awful tempests came on that I ever witnessed. The thunder and lightning made my very heart tremble within me, and the torrents of rain that came down, drenched us entirely. I had much ado to keep the children dry, by covering them with everything I could get together, and setting up a blanket on sloping sticks, over the place where they lay; but the poor things were so weary that they slept without heeding the roaring thunder, or the rain; and so we passed the first night in the bush." The next day, she said, they set to work quite early; her husband chopped down the trees, and cut them into lengths, while she tended the children, and did what she could to help. Then they put up the hut. She with the aid of a handspike helped to roll up the logs, and lay the foundation of their little dwelling; and when the walls were raised, she stood on the upper logs, and helped to haul them up with a rope, then her husband notched and fixed them; so that by dint of hard labour, their outside walls were raised ere night; and a few cedar, and hemlock boughs closed them in, till they were able to lay a roof of troughed sapwood the next day. After that they raised a wall of stones and clay, against one end, which served for a chimney, with a square hole cut in the roof to let out the smoke. They next chopped a bit of ground for potatoes. I forget now how they got on, but I think badly, and suffered from want of food during the winter. In the spring the wife fell ill with intermittent fever,[3] and was reduced to the most deplorable condition. She also lost one of her children that year. Her husband was at last obliged to leave her to get work at some distance, that he might procure food to keep them from absolute starvation. Just imagine the dreadful condition to which these poor creatures were reduced, when the husband was forced to leave his sick, helpless starving wife and children alone. It so chanced that the person to whom he applied for work, was a good and charitable man. He noticed the anxiety of the distressed husband, and asked the cause. This was soon made known, and without waiting for farther proof, the master instantly hurried him off to the relief of his suffering wife, loaded with food and necessaries for her and the children. "Oh, madam," said she, "sure never was sight so welcome to my eyes, as that of my husband, when he came in, and set before me, first one thing and then another; and I believe that want of food was one cause of my illness, for in a little while, I got well and strong. Our good master would never let my husband go home of a Saturday night, without something for me; and his dear wife would fill a basket with cakes, and butter, and milk, and eggs, and all sorts of nice things, for me; and never as long as I live, shall I forget the goodness of that blessed couple to me and mine."

The above sketch was written some years ago, and appeared in that excellent work, "Chambers's Journal." It was an extract from my 'Forest Gleanings,' and is so illustrative of Canadian scenes and characters, that I have not scrupled to restore it to its original place among them. It may not be uninteresting for my readers to know, that Bridget Jones, the heroine of my narrative, (and she was a heroine, though one in a lowly station,) has bettered her condition, by leaving the hemlock rock, on which her husband formerly toiled so fruitlessly, thinking it better to sacrifice the small sum they had paid in advance upon the lot, than expend years of labour on that which would yield them so poor a return. They are now living in Douro, and doing well, the children growing up to be useful. So grateful is this kind-hearted woman for any kindness or sympathy shown her, that she never failed coming to see me when in the neighbourhood, and would bring little offerings of maple-sugar, molasses, or fowls, as tokens of good will to the children. The little orphan girl, now a young woman is, I have heard, in service in a good situation in Toronto. I trust she will in her prosperity ever remember her kind foster-mother— "Mammy Jones."

1   Smith Township.

2   Mark 12:41–44.

3   Ague.

MY IRISH MAID ISABELLA—
A NIGHT OF PERIL

"My Irish Maid Isabella—A Night of Peril" is taken from
Traill's journal for 1836 and is here published in its original
form for the first time. This digressive sketch refers to
events in 1834 and 1835 and is of special interest as Traill
could have included much of the material in *The Backwoods
of Canada* had she chosen to do so. Curiously, a shortened
version of the sketch, under the title "A Night of Terror in
the Backwoods of Canada: A True Story," appeared in the
Canadian Monthly and National Review 1 (February 1872),
138–41. Its author was Mrs. M. E. Muchall—Traill's third-
born daughter, Mary—and it is told from the point of view
of an elderly woman and former pioneer. The events recall
a time prior to Mary's own birth (1841); as well, the shift in
authorship may indicate both Traill's desire to help her
daughter make headway as a writer and her desire to distance herself from somewhat problematical material. Mary
Muchall's interpretation, which is more like a unified story,
leaves out Traill's fascination with Isabella Gordon's Irish
background and experience, the fact that during the attack
her mother had a young baby in her arms, and the second
anecdote of intrusion into the Traill house when Thomas
Traill was again absent. Isabella Gordon was in fact Traill's
nurse and servant during much of 1834, and the Irish
shantymen were likely the same group or family that the
Traills hired in 1833–34 to clear the "thick pine forest" on
their property (see "The Canadian Lumberers") on Lake
Katchewanook. Both the richness of biographical detail
and the sketch's sense of immediacy have led us to present
it virtually as Traill wrote it in her journal. See the Traill
Family Collection (nos. 8691–8713), National Archives
of Canada.

The character of Isabella Gordon, my Irish nurse, will not be without interest to my readers. She had in her younger days lived in the family of my brother's father-in-law as nurse to one of the young children, but was unwilling to emigrate with the R——s to Canada when the family came out in 1832. But when Mr. R—— was preparing to return back to his Douro home in 1833, she proposed joining a party of Irish friends from Belfast, and came out under his special care, and hearing that I was in need of a nurse for my little boy then only a month old, she applied for the situation and was accepted.[1] She soon grew greatly attached to her infant charge, and under her care I grew strong and healthy once more. It was a sad loss to me when at the close of the summer, she left me to join her brother in York whom she had lost sight of for many years. She promised that if things did not turn out well between them, that she would return to me which she did the following December to my great joy and helped us to move in to the new log-house which with her help was soon made most comfortable.

Isabella was no common character. There was something in her face that bespoke intelligence, spirit, and decision. She was not young, probably between thirty and forty, but her lithe, active figure, dark sparkling eyes, and clear brunette complexion still gave you the idea of youth rather than of mature age. She left her native country under the conviction that her life was not safe from the following cause. She had been living in Belfast for some time, earning her scanty meals by her needle for like many of her country women she was a skilful seamstress, knitter and spinner.

Her father had been a travelling schoolmaster who went from place to place teaching or sometimes he kept a night-school or day-school or, it might be, earning a supply of food and clothing by his wits; he was a stanch protestant, [and] had kept an Orange Lodge, but at the time that I speak of he had been dead some months, and Isabella had to support herself and seek a poor shelter in the suburbs of the city. Nor was she at first aware of the nature of the place she had got into till one night while sitting in the dilapidated chamber she had hired, when looking through a broken lathed wall, she found herself close to a set of "ribbon-men," a wild set of disloyal men, who held their nightly meeting in an upper room next to the one she occupied.[2]

There she became privy to their wil[d] designs and deadly plans of revenge, arson, and murder. One night she learned their plan was on a certain night to disguise themselves, two or more of them, and murder a clergyman and his wife and children and to conceal the barbarous deed they would fire the holy place. Horror-stricken, she secretly left the house and going to the magistrate late as it was, put him in possession of the dreadful secret. He having solemnly sworn not to give her up as his informer, the warning was given, and the victims saved, but from that hour this brave woman felt that she held her life at the chance of being discovered by some of the villains whose plot she had revealed.

She led a haunted life, to use her own expression, and gladly accompanied her former master to Canada, and being recommended to me as a faithful and careful nurse for my baby boy, I gladly hired her, and found her all I could desire. Only that she was so fond of my darling boy that she shewed positive jealousy of his love for me his mother. She hungered for love; and desired to have it all her own and sometimes I thought that she liked to rule me as well as her infant charge. She was prudent and wise in many ways.

She had a good clear voice which her father had trained. She used to sing my boy to sleep with some of the Irish songs which she had learned in her youth, and some of these lyrics were wild and mournful, descriptive of the state of her country and its troublous times. She would with mischievous looks sing "Protestant Boys," "The Enniskillen Dragoons" and "Croppers hill down" just in the hearing of our Catholic choppers, or any Orange ditty she could think of to annoy them. And after she had roused up "a *bit of the Devil in the boys*," as she said, she would then give them some specimens, on the contrary side—some of these Irish songs were wild and pathetic, and when I asked her where she had learned them she told me that her own mother was a down-right papist and that her uncle, her mother's brother, had been hung in the Rebellion of ninety-eight. He was out with Lord Edward FitzGerald and was taken at the Bridge of Waterford and hung as a traitor.[3] One of her songs was made on this rebel uncle—she sang it with much feeling. I remember that the verses described the apparition appearing on the banks of the Liffy to encourage his disheartened comrades, and the last lines were thus to a slow solemn air—

"And fear not, he said, though my face it is wan
It was I who just died for the dear rights of man,
To witness your triumph I came from the skies,
Like the moon in *her* beauty, and the croppies shall arise!!"

"It was a fair day in May, the moon shining clear
It was down by Liffy Barracks a stranger did appear."

Isabella was thoroughly Irish in manners but there was a strange mixture of races in her. Sometimes she would dwell upon the wrongs of her mother's people and move me to pity. She was, she said, more like her mother who was from the South of Ireland and she bore more of the warm dark complexion which characterizes some of the natives of the South with the black hair, fine features and foreign aspects of the Italian or Spaniard, while the Northern men are generally fair and ruddy, and look as if they came of a different race entirely. Our seven stalwart choppers were from the South and were of the darker race. In spite of the difference in their religious creeds there was a likeness in features and complexion between these men and my protestant maid Isabella; they might have been near relatives. Perhaps they were!

They lived on fair outward terms, but Isabella watched them narrowly. She knew what they were, she said, and trusted them but little. "Mistress," she would say, "you do not know my *country-men—I do*." She spoke bitterly, poor soul; she had had sad experience of the Roman Catholics—perhaps in her own way she was as intolerant as the greatest bigot among them.

Isabella used to tell me of the terrible scenes her father had witnessed during the Irish rebellion, and though himself a stanch and loyal protestant, he would bear witness to many an act of atrocity and fiendish cruelty; he had been an active militia man himself but he would horrify her young blood by relating terrible acts done by the soldiers, but then though these things were all charged by the rebels upon the regulars and British troops, he knew that it was the hatred of Irishmen against Irishmen that was really the cause. Retaliation and Protestant against Popery—that was at the bottom of half the devilish acts. She was her father's own Protestant child and hated Papists. When she was young, her mother, a Roman Catholic whom she never loved, had taken her down among her own people in the wilds of Conemara, but this visit had opened the young Isabella's eyes to much that she learned to abhor. Her mother died of famine fever when they were [there], and the girl made her escape back to her father.

"Mistress, get up the blood of one of my countrymen and it is not easy to say what they will stop at."

"In those days it was blood for blood and no mistaken mercy for an enemy. No, mistress, there was little of the milk of mercy then among the people for all were opposed, man against man. My mother's people were sworn against my father; the bitter hatred was in their hearts. At that time it was, a man's foes were often those in his own household if they did not follow him in politics and belief. And in that they were blind as bats."

"I suppose it was the love of liberty that they fought for," I said.

"What liberty could they have under popish rule," she muttered. "They are a set of knaves. Poverty and the restlessness of the blood," she said. "Nature's poor misguided creatures, taking into their hearts and bad men stirring up strife."

"And yet," she added, "they are a fine people—kind, warm-hearted, clever in their ways, patient of wrong till the blood be up and then—, but Mistress I am an Irish woman born and bred and like my people I can both love and hate them," and she had a flash in her dark eyes that bore her out.

Isabella was no common vulgar person and had a power of strange eloquence when the subject touched her own people and their wrongs. For though she railed at the Priests and attributed much of the misery of the Irish to the state of ignorance, superstition and subjection they were kept under, yet if I had taken up the subject and even fully agreed with her she would have flamed out in vehement language defending them and asking me what I, an English woman, should know of the Irish and Ireland. Poor Isabella, it was just thus: "I, if I choose to, can abuse my people and my nation but no one else shall in my hearing." So I rarely ventured on more than some slight remark when I saw how excited she became if I said any thing that stirred her Irish blood.

And now having dwelt at some length upon the character of Isabella, I will give an instance of her ready wit under very dangerous, trying circumstances in which I owed to her my safety, from a great peril. The very bare recollection of it filled me with terror for a long time afterwards.

It was in the month of January, that my husband was obliged to go to the far distant town of Cob[o]urg on a matter of business with his agent through whom he drew his pay from the War Office. At that time the facilities for travelling were few—there was no stage and no boats, the Rice Lake being frozen only partially and unsafe for crossing, no horses for hire and the only means of travel was just on foot. A distance of forty miles through a wild forest road in mid-winter was no joke. The journey generally took a week to perform before the traveller would reach home again but just as he was starting on his pedestrian tour, the eldest of the choppers Mick came in and asked for an order to be given in writing for goods on the store in P—— and some cash in hand for current expenses.[4] This was quite the usual way of paying work-men in those days. The order was written and after a while the men from the shanty left, some four of them, and we had a quiet day.

Patrick, the second eldest of the B—— family, was remarkably handsome with a tall fine figure and gay rollicking air, a contrast to his eldest brother, Mick, who wore a gloomy and treacherous expression with strong marked features—a fine outline but forbidding.[5] He had a sort of brigandish look so that one might have fancied him the chief of a band of foreign outlaws. Of this man I had an instinctive dread, though he was always courteous and obliging.

There was nothing low or vulgar in the appearance of the B—— brothers. Still, I never liked to see Mick come into the house, which he often did on one errand or another, and the handsome Pat affected to be in love with Isabella but, though she would laugh and chat with him coquettishly as Irish women will, she disliked him in her heart and suspected his motives. He often asked her questions about my husband and myself and if we were not rich—he had seen silver, and other articles on our table, and thought the oaken iron-bound [cant]een was full of gold and valuables. All these remarks awoke suspicion in my faithful servant. She doubted Pat's blarney, but she did not let him see it.

Only one of the younger boys, a lad about sixteen came in for medicine as he was ill, and Isabella gave him some and also a bowl of good soup. I was always sorry for Johnnie, he was a gentle well behaved lad and was studious too as his great desire he said was to become a *priest*. He had been often cruelly beaten by his elder brothers who thought him lazy when he had ague and was too weak to work, and this poor boy was an object of interest and compassion to me, if not to Isabella, who was always sceptical of her Catholic neighbours.

But to resume my story. The choppers were away that night and all the next day. It so happened the second night that we were up late; Isabella had ironing for baby to finish and I had a little cap to trim for him. It must have been about eleven o'clock when we were made aware of the return of the shanty party by the heavy tramp of their feet passing the house, and then a burst of loud voices, and the sound of violence, shouting, and struggling on the road.

"Those men are fighting and I dare say none of them sober," was Isabella's remark. The row in the shanty awakened my boy and I went into the parlor. As I took him up to soothe him the outer door which led into the kitchen was opened (there was neither bolt nor lock on log-houses in those days) and Mick B—— entered the house.

At a glance we saw by the wild glitter of his dark eyes and the marks of bruises on his face that he had been fighting, and was not sober—*not drunk*, but excited by the whiskey he had taken and the passion that was expressed in his face. He walked straight up to where I stood with the babe in my arms, and catching hold of my wrist tried to force the child from me. Its little arms clung to my neck as if for protection while in an agony of terror I clasped the child so tightly that I wonder it was not killed. Not a word could I speak! I was paralyzed with fear while that terrible man's wild eyes were upon me and his iron grasp upon my arm— but Isabella was perfectly cool. Standing a little *behind* him she made signs to me not to shew my fear, and in a bright cheerful voice she said, "Why, Mick, who would have thought of seeing you so late? Is any thing wrong in the Shanty?" to which question he replied, "Oh, no. I came to keep you women company. I couldn't let two pretty young women stay here alone all night."

"Well," she said, "that was very thoughtful of you, but the Mistress and I are just sitting up late for we expect the Master in every minute."

He cast his eyes on her as she said this with a mocking glance and laughed a scornful laugh of derision as he said, "Then I may tell you that you may take it out in expecting him. The Master is in Cobourg and won't be home for some days to come."

She replied, "Don't you know that we got a message to say that he got a friend to do the business for him in Cobourg and that he would be home this night."

Alas, the man knew that this was not true. Then swift as thought she passed behind our unwelcome visitor as a fresh burst of noise came from without and, going to the glass door of the parlor which commanded the view of the Shanty, clapped her hands and cried out in excited tones, "Run, Mick, run! O, run quick! They are killing Pat!" This time he *was* deceived by her and, leaving hold his grasp of my wrist, he darted from the room and made for the scene of strife and riot. Isabella instantly dragged a heavy sea-chest that was in the outer room across the door-way, and secured the latch of the door by inserting a carving fork above it while I burst into a fit of hysterical crying and was seized with so violent a fit of trembling that I sank down on the couch unable to speak for some minutes. The horror of the situation had overwhelmed me and I still feared the return of the hateful and terrible object of our dread.

When I had at last recovered myself I observed Isabella's precautions and remarked almost desperately. "What use are these barricades against the force of a man like that? He can open any window, or come in at the glass door." I felt all my fears return at the thought of our undefended state, powerless to resist this fearful man. But my brave Irish maid was not daunted. "Mistress," she said, "he will not come back, and I will keep watch and if I see any movement on his part you open this door, and go out straight away to the Shanty and claim the protection of the men that are there."

"What?" I cried, "Put myself in the power of Mick B——'s brothers and those other wild men his comrades— I daresay as bad as himself?"

"Yes," she replied: "They would not suffer a hair of your head to be touched. I know my countrymen, Mistress, better than you do. They are often wild and rough, and will do desperate deeds when their blood is excited by religious zeal or politics, but they are at heart generous and kind and noble men, and if a weak woman or little helpless child appeals to them for help and throw themselves on them for protection they would not see them harmed." And she added: "Those men will not let Mick come back."

Neither did they. Isabella was right. When Michael, one of the younger lads, came in the following morning, he told Isabella that the men had suspected some bad design on Mick's part and that they had got him unawares and bound him down with ropes, and kept guard over him and Pat who was too tipsy to oppose them, and they are both asleep now and will be quiet after this frolic.

The next day I went over to my brother's house, who when he heard of our fright sent one of the men of his household to stay every night till my husband's return.[6] Glad indeed was I at the end of the month to see the choppers' shanty broken up, and the Irish men take their leave of our clearing. Nor did I ever see any one of them again. I heard afterwards that the whole family had left for distant parts. The overbearing assumption of the elder brother had caused many quarrels in the place where they lived. Isabella used to laugh at Mick's boasting of his long line of Kingly ancestors; though she admitted he might have come of a lordly race of Irish Chiefs from the look of him. "Bad luck to him and his beggarly pride," she added.

I lost my clever Irish servant the following year. She went back to her native country in charge of an invalid child, and I never heard of her afterwards.

The night of terror when I was so alarmed by the midnight visit of the Irish chopper was not the only fright I had. The second time I was entirely alone in the house. On the first occasion I had my courageous Irish servant with me.

It was in the summer of 1835 when it happened that business in a distant quarter delayed my husband's return home one night. The very same day my female servant Mary received a pressing message from her mother who was taken suddenly ill and left me early in the morning.[7] The hired man had the ague and also left. I was consequently left alone with no one in the house but my baby boy, who was about eighteen months old. Still, the weather was lovely and there was bright moonlight. I was well and had no anxiety about the matter of being alone for one or two summer days and nights; in fact, I went to bed a little wearied with the additional fatigue of the household work and attending to my little one. I was awakened, it might be about midnight, by the sharp click of the latch of the outer door and the heavy tread of a foot crossing the kitchen floor, and through the open seams of the partition wall I discerned the figure of a strange man in a working dress standing in the kitchen.

I then felt my lonely helpless state, and for a few minutes fear took possession of me. "What if the child should awake and cry?" But he slept the sleep of innocence. I slipped out of bed, noiselessly dressed myself, and as noiselessly opened the window, ready to make my escape should the strange visitor make any move to search the house and find out my room. I had a wrap ready for baby in event of my having to take him up and flee with him. Then I sat and watched—watched with the trepidation which is born of fear. It was not long before I felt reassured by seeing the unwelcome, unknown guest take off his coat, roll it into a bundle to serve for a bolster, and stretch his tired limbs upon the floor. His heavy breathing soon satisfied me that it was the shelter of a roof from the fear of prowling wild beasts and protection from the heavy night dew that had induced him to come into the house uninvited and truly unexpected, but with no evil intention. Possibly he did not even know that there was only a helpless infant and his almost as helpless mother within its walls.

Sleep however was impossible under the circumstances. I sat near the open window and felt the cool air restore my bewildered senses. It was a lovely moonlit night—no sound was there to disturb me save the distant whistling monotonous weird cry of the Whip-poor Will from the neighbouring forest or the chit-chit-chit of the little, striped, ground squirrel scolding some night hawk or predatory owl that was ready to pounce upon its harmless defenceless prey. As the morning dawned, a shiver passed over the beech trees rustling the stiff shining foliage at the edge of the forest and sighed with soft cadence through the thready needles of the dark plumy heads of the pines. These sweet natural sounds were music to my ears who loved Nature in her wildness. They always soothed and comforted me.

Not long after the day broke the sleeper rose, donned his garments softly, unclosed the door, and soon his heavy tread passed on to the woods and he was lost to sight. I never knew who my midnight visitor was, but guessed him to be some emigrant making his way to the distant "English-line" some ten miles off that had been recently settled by a party of Wiltshire labouring people from the Downs of Marlborough & Frome, and some from the Marquis of Bath's lands. Good honest hardworking folk they were.

∽

1   Reid returned to Ireland and England in 1831–32 to deal with business matters (see *Letters of a Lifetime*, 17, 63). For further details about Reid see p. 77, note 1. Catharine's first child, James, was born in June 1833.

2   Ribbon-men, also known as Whiteboys or Defenders, were members of Catholic peasant secret societies opposed to the actions of the landlord class.

3   The Society of United Irishmen, founded in 1790 in the cause of Irish independence from Britain, planned a general uprising for May 23, 1798. However, the society's leaders, including Lord Edward Fitzgerald, were arrested prior to this date and the intended rebellion became only a series of local insurrections through the summer of 1798.

4   Peterborough was about eleven miles south of the Traills' farm.

5   Traill identifies the Irish shantymen brothers as B——. Mary Muchall, writing over forty years later, names them as Burke, though she changes several first names.

6   Sam Strickland's farm was about one mile south of the Traills' homestead.

7   Mary was likely Mary Pine (Payne) whose family had settled in Dummer Township.

Rebellion

THE MACKENZIE REBELLION

"The Mackenzie Rebellion" is a section from Traill's
journals of the year 1837–38 and is unusual in that, charac-
teristically, her journals are given over to very detailed
observation of the flora, fauna, landscape, and climate of
the Douro area. Here, however, the immediate events of
the Rebellion of 1837 provide a narrative frame that allows
the opportunity for comments upon the beauties of the
Canadian winter (set against "the monotony of our winter
landscape"), the celebration of Christmas and New Year's
in the backwoods, and the curious patterns of weather that
Traill had observed over her five winters in Upper Canada.
As is often the case in the journals that survive, an entry
will begin as if it were a letter—perhaps it was a draft of a
letter she actually wrote—to an English friend or to family
members. Traill's account of the Rebellion—fervent and
patriotic in the moment and more contemplative and astute
in its later sections—is interestingly compared with what
Sam Strickland had to say in *Twenty-Seven Years in Canada
West* (1853) and what Susanna Moodie recalled in *Roughing
It in the Bush* (1852). For factual accuracy and immediacy,
Traill's diary format provides a more reliable description of
the unfolding of events than either Strickland's or Moodie's,
both of which were written years after the events.

   Along with "Bush Wedding and Wooing," this
"chapter" was included as an addition to Edward S. Caswell's
1929 edition of *The Backwoods of Canada* for McClelland and
Stewart, the first edition of Traill's book to be published in
Canada. Chronologically it was conspicuously out of place
there because the events described in *The Backwoods* conclude
in May 1835. Caswell chose it from among several sketches
and pieces submitted to him by Traill's granddaughter,
Florence Atwood.

1837—The sight of your beloved handwriting, my dear friend, warmed my heart, though I do assure you its affections had not grown cold towards you. Accident, I suppose, prevented my two former letters from reaching you, and now I must recapitulate some of their contents to satisfy you on some heads, relative to my present situation. You tell me that the date of my last letter was June, 1834, and ask me what I have been about since then. Let me see, the events of three whole years, to be summed up on a sheet of foolscap paper—I am afraid before I have finished the review of those three last years I shall be inclined to twist the sheet of foolscap into a cap for my own head. However, I shall endeavour to gratify your wishes, and give you some account of our proceedings in the backwoods—and such little domestic details as I think may be interesting to you, my old friend—notice I did not say *aged*, so do not look dignified at the word but remember that it refers to the years of friendship and *not* to *your* years. First, before I say anything to you of our out-of-door improvements—let me introduce to your attention my little flock within. When last you heard from me I had only one child, now I have three. James has grown stout and healthy—and the image of my brother Tom—his sister, Katherine—Katie, as we call her— a fat, rosy, roly poly, very amusing, but though twenty months old cannot speak more than ten words distinctly. The youngest darling, my little Harry, is one of the sweetest pets of six months old, just beginning to amuse and to be amused. Well, these are all my treasures, and though Dame Fortune has not overwhelmed us with her gifts in the form of gold and silver, much riches has she given us in our little ones, for they are very precious to us, alike our care, and our joy. Little Katie lies at my feet fast asleep, her cheek resting on a fawn skin that was given me by a squaw last summer, and which the dear child is so fond of that she takes it to bed, and when awake is either sitting on it or hugging it in her arms, as if it were a kitten or some live pet. Jimmy is bringing in wood for the stove, and Baby is sweetly sleeping in his wooden cradle near me. Do you remember the old Christmas carol?

> He neither shall be rocked in silver or in gold
> But in a wooden cradle that rocks in the mould,
> He neither shall be dressed in purple or in pall
> But in fair linen as are babies all.

So you see my wooden cradle was used in olden times, and here in the backwoods we have but returned by necessity to one of the usages of our forefathers.

After five years' residence in the country you will naturally conclude that we have overcome every difficulty, and are revelling in all the comforts and luxuries that you read of as being so quickly acquired by settlers in Canada. We are, I can assure you, as yet far behind the old settlers, and some years must elapse before we arrive at the same state of comfort as they enjoy who live in the long settled tract of country on the St. Laurence or other navigable waters. Many circumstances have combined to keep us back and depress the energies of the settlers in this township. The want of emigrants during the last three years has been one great cause, and we attribute this in the first place to the dread of cholera, which visited us in '32 and again in '34; then the dread of civil commotions, which we consider to have been quite unfounded in our Province. The high price of crown lands has also been a bar to emigration.

All operated against the prosperity of the country— also the want of good roads, or navigable steamers for the conveyance of commodities to market. The judicious and energetic administration of our excellent Governor did much to restore the confidence of the Colonists, and the passing of several Acts, and large sums voted for the improvement of the roads in our district, and for opening the navigation of the Otonabee from Peterborough to the Bay of Quinte, put the settlers in good spirits, and when carried into effect will do much towards promoting the welfare of these districts.[1] Since my former letter an Act has passed for dividing the Newcastle District. This will raise Peterborough to the dignity of a District town,[2] and many official situations are consequently established, and several public buildings are to be erected as soon as the division of the District takes place; but this requires funds, and the depressed state of the money market has put a stop for the present to many important works that were expected to be put into operation. You see matters go but slowly with us; we creep up the hill a few paces, and then slip back nearly to the point from which we set out—but still we *do* contrive to get forward a little bit, and are always upheld by the hope of climbing still higher, till we finally reach the summit of Colonial prosperity. The price of grain has been very high during the last years, which has been a great thing for those who had it to sell. It appears likely to be a high price this winter also. During the latter part of the summer, just before the harvest commenced, flour rose to twelve dollars a barrel, and in some cases even higher than that, and pork was eighteen dollars a barrel. Owing to the extreme wetness and lateness of the harvest, many of the small growers were without flour, and were obliged to substitute barley flour for wheaten, and use potatoes, as the enormous price of grain made them unwilling or unable to buy till they were able to thresh a small quantity of the new harvest to supply present wants. Owing to the warm, moist weather and heavy rains after the wheat was cut, a great deal of the grain sprouted in the sheaf, and even in the ear, uncut. Our crop fortunately was not injured; it was good in quality, but the return was short, owing to the wheat having been winter killed a good deal.

How strange would our rough style of farming appear to the British farmer; how different from the smooth garden-like enclosures of the eastern part of England are our Canadian clearings. But the state of the ground, climate and want of labour make all the difference, and experience teaches us that to pursue the regular and approved method of cultivating the land, such as is practised at home, would only involve the emigrant in loss and disappointment. When a farmer from the old country comes out, he looks aghast at the wild rugged appearance of our fields covered with stumps from three to four feet high, and the surface of the ground interlaced with roots. Around these stumps a number of wild shrubs appear, in the course of a year or two—wild raspberries, and gooseberries and a number of other fruits as well as a luxuriant growth of strawberries—but it is some years before the fields begin to look smooth.

We go on but slowly clearing from eight to ten acres a year; this gives us a crop of wheat and potatoes, oats and sometimes turnips and Indian corn. More than two crops are seldom grown in succession, but the clearing of the former year is generally sown with grass, and remains in pasture for three or four years and is then ploughed up. By that time most of the smaller stumps have decayed, and can be easily pulled with a yoke of oxen. But it takes a much longer time for the oak and pine to decay, and they will remain for years. I have been told that there are pine stumps still undecayed, though exposed to the vicissitudes of the elements for forty years.

These are but a few of the drawbacks we have to contend with, so you will perhaps understand why we have not made such progress as you infer, and we are not yet living *exactly* in the "lap of luxury," but withall are happy and contented, and always look with hope to the future.

Thursday, December 7th.—This morning my brother Sam came over to communicate the startling intelligence that an armed force was on the march for Toronto. Despatches had just reached Peterborough to that effect, with orders for every able man to hasten to the Capital to assist in driving back the rebels. They are headed by Mackenzie and Lount. God preserve us from the fearful consequence of a civil warfare. It seems we have been slumbering in fancied security on a fearful volcano, which has burst and may overwhelm us. Let us devoutly and earnestly ask the assistance of Him, whose arm is powerful to save. Assured of His help we need not fear, for greater is He that is for us, than those that are against us. "The hand of the Lord is not shortened that it cannot save." Surely ours is a holy warfare; the rebels fight in an unholy and unblessed cause. My dear brother has already left home for

Peterborough, and my beloved husband goes at daybreak. It is now past midnight; the dear children are now sleeping in happy unconsciousness of the danger to which their father and relatives are about to expose themselves; they heard not the fervent prayer of their father as he kneeled beside their bed, and laid his hands in a parting blessing upon their heads. O, my God, the Father of all mercies, hear that father's prayer, and grant he may return in safety to those dear babes and their anxious mother.

Friday night, Dec. 8th.—My heart is lonely and sad; this morning was only beginning to dawn, when Mr. Traill departed; he went off in good spirits, and I rallied mine till the snow drifts that were whirling before a keen sweeping wind hid him from my sight. I sent word to my sister Susan, telling her and Mr. Moodie what had happened. They both came down to dine with me. Moodie is resolved—in spite of his lameness, from a recent fracture of the small bone of his leg—to go down to Peterborough. I hope he will be detained on home duty, for he is quite unfit for moving. This has been a day of suspense, no word from my husband; I know not whether he marches forward to Port Hope, which seems to be proposed as a rallying point of rendezvous. It is said a steamer is to meet the volunteers there to convey them to Toronto.

Saturday 9th.—Moodie came in to adjust his knapsack, and bid me good-bye. God bless him and restore him to my dear sister and her little ones. Snow has been falling at intervals all day, much suffering must have been endured by those who were encamped, or on the march. Sibbons came in about three o'clock and brought me a kind note from Mrs. Stewart;[3] she had seen my husband and brother, previous to their leaving the town, which they did under the command of Captain Cowell.[4] A report has reached us that 400 Indians had come down on Toronto and slaughtered a number of the inhabitants—this seems to be unfounded. Five hundred Mohawks and Hurons have joined our party, and Colonel Anderson from Rice Lake has led up 170 Rice Lake Indians.[5] Parties are arriving constantly from the back townships. Colonel Brown's troop, 4th Northumberland, are to go off to-night.[6]

Saturday night.—The day has been piercingly cold, dark and gloomy; just at dusk I went to see my sister-in-law Mary, to hear if she had had any news.[7] The cold was so intense, and myself so agitated and unwell, that when I reached my brother's warm parlour I fainted. No news; no news of Sam and my dear husband, or *anyone*. All in painful suspense and anxious fears. *Later*—have just received a hasty note from Mary. One of her brothers had ridden up from Peterborough, no post in, no despatches up to eight o'clock—rumour speaks of a Colonel Moody having been killed and six men at Toronto.[8] This is bad news. The muster of loyal men continues hourly to increase—Cowell sent 400 men, and Cobourg proved loyal beyond expectation—much fear had been entertained of the disloyalty of this town, but to their honour, be it recorded, that they proved faithful on trial.

Sunday evening.—I became so restless and impatient, I felt in a perfect fever. Snow has been falling thickly, the ground is quite covered; this change will prove beneficial to our friends. I resolved on despatching Marten (the hired man) to hear if Moodie went on or was on guard at the Government House, on account of his lameness—it will relieve poor Susan of a load of care, if we hear this is the case. About three o'clock I noticed a person on the road, slowly making their way through the snow, which by this time was several inches deep. I watched the traveller up to my brother's house, and felt certain she was the bearer of news from below. Soon Mary sent the lad Tom over, with the glad tidings that the rebels were all dispersed and twenty of them killed on the other side of Toronto. Miss Reid had walked up by herself from Peterborough, through the snow—a distance of nine miles—with a devotion of purpose that reflects great credit on her heart, being anxious to be the bearer of the first good news to her sister Mary. What a change of feelings has a few words wrought in me; I no longer feel that dead weight on my heart—or that restlessness, that kept me constantly moving. The feverish impatience that made me chide the dear children for their innocent mirth has gone; I could now listen to them and take part in their amusements. I sent off Marten to Susan to let her share in our good news.

Mr. Moodie rode out this morning at the head of two hundred men from Smithtown. He would not remain in Peterborough on guard, but in spite of his lameness went on to join the rest of his brothers in arms. Ten thousand well-appointed militiamen are now in Toronto, and hundreds hourly flocking in. It is a glorious thing to think how few traitors, and how many loyal hearts, the Province contains. I feel now a proud satisfaction that my dear husband was among the first to volunteer—and with him my brother and brother-in-law. Two spies were taken up in Peterborough and sent in charge of Moodie and his two hundred men to be safely lodged in the jail at Amherst.[9]

The Saturday night's mail did not come in till ten; it brought the news of a skirmish having taken place, in which twenty of the rebels paid the forfeit of their lives. Reward of £1,000 is offered for Mackenzie and £500 for either of the other leaders—Lount, Gibson, Lloyd and Fletcher.

God be praised, who has confounded the malice of the enemies of our adopted country. To His name be the honour and the glory, now and forever. I shall lie down this night with a light heart. This morning I sent up Marten in the ox-sleigh for Susan and the dear children to spend the day with me. In the afternoon I had a letter from my dear husband from Cobourg. Up to Saturday they had been detained in that place, for on account of the tempestuous state of the weather, the steamboat did not arrive, but the whole party were summoned to meet the men at the Court House and march forward to Toronto. My brother and husband are under the command of Captain Cowell. He enclosed a printed proclamation of the Governor's. At the end of his address to the loyal militiamen of Upper Canada he says,—"The party of rebels under their chief leader is dispersed and flying before the loyal militia—the only thing that remains to be done is to find them out and arrest them."

I left the dear children all soundly sleeping and accompanied my sister Susan home in the ox-sleigh; we made a merry party comfortably nested in our rude vehicle, with a bed of clean straw, and a nice blanket over it, with pillows to lean against; well wrapped up in our Scotch plaids, we defied the cold and chatted merrily away, not a whit less happy than if we had been rolling along in a carriage with a splendid pair of bays, instead of crawling along at a funeral pace, in the rudest of all vehicles with the most ungraceful of all steeds; our canopy, the snowladen branches of pine, hemlock and cedar, the dark forest around us, and our lamps the pale stars and watery moon struggling through 'wrack and mist' and silver-tinged snow-clouds. Here then were we breaking the deep silence of the deep woods with the hum of cheerful voices and the wild mirth that bursts from the light-hearted children. No other sound was there except the heavy tread of the oxen and the lumbering sound of the sleigh as it jolted over the fallen sticks and logs that lay beneath the snow.

Nothing can surpass the loveliness of the woods after a snowstorm has loaded every bough and sprig with its feathery deposit. The face of the ground, so rough and tangled with a mass of uptorn trees, broken boughs and timbers in every stage of decay, seems by the touch of some powerful magician's wand to have changed its character. Unrivalled purity, softness and brilliancy has taken the place of confusion and vegetable corruption. It is one of the greatest treats this country affords me, to journey through the thick woods after a heavy snowfall—whether it be by the brilliant light of the noonday sun in the cloudless azure sky, giving a brightness to every glittering particle that clothes the trees or surface of the ground, or hangs in heavy masses on the evergreens, converting their fan-shaped boughs into foliage of feathery whiteness and most fantastic forms—or by the light of a full moon and frosty stars looking down through the snowy tops of the forest trees—sometimes shining through a veil of haze, which the frost converts into a sparkling rime that encases every spray and twig with crystals. The silent fall of the lighter particles of snow, which the gentlest motion of the air shakes down, is the only motion the still scene affords—with the merry jingle of our sleighbells.

December 12th.—Enjoyed a quiet day; no news of the rebels this day. I suppose our gallant volunteers are in Toronto by this time—where it seems probable they will be detained till public confidence is restored.

Nine o'clock p.m.—While preparing for my tea, I heard the parlour door open, and looking up was greeted by my dear husband, a sight that was as welcome as it was unexpected. It seems that the party of volunteers—of which my husband was one—had proceeded only as far as Port Hope when their Colonel, Alex. MacDonnel, received a despatch countermanding their further progress.[10] According to report, Silas Fletcher, one of the proscribed leaders, and several others had been taken prisoners. By the confession of some of them, it appears the plan originally proposed was to march to the Capital at night, seize the Governor and any of the men in office whose principles were opposed to theirs, take possession of the arms and ammunition and the public money. Taken by surprise, naked and unarmed, the inhabitants could have made but little resistance against even a few hundred men, well armed and bent on accomplishing their purpose, but fortunately the leaders of the rebellion were not unanimous in their opinions as to the fittest time for the assault, and Mackenzie was prevailed upon to sit down quietly and encamp beyond the city, thus giving the Governor time to make preparations for defence, and to rally round the standard of loyalty—the militia of the province—and well the summons was answered. From every part of the country came men of all ages and degree, anxious to prove their attachment to their Queen and the established government, by whose laws they were protected, and to protect their homes. It is currently reported that Sir Francis himself went out at the head of 300 militia and had a skirmish with the rebels, but till we hear further particulars we do not know if this is correct. Sixty prisoners were brought in—taken between Lake Simcoe and Toronto—among them the son of the rebel Lount.

December 14th.—It is reported that Mackenzie is somewhere in the township of Mariposa—endeavouring to raise fresh troops, either with the view of renewing hostilities in the Upper Province, or making his way down to aid the insurgents in the Lower. The latter scheme I should think the most probable as by this time he must consider any attempt to raise a revolution in this Province as a forlorn hope. Among other rumors it was said he was skulking in some of these back townships—one man asserts that he passed through Smithtown disguised as a woman—a story that savours more of romance than probability, and by no means agrees with his being in Mariposa. The latter report is confidently believed and a meeting of the Volunteers is to take place early to-morrow, to go on an expedition in search of the traitor. My husband goes down to attend the meeting and, if required, to join Captain Cowell and his volunteers.

Again I am left alone, but this time parted from my dear husband with less feeling of dread, and in reasonable hope of his sage and speedy return. *Nine o'clock.*—Moodie just rode his horse home with the distressing intelligence that Mr. Traill had fallen and sprained his ankle, so severely as to be unable to get further on his way home than our friends the Stewarts, where I am certain he will be paid every kind attention.[11] I am to send Marten with the horse for him in the morning.

16th.—My husband returned today, but so hurt as to require assistance to dismount from his horse. His foot and leg are dreadfully swollen and discoloured. This accident will, I fear, make him an unwilling prisoner for some time to come.

19th.—A bright cold day; thermometer below freezing in the parlour at five o'clock this morning; the lake frozen over with the exception of a narrow stream of dark blue water, confined between two fields of ice, all rough and crested, as if with mimic billows, and glittering as from the reflection of a countless host of stars. Nothing can be more splendid than the appearance it presents this morning. The few young trees that fringe the margin of the frozen water are covered with hoar frost, and look like snowy feathers growing gracefully above its motionless surface. As the mist gradually withdraws from the bosom of the waters, a new and lovely sight breaks upon the eye. The two small islands on the little lake are seen, slowly emerging from the mist, clothed with the most dazzling whiteness, contrasted with the gray tinting of the snow-clouds that border the horizon, or the dark shade of the troubled waters and the floating fragments of ice from the upper lake which are seen hurrying down the current, and as the sun's rays strike them they assume the most beautiful appearance, like globes of burnished silver, hurrying on with surprising rapidity, till you could fancy them a flock of silver swans chasing each other at play on the waters. Such pleasing sights as these in some degree break the monotony of our winter landscape, which for so many months would otherwise weary the eye and make us pine for other sights than the unvaried snow scenes of our Canadian winters.

25th, Xmas Day.—Christmas Day in the backwoods is not like Christmas Day in merry old England, for the heart of the emigrant yearns for his Motherland and for the old familiar friends that were wont to meet round the fireside, for the home of his childhood, that he has left, perhaps, never to look upon again. Our Christmas meetings are at best but a melancholy imitation of those social hours, and their chief charm arises from the retrospect of the past, and from the long train of affectionate remembrances that crowd thick and fast upon each other, and because we know and feel we are not forgotten, and that as often as that season returns there will be kind voices to name our names and sigh that our place is vacant in the family circle.

Dear sister Susan and Mr. Moodie with their little ones came to spend the day with us. A ride in a little hand-sleigh over the snow made the dear little flock as happy as could be, and they went home in the evening in the ox-sleigh, half asleep and tired out with what was to them a joyous Christmas Day—a day to be marked with a white stone in their little memories of happy seasons.

The party of volunteers returned from Mariposa and Opps—no trace of rebels there. We hear that Mackenzie is trying to stir up the Americans on the other side, and promises them large rewards for their services in endeavouring to tear from us our Government and laws, and force us to become a free and independent people. Surely our freedom would be a blessed gift so obtained!! And with the traitor Mackenzie for our President our independence were most honourable and admirable!! God forbid we should change our dependence on a gracious Sovereign to become the tools and victims of the most despicable of rebels. It is commonly reported that Mackenzie offered a reward of 3,000 pounds for the head of Sir Francis—at all events he considers it worth 2,000 more than his own. Our gallant Lieut.-Governor did go forth at the head of the party that attacked the rebels, and after having put them to flight returned to the city with many prisoners, amid the greetings and tears of a grateful multitude. Shall we not lift up our hearts in thanksgiving to Him who hath given us the victory over our enemies.

January 1st, 1838.—How mingled are the feelings with which we welcome the birth of another year—a new era seems to have dawned upon us. What mingled sensations of hopes and fears arise while we write the new date, and though in point of fact every new day of our lives is equally valuable, and ought to be as great a cause for grateful reflection—and the day past as the year past—an occasion for repentance and humiliation of spirit, yet there is as it were a solemnity in the closing and dawning of the year that is unlike what we feel on ordinary occasions. Oh, Lord God, who hast kept us safely to the beginning of another year, grant us Thy blessing and prosper, I beseech Thee, all undertakings of the New Year. Committing ourselves to Thy care, let us be contented with our lot whatever it may be, and humbly say—Not our will, but Thine, be done, O Lord.—Amen.

I spent the day with my dear sister; while I was there Mr. Moodie shot a huge hawk, the great American hawk; it measured about three feet from wing to wing. The only difference I can see between this and those described by Wilson and Nuttall is that there is no brown marks—the breast and lower part of the body being interlined with irregular bars of very dark slaty hue on a white ground, like broad and beautiful pencilling.[12] This was the largest hawk I have ever seen, with the exception of one that was hovering over the lake about a month ago in pursuit of one of my geese, and which appeared almost equal in size to a small eagle. The goose with instinctive fear dived down whenever her fierce enemy was about to strike her. Though painfully interested for the safety of my goose, I could not help admiring the graceful evolutions of her assailant, now wheeling round and round, narrowing the circle till he reached a centre from which to sweep downward, and when baffled rising slowly again higher and higher till he again seemed to poise his frame and float steadily for a second or two before he again commenced his gyrations. The shouts of our boy Marten, however, caused him to turn in another direction, and he slowly and gracefully withdrew and sailed off towards the head of the lake quite calm and collected as though he disdained to exhibit fear or annoyance at his disappointment.

January 7th, 1838.—What a change of atmosphere we have experienced during the last week! The thaw had indeed commenced during the last week of the old year, and now not a speck of snow is to be seen on the fields. For the last three or four days the days have been warm and pleasant, with spring-like skies, with the variety of some warm showers of rain.

8th.—The wind and rain were tremendous last night till past two—towards sunrise it changed to heavy snow. To-day it freezes in the shade, thaws in the sun, but promises more snow and frost again. The second and third of January were almost too warm for fires. This January thaw is customary, but for the last two winters we have seen nothing of it. This may account for the cold late springs and wet summers of the last two years; so if my augury be right we may expect the seasons are returning to their old course.

And now having but little to note in my journal of a domestic nature, let me endeavour to take a short review of public events. The Lower Province seems to be comparatively quiet, since the defeat at St. Eustache and Grand Builè, but where are Mackenzie and his rebellious followers? His first retreat was to Buffalo, where it appears he was received with enthusiasm by the greater portion of the Buffalonians. After haranguing them in the theatre, numbers of adventurers joined his standard; however, the authorities gave him notice to leave the place in six hours time, which he did, and withdrew to an island in the Niagara river called Navy Island, where he has been supplied with ammunitions and every necessary, with a considerable increase of men from the American shores.

But what says this for the popularity of his cause? Were he speaking the voice of the Canadian people how comes it that he is obliged only to republican neighbours for men and the munitions of war? If it be the great desire of the mass of the people why do they not fight their own battle and not be obliged to the Americans for redressing injuries—if injuries there be—to redress? But it is not the voice of the people, it is but the factious cry of the discontented few. And shall we then allow a few traitors to impose new laws and change the form of government? And shall we allow the Americans to force their republican form of government upon us against our inclinations? The Canadians are not oppressed—and if they be, let them stand forth in their own defense after having appealed to their Sovereign for redress, if redress be required? Mackenzie raised the cry of rebellion, and the answer has been the rallying of thousands and tens of thousands of valiant men round the standard of their young Queen—with the thrilling cry echoed from lake to lake and forest to plain, "Long live Victoria and the British Constitution." Has not this trial of strength been sufficient to prove that the greater part of the Canadian population, and decidedly its most respectable members, are opposed to change, at all events to such a change as Mackenzie and his allies would introduce? Some few of his adherents, such as Van Rensselaer and Van Egmond, and others of the respectable class of American citizens may be actuated by a mistaken enthusiasm, and with what they may consider laudable ambition, are desirous of having their names recorded in history as the benefactors of an oppressed people struggling for freedom, the first to lift the sword in their behalf—in short, to be the Washingtons of Canada. But the cases are not parallel—we are not oppressed, our taxes are light, and we enjoy every liberty that free-born Britons can desire—our safety, our dependence, our population are from the Mother Country, and shall we like ungrateful children, while yet dependent on her for support, withdraw ourselves from her arms? But to return to facts. The rebels, encouraged by their increase of men and ammunition, seemed to imagine themselves already crowned with success, and Mackenzie with his usual audacity publishes a proclamation, in which he speaks of the Canadian Government as at an end, and offers a reward for the apprehension of Sir Francis Bond Head, with many other absurdities of the same kind. The States' authorities have done all they could to restrain the zeal of their people, but it is not easy to keep down the spirit of liberty and speculation. The American mob want their neighbours to be like themselves, whether they like it or not, and then they are flattered by the rewards held out to them in event of success.

The capture of the steamer *Caroline*, which was boarded, fired and finally sent down the rapids and over Niagara Falls, has given great offence, and the Governor of New York talks very big about the lawlessness of the deed. The Provincial papers give the history of this daring, but as we think justifiable, event. Much excitement existed for some days, and the conjectures whether or not we shall be involved in a war with the United States seemed to occupy our minds. But the Navy Island bubble has burst. The bombardment of the Island has taken place and about 100 of the insurgents were killed, and the rest fled with haste. Lount was taken in the attempt to cross the Niagara to the American frontier, and has undergone an examination at Toronto. He appears, by all we can learn, to have been a misguided, but in his general character an amiable man. Gibson, another of the leaders, has also been taken.

On taking possession of the Island it presented a melancholy spectacle: the earth ploughed up by shells, trees uptorn. In one spot was a pit, in which nearly a hundred dead bodies were lying, (the victims of intemperate zeal or wretched cupidity) that had been killed during the bombardment of the place. So wretched were the fortifications that had been thrown up that they could not have stood the charge of the cannon. The wretched huts that had sheltered Mackenzie and his men were represented as no better than pigsties.

Colonel Van Egmond died in the hospital at Toronto some days since. He was a veteran of seventy years of age. He was in ill health, but it is supposed that mortification and chagrin hastened his death. What had a man of his age to do with aiding a rebellion so uncalled for as that of Mackenzie? Had it been in defense of his country or against the oppression of a tyrannical Sovereign that the white-haired man girded his sword upon his thigh, we would have venerated the feeling that had prompted him to go forth, but such a motive did not, and could not, have actuated him.[13]

⌒

1   Sir John Colborne, lieutenant-governor of Upper Canada, 1828–36.

2   Peterborough became part of the Colborne District in 1841.

3   Solomon Sibbons—Edward Sibbings of Lot 22, Concession 5, in Douro Township was a "Suffolk settler of low degree."

4   Captain Cowell—Captain James Gifford Cowell of Peterborough (d. 1840), captain of the 2nd Northumberland militia.

5   Colonel Anderson—Major Charles Anderson (1786–1844) of Rice Lake.

6   Colonel Brown—Lieutenant Colonel Robert Brown of Peterborough commanded the 4th Northumberland militia.

7   Mary (Reid) Strickland.

8   Colonel Robert Moodie was shot by rebels and died on December 4, 1837.

9   Now a part of Cobourg, Amherst was the site of the courthouse and jail.

10   Colonel Alexander MacDonell of Peterborough commanded the 2nd Northumberland militia.

11   The Stewarts' home, Auburn, was located about two miles north of Peterborough on the Douro side of the Otonabee.

12   Likely *Wilson's Ornithology: With Additions including the Birds Described by Audubon, Bonaparte, Nuttall, & Richardson* (n.d.).

13   Colonel Anthony Van Egmond (1771–1838) commanded the rebels at Montgomery's farm; he was captured and jailed and subsequently died in hospital in early 1838.

THE INTERRUPTED BRIDAL.
A TRUE STORY OF THE FIRST
REBELLION IN THE COLONY

This story appeared in a new London magazine, *The Home Circle* 1:1&2 (1849), 6–7, 19–21, as a result of Agnes Strickland's agency. It incorporates Traill's own experiences with stories heard about other families in early December 1837 when Sir Francis Bond Head's Proclamation suddenly reached the backwoods north of Peterborough. Highly conventional from its use of names to its depiction of attitudes, the story makes two significant contributions. First, Traill offers a picture of Agnes Denham as a capable and well-trained backwoods girl, rich in "useful knowledge" and unattracted to the "superficial graces." In its presentation of aspects of a bush wedding and the tapping of communal resources, the story validates the approach to life that Agnes incarnates. Secondly, in dramatizing the response to the proclamation, Traill captures the solidly British patriotism of the backwoods settlers. "We are all, every one, concerned in it," says Agnes's father. Indeed, in Traill's recreation part of the appeal of loyalty for her and her characters lies in the settlers' sense of commitment to their "youthful sovereign," Victoria, who had taken the throne in 1837. The piece was republished as "The Volunteer's Bride" in *The Maple Leaf* (May 1854).

George Hilton was one of the smartest backwoodsmen in our district; he could turn his hand to anything, and was strong, active, good-tempered, and energetic. Before he was three-and-twenty years old he had cleared a hundred acres of his farm, brought fifty into cultivation, and built a capital log-house upon his estate. The interior of his domicile was fitted-up with more taste than is usually seen in the dwelling of a bush-settler; but all the carvings, mouldings, and decorations were the work of his own hands, and he had taken the greater pains with them because he was preparing for his bride.

A settler is nothing without a wife; and George Hilton was considered an enviable man when it was known that he had persuaded Agnes Denham, the eldest daughter of an emigrant lieutenant from the mother country, to share his fortunes; for Agnes was not only one of the prettiest girls in the township, but the most amiable and well-conducted. Accomplishments are not particularly requisite for the daughters of large families in the bush, and Agnes Denham had acquired quite as many of the superficial graces of life as were necessary. She was well read, wrote a clear, distinct hand, danced with spirit, sang pleasingly without any acquired affectations, and could accompany herself on the guitar. Her stock of useful knowledge was far more extensive; she could make bread, cakes, pickles and preserves, candles, soap, and maple-sugar, and was a proficient in needle-work of the domestic kind. She was, in short, the very girl to make a sensible man happy, never having had any time for folly or foolish dissipation. Her parents knew not how to spare her, for she was the sunshine and comfort of their home; but when they were assured of her affection for George Hilton, they raised no objections. The course of true love for once flowed smooth as a summer stream, and it was agreed that the bridal should take place on the day when she should complete her eighteenth year.

Agnes's cheerful temper and affectionate disposition had made her a general favourite in the neighbourhood where she lived; and her female friends took the present opportunity of evincing the lively interest they took in her approaching happiness, by rendering her every assistance in their power in preparing her wedding-dresses, and the thousand-and-one little essentials for so important a change as that about to take place.

Agnes was anxious to save her parents as much expense as she possibly could in her outfit, and resolved that there should not be any milliners' bills to pay on account of her marriage—so it was unanimously agreed by her young friends, that they should give Agnes all the help they were able in completing her wedding toilette; and many a pleasant day was passed by the little bride-elect and the chosen few who were admitted into her counsels, in cutting-out and contriving, fitting and trimming, and admiring the bridal finery, as each article of dress was completed and consigned to the packing cases that were destined to receive the treasures.

And many were the little offerings of affection that were presented by loving generous hearts—which, if they lacked something in costliness of material, were rendered charming in the eyes of the little bride by the kind manner in which they had been wrought and given.

There was the bridal handkerchief, delicately embroidered and edged with the finest lace that gentle and ingenious hands could fabricate; the pretty manchettes and collars, berthès and reticules, were all the labours of kind fingers eager to contribute something to please and enrich her little wardrobe; and not the least admired were the sprigs of myrtle and white rosebuds tastefully made by George's youngest sister, and which, though from the hands of only an amateur *artiste* in this species of fancy-work, looked almost as natural among the shining ringlets of Agnes and her bride-maidens, as if they had been plucked from the garden and green-house.

But the best of the fun was making the bride-cake. There was a regular "Bee" for the occasion, conducted, however, with a secrecy and mystery quite befitting so delicate a matter. What will my youthful readers, meet to be made brides themselves, say to such an innovation of all rules of orthodoxy in wedding preparations? A home-made bride-cake, and the bride one of the compounders thereof!—who ever heard or even dreamed of such a thing? True for you—as the Irish say—but remember, ye fair and fastidious critics!—Agnes Denham's was a "Bush Wedding." The grand difficulty was in the icing [of] the cake. It was quite amusing for a looker-on to watch the curious anxious faces peeping over one another's shoulders into the various cookery-books, English and American, that had been privily borrowed from the most accomplished housewives in the neighbourhood.

The gentlemen were, of course, excluded from these mysterious conferences, the only piece of broadcloth admitted into the secret consultations was little Harry—Agnes's youngest brother—who, after having listened with breathless interest to some discussion going on among the fair bevy of confectioners, respecting the difficulty of finding some suitable instrument for laying on the icing, hastily retreated to the workshop, and soon returned with a triumphant air, bearing in his hand a sort of flat trowel which he had carved out of a clean shingle—declaring "he was confident it would answer the purpose admirably."

Harry's expedient was highly applauded by all present, and adopted forthwith. Then there was such anxiety about the baking of the precious compound, and the turning of it out of the bake-kettle, when done, so as not to injure its fair proportions. All the females of the house, from Mamma down to Biddy Fagan, the Irish maid, were in a fever till this important affair was concluded. The cake exceeded all expectations; it was neither broken nor burned, and the ice looked almost like snow itself—the house was filled with the odour—the cake was indeed rich and rare to sight and sense. In short, it was a splendid achievement in the way of a home-made bride-cake; and, as the boys all declared, looked gloriously when decorated with the wreath of white roses which Caroline Hill placed upon it.

It was arranged that the ceremony was to be performed at five o'clock, and arrangements were made for a dance after tea. After supper, the young couple were to go quietly home to their own house, which was scarcely a mile off.

Never did Agnes look more lovely than when she entered the little parlour, leaning on her fond father's arm, dressed in white muslin, white ribbons, and the simple white rose-buds among her dark and shining locks; these were her only ornaments. Some delay had been caused in the marriage by the unusual absence of Edward, Agnes's eldest brother, who had been despatched in the early part of the day on some errand to the town, having promised to return by dinner-time, and long before the ceremony was to take place; but hour after hour had passed, and at last his place as grooms-man was given to his cousin, Frederic Lacey. A vague misgiving that some untoward accident had caused the delay, had at times glanced over the minds of more than one of the party, though no one gave utterance to their fears, lest they should cast a gloom over the minds of the young couple; and the solemn service commenced. Just as the ring was being placed on the finger of the bride, a sudden bustle was heard in the entrance, and Edward Denham hurried into the room, his cloak and cap covered with snow, for it had been snowing heavily for some time. The clergyman raised his finger as he entered to enjoin silence, and with more than usual gravity pronounced the last prayer and benediction. It was over; and then came a buzz, and whispering murmur, and sudden exclamations of dismay and terror from the females, of excitement from the men, as they gathered about Edward to hear the news he had to communicate.

Agnes had been so naturally engrossed by her own feelings and the peculiarity of her situation, that she had hardly noticed her brother's return, till she found herself suddenly deserted by all her companions, and became conscious that she stood alone in the centre of the room; even George had left her side. And now she perceived that looks of sadness and interest were directed towards her by several of the group, and a sense of some dreadful calamity, in which she or some one dearer to her than herself, was somehow involved, came over her. "What can it be? Oh, do tell me what has happened!" she exclaimed at last, casting her eyes imploringly upon her father's face.

"Only, my child, that George must leave you this very night—this very hour, were it possible."

She clung, speechless with terror, to her father's arm.

"Listen to your brother, Agnes; that paper will explain all. It is the Governor's proclamation."

"But George! Oh, how can he be concerned in it?" gasped out the trembling bride.

"We are all, every one, concerned in it, my child; not your husband only. Rebellion has broken out in the province. Toronto is threatened with fire and sword; and every man, be his station what it may, is called upon to arm himself and obey the mandate of the Governor, to enrol himself under the banner of his sovereign, and march to the defence of the capital, or be marked as cowards or traitors. Your brother is the bearer of this declaration."

Silence was now commanded, and standing forth in the midst of the ring that formed round him, Edward, with loud and distinct voice, read the proclamation of the Governor. Very different was the effect produced on the minds of his audience; for while some of the young ladies wept and turned pale, the servants, who occupied the open doorway, cried, and almost screamed aloud. The old men and fathers looked grave and stern; while among the young men all was excitement and energy; even the newly-made bridegroom, forgetful of his agonised partner, partook of the general enthusiasm, and stood with flashing eye and animated tone eloquently declaring his readiness to join the gallant band of loyal volunteers. It was not till he caught the pleading glance of his pale bride's dark eyes fixed so mournfully upon his face, that a sense of her desolation of heart struck him; and as if to atone for his seeming forgetfulness of her, whom but a few minutes before he had so solemnly vowed to cherish, in joy or sorrow, he hurried to her side, and tenderly drawing her arm through his, led her to the sofa, and placing himself at her side, strove with all a lover's fondness to soothe and comfort her; but it was a hard trial for them both, and the very suddenness of the shock and the vague notion of the perils that threatened her husband, added to the anguish of the parting.

This was not a time indeed to talk of marrying and giving in marriage. All was now hurry and excitement. Every bosom responded to the loyal appeal—every hand was warmly linked in one bond of loyal brotherhood, young and old, the weak with the strong, swore to fight bravely in defence of their hearths, their altars, their adopted country, and their youthful sovereign.

"Come, my friends," said Capt. Denham, Agnes's uncle, an old veteran U. E. Loyalist, the most collected person in the room, "let us drink health and happiness to our little bride and her husband, and give three cheers for Queen Victoria! and then for business, for there is much to do."

The toast was given, and enthusiastically drunk by every one present; even the women caught the spirit of loyal feeling, and forgot their fears and griefs, while the rafters of the old log-house rung with the auspicious name of their beloved Queen.

"Now, girls," said the old veteran, "no more tears, no more doleful looks; come, quick, stir yourselves,—get us a good cup of tea, and then look to your brothers' knapsacks. And you, my little bride, come hither, and attend to your old uncle. Remember that you are now a soldier's bride, as well as an old soldier's niece, and you must overcome all childish regrets, and be my own brave girl; you are not the first young couple that have thus rudely and suddenly been separated by the mischances of war; let me see that you are not unworthy of the high character that you have so long held in your uncle's opinion. And hark you, Agnes, when George comes back we'll have a good frolic, and you shall dance the first set with uncle Fred."

The cheerful tones of this dear old relative, whom Agnes loved almost as a father, did more to cheer and quiet her disturbed spirits than even the tender soothings of her young husband, and Agnes soon busied herself in assisting in the requisite preparations for the evening repast, and tried to forget the singularity of her position; and well and bravely did she battle with the choking tears and sighs.

The evening meal was hastily concluded; and now so changed was the scene, that you would have supposed there were preparations making for a siege rather than a bridal. Guns, pistols, old rusty firelocks that had hung for years unheeded upon the rafters, more for ornament than use— every weapon of offence or defence, were handed forth; rifles, that had only been employed against the wild animals and feathered game of the woods, were now to be employed in more deadly warfare, and it was astonishing with what coolness and determination these things were examined and discussed by the young people.

As to the females, they were deeply occupied in selecting such changes of linen and other matters as could be collected at so short a warning; and uncle Frederick's advice and opinion was continually in requisition to decide upon the necessary and unnecessary articles to be packed up.

Nor was Agnes idle. She sat down to fix the thongs to a pair of moccasins for George, and assisted him in adjusting the wrappings for his feet, as familiarly as if she had been a wife of years' standing; and a pretty picture she would have made as she sat on the ground at George's feet binding the strings round his ankles, while her bridegroom bent down with admiring fondness on her slight form, set off, as it was, by the full flowing muslin dress; her pale cheek shaded by the clustering ringlets of her dark glossy hair, among which, half-hidden, peeped forth the simple emblem of her bridal state—the pure white rose.

The morning broke through heavy snow-drifts and piercing winds—a day as melancholy as the hearts of the mothers, sisters, wives, and friends, who were then about to part with those so near and dear to them, perhaps never again to meet. It was not till the last waving hands could no longer be distinguished through the blinding snow-shower and dim grey twilight, that the anxious household felt how really terrible the separation was under such circumstances as the present. Their very ignorance of the state of affairs in the country increased the feeling of uneasiness that prevailed; all was horrible uncertainty and fearful conjecture.

And how fared it with our poor Agnes at this trying moment? She had borne up courageously, beyond even her old uncle's most sanguine hopes, till the last; but when the object of her affections was no longer visible to her aching eyes, she flung herself into her mother's arms and wept, till worn out with excess of grief—the more violent from having been so long repressed—she at last sobbed herself to sleep upon her mother's breast, like an o'er-wearied infant. Her young companions laid her on the sofa, and sorrowfully went to their task of restoring all things to their former state, and resumed once more their every-day garments, laying aside the bridal finery for some more auspicious day.

And now it was that the family, like hundreds similarly situated at this period, began to feel the helplessness of their condition. A second peremptory summons hastened the departure of all the men-servants. Nor did Mr. Denham and uncle Frederic hesitate to obey the call; they were neither too old nor too infirm to carry arms; and leaving the family to the care of the female servants, and old Michael Regan to tend the cattle and be their hewer of wood and drawer of water, they also departed.

But, unfortunately, old Michael was seized with a very inconvenient fit of military ardour, and hurried off to join the volunteers at H——, seeing afar off visions of plunder and visions of glory; his departure was a signal for the two faithless damsels, Biddy and Catharine, to depart also; declaring that they dared not stay for their lives, now all the men folk were gone, for they were sure the rebels and Yankees would be up directly they heard the master and all the men were away—so off they went and returned no more.

In this dilemma it was in vain to look for help from neighbours or friends; all that could be done was to rely upon their own unassisted efforts. Harry now found himself a person of no small importance. On this little fellow devolved the heavy tasks of supplying the house with wood and water, feeding the cattle, and many other things; and in these matters he was often obliged, though reluctantly, to accept the help of his sisters and the other bridesmaids who had remained from the day of the wedding, not deeming it safe to return to their more distant homes. There were other girls in the neighbourhood whose unprotected state had moved the maternal compassion of Mrs. Denham to offer them an asylum till they should be enabled to return to their lonely and desolate homes; and but for the tormenting state of anxiety that was endured as to the fate of those who had left them, so large a party must have been merry and cheerful. As it was, they alternately helped to comfort or alarm each other, as rumours of the distant rebellion reached them through some of the poor distressed women, who ventured to the town from time to time to gather news of their absent sons and husbands.

Three days of agonising suspense had followed the report of Colonel Moodie's death,[1] and the expectation that the rebels were about to enter the capital, when Agnes noticed a dark figure moving slowly along through the deep snow-drifts that blocked the untracked road across the clearing. Who could it be? was a matter of conjecture not unmixed with interest to those to whom every stranger was now, in some shape or other, connected with the fate of their country and absent friends.

It was evidently a female, from the dress and faltering movements, and Harry was despatched to offer what help he could to the weary traveller, and hear the news. In a few minutes the good-natured boy ran in, bearing in his arms a bundle, which he put into Agnes's arms, while, with a face radiant with joy, he exclaimed—

"Agnes dear, joy! joy! the war is over, the rebels flying; George will be back soon. Hurrah! Hurrah! for Sir Francis

Head and the gallant volunteers! But take care of the poor baby, while I run out for the mother;" and away flew Harry, leaving a half-frozen babe in his astonished sister's lap, while, with a gallantry and feeling hardly to be expected in a little fellow of ten years old, he hastened to lend his arm to the young mother, who, defying the dreadful state of the weather and snow-blocked roads, had left her home, which was some miles higher up the road, and taken her young infant in her arms, and travelled to the distant town to enquire for her husband. She had none with whom to leave her child—no person to assist her in her almost perilous undertaking; but what will not woman do, what cannot woman bear for the man she loves,—the husband of her heart, the father of her child? She said, "joy for the good news she brought had kept up her strength and spirits for many miles of her journey, but her clothes had become so heavy with the accumulation of ice and snow, that she could go no further, and was fearful lest, as the day grew colder, the baby might be frozen in her arms."

How was the poor half-frozen traveller cherished, admired, and applauded, by the whole household! What an angel of female heroism and self-devotion did she appear in the eyes of the delighted Agnes!

What a revolution from doubt and dread to joy and rapturous delight, had been effected by a few brief words—"The rebels are dispersed, and flying in all directions; the gallant band of loyal volunteers will be home directly." Agnes repeated these welcome words over a thousand times, and laughed and wept by turns; but now her tears, like those of the wives, sisters, and friends of our brave Canadian volunteers, were tears of joy.

Every hour now brought up fresh news of victory and return.

It was late in the evening of the following day, when, just as the family were gathered round the fire previous to retiring to rest, a quick step was heard on the crisp snow on the footpath beneath the window.

"Hark! some one is coming with news for us," exclaimed Harry, starting up, and hastening to unbar the door.

"It is Papa!" cried Ellen.

"It is my own George—my husband!" burst from the lips of Agnes—

"For lover's ears are sharp to hear."

The next moment the arms of George were clasped about the neck of his bride.

We will not describe their greeting.

The next morning brought home all the volunteers of our district, and the long delayed nuptial *fête* of George Hilton and his bride took place on a day of public rejoicing for the return of our brave defenders.

The wedding-cake, which had remained whole while the Canadas were in some danger of tumbling to pieces, was getting somewhat stale by that time, I guess; but it had been carefully stored by the thrifty mother of the bride, and when it was placed in the centre of the supper table it looked better than at its first appearance, for it was garlanded with victory-laurels and ribbons of the loyal colour, which looked very lively among the white roses and orange blossoms, its original decorations. It was cut up with three cheers—one for the bride, one for the bridegroom, and the third for the colony and its brave volunteers.

～

1   See page 128, note 8.

Canadian Lumberers

Like many of Traill's sketches that appeared in British
magazines in the 1830s and 1840s, "Canadian Lumberers"
was meant to be part of a sequel to *The Backwoods of Canada*,
a book that would provide more pioneering detail and a
richer range of human interest than Traill had been able to
include, given her limited experience of Canada, in the earlier volume. "Canadian Lumberers" appeared in *Chambers's
Edinburgh Journal* 7 (December 20, 1838), 380–81. While
ostensibly a sketch about lumberers and loggers, it is typi-
cally digressive, ranging outward to include her five years'
experience with ague or intermittent or malarial fever, the
uses pioneers make of their cellars, and the susceptibility of
the local Indians to new illnesses, particularly the influenza
epidemic of 1837. Indeed, with its record of the changing
landscape of Douro Township as the forests of pine were so
quickly cut down and her lament that, as European illnesses
deplete the Native population, "The time will come when
the smoke of the wigwam will no more be seen among the
forest trees," the sketch provides both a close personal
observation of the changes taking place around her and the
beginnings of Traill's attempts to measure and account for
the losses she had witnessed.

The latter part of the last winter[1] was busily employed by us in drawing saw logs to the lake, having made an engagement with a gentleman to supply him with five hundred pine logs, for which he engaged to pay us half a dollar a log. These logs were to be twelve feet in length, and not less than sixteen inches in the square; many of them, however, far exceeded this standard. A fine clean pine will yield from five to six logs; the largest of these will frequently measure from three to four feet in diameter; but no difference is made in price between the very large and those that are just within the limits—they are taken one with another.

After the logs have been sawed to the proper length, they are placed on a wooden truck, a sort of rude lumber sleigh, or else simply fastened to the oxen by means of the logging chain, and thus conveyed over the snow to the ice; when the whole number are collected together, they are surrounded by a circular enclosure of timbers securely pinned together, to prevent the logs from floating away when the waters of the lakes rise, which they do to a considerable height after the melting of the snow and breaking up of the ice has swelled the tributary streams and springs.

After the owner of the logs has been duly advertised that the boom is completed, and you have called in two competent witnesses to bear testimony that the logs have been properly secured, you are no longer accountable for any accident that may happen to them. The proprietor, if he be a prudent person, then sends up some person to number and mark the timber, and at the proper season employs lumberers to form them into rafts, and guide them down the river to their destination.

It is a pretty sight of a cloudless summer day to watch the large pine rafts on our lake floating slowly down with the current, sometimes towed along by men in canoes, or else guided with long poles by the lumberers, who are stationed upon them. Now and then you will see a little hut or shed erected on the rafts, from which the thin blue smoke curls upwards, and floats like a gauzy veil among the branches of the trees that skirt the neighbouring shores; and the ear may catch at times the voices of the raftsmen singing and making rude melody, or hoarsely calling to their fellows. These sounds, when softened by the water and the distance, are far from unpleasing, and have the effect of soothing and cheering the spirits, while the eye is relieved by the sight of the busy crew, and the huge mass they are so gently guiding over the calm blue waters.

I have seen five or six such rafts pass down in one day. The men employed in the business of rafting earn great wages, and so they ought to do, for they are exposed to many hardships, and every vicissitude of weather, besides being often in the water up to the knees, and sometimes to their very waists for hours together while forming the rafts. When employed by timber-merchants to cut and square the pines, besides forming the rafts and conducting them down the river to the St. Lawrence, they build themselves rude dwellings in the woods near the water side; and here, secluded from the world, and shut out from the society of their wives, mothers, and sisters, they pass weeks amid the solitudes of the lonely woods and unfrequented waters of these lakes. Yet, even in this savage sort of life, there seems to be a charm, for the raftsman will dwell with infinite satisfaction on his life of peril and hardship, talk with enthusiasm of the gigantic trees he has felled, of the dangers he has escaped, of the game he has killed, or the fish he has speared. In short, he seems to pity those who are confined to the inglorious labours of the farm or the store, while he can roam free like any of the wild denizens of the forest.

I had often heard and read of the lawless conduct and wild manners of the men engaged in the occupation of lumbering; but I must say that the few men of this class that I have spoken to, were for the most part well-behaved, civil people, with much of the milk of human kindness in their hearts. Some of them were native Canadians; the rest were Irish.

I well remember one fine June morning—it was our second spring in this country—I was sitting on a log beside the garden gate, holding my little boy upon my lap, who was suffering under the influence of an ague fit, and I was glad to warm his chilled frame in the warm sunshine.[2] A party of lumberers from a raft, having landed at the shore of our lake, came up to me, and with great politeness asked my permission to take a live coal from the kitchen fire. This small boon was readily granted, and while one of the party was securing the coal between two cedar chips—for the better conveying it in safety to the lake shore, where they desired to kindle a fire by which to cook their frugal meal of salt pork and potatoes, or flour bannocks, baked in a frying-pan over the embers—the rest of the party drew near to the place where I was seated, and scanned, with compassionate eyes, my suffering babe. These rough men had kindly hearts, and expressed the tenderest sympathy for the child, and not less so for my anxiety on his behalf, cheering and soothing me with such expressions as genuine benevolence suggested. One took the little fellow's thin wasted hand in his, another patted his pallid cheek, and each in turn recommended some favourite remedy which had proved infallible in ninety-nine cases out of a hundred; but these receipts were all of too stimulating a nature to be ventured upon in the present instance, and I shook my head doubtingly when they told me of such doses as red pepper steeped in whiskey, to be taken fasting; or a teaspoonful of black pepper mixed in a glass of proof spirits, to be taken with the coming on of the cold fit; or decoction of strong green tea, &c.&c.; these remedies might have their beneficial effects on persons living the life of lumberers, but I dared not administer such to a tender infant. The inner bark of the root of the sumach they also mentioned as a specific, and I have since seen it tried with success in several instances. They had all suffered from ague and lake fevers, they said, but now they had become so inured to the changes of heat and cold, wet and dry, that they were quite hardy, and would as soon be in the water as out of it.

These good men strove to comfort me by the assurance that the ague would not trouble us after the present year, or if it did return next spring, it would be of a much milder character. The first year of the emigrant coming out to Canada, he is generally safe from the attacks of the ague and lake fever, unless exposed to some peculiarly unwholesome atmosphere, such as the low shores of swampy weedy lakes; but the second spring he rarely escapes; and the months of May, June, July, and August, are too often spent under the depressing effects of this distressing complaint. The working season is thus frequently lost, and many most melancholy instances of severe distress have fallen under my knowledge, where the poor emigrant's little means have been utterly consumed to supply a starving family of sick children with the merest necessaries of life. The cow, the pig, every article of clothing that could possibly be dispensed with, have all gone in turn, till misery, and want, and despair, have almost brought them to the verge of the grave. I heard one poor woman relate, with tears streaming over her pale face, such a tale of woe, that the remembrance of its sad details yet grieves me. Her husband had been sick for fourteen months, and at last his sickness deprived him of his reason; and she, with several small children, could do but little in the rude labour of clearing the forest-encumbered ground; what they could do, they did; but the frost killed the potato crop, or nearly so, and breachy cattle made inroads into the ill-enclosed field, where they had contrived to sow and rake in a little spring wheat; this resource also failed them. Then came despair, and famine. For some days she declared they subsisted only on the wild leeks that grew in the forest; and, having been obliged to part with every spare garment, they beheld the coming on of the winter with unspeakable dread. To add to their distress, they were far from neighbours. The sufferings they endured for some time were of the most dreadful kind. This sad statement was borne witness to by a poor woman who chanced to come into the store at the time this poor creature was telling me her story. Since that time, I have met with many cases of almost similar distress arising from the loss of time occasioned by attacks of ague.

The prevailing opinion among the lower class of settlers is—and I must think it a strange one—that the ague should not be stopped, but be let to run its course for some time. If you put it away, they say, it is sure to come again worse than at first; and that it often does return after a week or ten days, is certain; but if vigorously attacked with doses of calomel and quinine, it generally disappears entirely from that time. I have known persons who seemed constitutionally liable to returns of ague, or a sort of nervous intermittent, in the spring, and these aver their belief in its having arisen from their not letting the ague have its course the first year they were attacked by it; and so deeply is this assurance, that it is in vain to contest it with them.

As far as regarded ourselves, the lumberers proved true prophets; the ague has never visited our house since that year. We always considered the rising of the water in the cellar to have been the primary cause of that season of suffering, and have taken precautions to prevent a recurrence of the evil. When we talk of cellars, I dare say you think we must have goodly stores of wines in them; but you are mistaken—for a cellar in a log-house is nothing more than a substitute for a root-house, and, in lieu of generous wines, is simply stored with potatoes, carrots, turnips, beets, and such like winter roots, with the addition possibly of barrels of pork and beef, or a firkin of salted butter; sometimes, if floored with boards, or paved, they are made to answer the purpose of a winter dairy; as it must be frost-proof, or the vegetables would be spoiled, it answers the purpose of keeping the milk well. I have known milk frozen into a solid mass in a closet beside a stove in a warm parlour.

I have often wondered that the Indians were not more liable to ague, from their constant exposure to weather and other hardships; but though bilious fevers often prove fatal visitors to the Indian villages, you seldom hear of the ague. Under severe attacks of illness, the Indian constitution appears rapidly to sink. I am inclined to think the seeds of disease are sown very early in infancy and childhood, first by unnatural confinement of the tender limbs and chest of the babe while strapped upon their wooden cradles—and afterwards from the hardships they endure. The older children are generally so miserably clad, that they must, and they do suffer greatly, from the vicissitudes of a climate where the sudden alterations from cold to heat, and from heat to comparative cold, are often very remarkable. Though you will sometimes see a boy of four or five panting under a heavy blanket coat in July and August, you as frequently notice the younger children and the little girls of that age shivering in cold wet weather, with no better covering than a thin cotton frock and cloth leggings; the latter merely clothe the leg from the knees downward, being fastened by straps and bands round the body. The result of such scanty clothing is, that the Indian children suffer from continual catarrhs, which must waste and weaken the constitution in time. While that terrible scourge, the influenza of 1837, passed slightly over the European settlers in this province, it proved fatal to many of the Indians, whose constitutions and peculiar mode of life made them sink more readily under its influence.[3] It is thus, by slow but sure degrees, the native race are fading from the land of their fathers. The time will come when the smoke of the wigwam will no more be seen among the forest trees, nor the sound of the Indian's rifle be heard ringing through the woods. Let us be thankful when we reflect that it is by the hand of God, and not by the sword of extermination, that the Indians are disappearing. Beneath a merciful government, their rights are protected; they are not driven into banishment, as the natives of the south are at this day, exiled, broken-hearted, and burning with just indignation at the wrongs that have been heaped upon their devoted heads.[4] The Indians of Canada fall asleep and are gathered to their fathers in peace, with the blessed light of Christianity shedding a peaceful glory above their graves.

෴

1   The winter of 1833–34.

2   James Traill was just over a year in age when the ague felled him and the Traill family.

3   The influenza pandemic of 1836–37, which prevailed widely in Canada, was one of a series of influenza epidemics to strike North America during the early nineteenth century.

4   Traill was clearly aware through newspaper reports of American violence to Native peoples and in particular the forced movement of tribes to remote reservations. In May 1830, the United States Congress passed the "Indian Removal Bill," which allowed President Andrew Jackson to initiate the removal of tribes residing east of the Mississippi River. The movement of eastern Natives to sites west of the river occurred over the next decade; among them were more than 60,000 members of the Choctaw, Creek, Chickesaw, Cherokee, and Seminole tribes. Designated by the displaced Natives as the "Trail of Tears," their relocation involved not only the physical hardships of the journey but also the emotional trauma inherent in their removal from their established homelands. See Grant Foreman, *Indian Removal, The Last Trek of the Indians*, and *Advancing the Frontier*.

A Visit to the Camp of the Chippewa Indians[1]

This sketch appeared in *Sharpe's London Journal* 7 (1848), 114–18, accompanied by a note identifying it as a "Letter from Mrs. Trail [sic], Authoress of 'The Backwoods of Canada,' to her sister, Miss Agnes Stickland [sic]." It is likely that, in writing her sequel to *The Backwoods of Canada*, Traill used a similar letter format, drawing material from her journal. Indeed, even in the journal she occasionally begins entries as if they were letters back to her Suffolk family.

Here she returns to material in Letters VIII and XVI of *The Backwoods*, offering a further description of the Nogan family, Ojibwa who were associated with the Curve Lake reserve. She switches attention from Peter Nogan (see also Naugon, Nogy, Noggan, Nogee, Nogie) who was the village chief (1831–60) to his brother Tom and his family. Informal in its structure, the letter/sketch moves easily from medicinal treatments for Mrs. Tom's papoose to the nature and quality of Native crafts to a canoe trip to Strawberry Island, just south of the Traills' homestead on Lake Katchewanook. In particular, her attention to Mrs. Tom's manner of disciplining her temperamental son provides a focus for the visit. The miniature canoe mentioned here that was sent to Agnes Strickland is still to be seen in the small museum at Southwold, the town in which Traill's sister lived out her final years. "A Visit to the Camp of the Chippewa Indians" also appears in *The Prose of Life: Sketches from Victorian Canada*, ed. Carole Gerson and Kathy Mezei (Downsview: ECW Press, 1981).

You ask me if I have seen anything of the Indians lately. I am glad you were interested in my former accounts of them, and will supply you with any little anecdotes I may collect, from time to time, for your amusement. I have not seen old Peter, the hunter, or his good-tempered squaw, since the death of poor Jane, the pretty Indian girl I told you of: she had been married about six weeks, when she fell ill with a bilious epidemic, which proved fatal to her and many others of the Indian village.

Last harvest Tom Noggan (old Peter's brother), his squaw, and their children, came to our neighbourhood, and encamped on the opposite shore, near one of my brother's little islands. The squaws came frequently to get pork and flour from me, and garden vegetables, in exchange for fish, venison, or baskets. For a few pounds of salt pork they will freely give you a haunch of venison, or dried salmon trouts. They are fond of peas, Indian corn, melons, pumpkins, or indeed any vegetables; sometimes they will follow me into the garden, and beg "*onion*," or "*herb*," to put in soup: potatoes they never refuse. They often beg for the shells of green peas, to boil in their soups and pottage, and will eat them by handfuls.

Mrs. Tom Noggan is sister to Mrs. Peter, and was once reckoned an Indian beauty—but no trace of comeliness remains; but their notions of beauty possibly differ somewhat from ours, for her brother, who bears the appellation of "Handsome Jack," is, to European eyes, a sad ill-looking savage. But, to return to my squaw. When she first came she was in very ill health, and had a poor, sick, brown baby with her, about whom she seemed very uneasy. The poor babe was suffering under the effects of a slow fever, that seemed to be wasting and withering up its weakly frame. Its tiny hand hung listlessly beside it, its skin was hot and damp, and its tongue deeply furred and ulcerated. The sorrowful mother besought me, in the most intelligible manner she could, to give it medicine to cure it. I first petitioned to have the poor thing unbound from its wooden cradle, and suffered to have the free use of its limbs, unrestrained by the close swathing bands that confined its narrow chest. I then administered to it, as the safest and readiest remedy, a dose of castor oil, and, in spite of my compassion for the poor little sufferer, I could not help being amused by the original plan the mother adopted to make the papouse swallow the medicine. As soon as I had put it into the child's mouth with a teaspoon, she gently shook its head from side to side, till she fairly got it down the poor thing's throat, reversing the old joke of "Before taken to be well shaken."

Mrs. Tom was very thankful for some white bread and rusks, and a bottle of new milk, with which I supplied her, from time to time, for the sick child. She generally came every day to show me the little patient, and I gave her some rhubarb and magnesia for it. Whether they were the proper medicines for its case I cannot say, or if it was the better food it got, and the release from its cradle, that agreed so well with it; but I had the satisfaction of seeing a wonderful improvement take place in a short time, and before the Indians moved their camp, little Moses was quite brisk, and as lively as a kitten.

When Mrs. Tom was so poorly, and came to trade for meal or flour, and I asked for baskets, she used to shake her head, and answer in a plaintive tone, "Got-a-none," "Go Mut-a-Lake,"[2] or "Buckhorn-a-Lake," meaning she had got none till she went to Mud Lake or Buckhorn Lake. The former place is where the Indian village is situated at present; but, on account of the unhealthiness of the site, it has been judged expedient to remove them to Buckhorn Lake—one of the largest of our beautiful chain of Otonabee lakes. This sheet of water takes its name from the singular indentations of its bays and peninsulas, which they say resemble the horns of a deer.

The Indian women manufacture their baskets from the inner tough rind of the bass, which you know is a large species of the lime or linden, and from the blue beech; having stripped off the hard or outer bark, they then divide the inner or white rind into strips, and beat it with a tomahawk to render it pliable, keeping it wetted frequently whilst they are at work; these they dye black, or red, green, blue, or yellow, to fancy, with indigo, logwood, butternut, hickory, blue beech, redwood, and other dyes, with the uses of which they are intimately acquainted; but they are not very communicative on the subject, and will not tell you how they give those bright hues to the porcupine quills.

The winter and spring passed over without our seeing anything more of the Indians, with the exception of three squaws, who came in one cold day; and though I showed them some attention, they were apparently very insensible to it, and on my declining to purchase some ill-wrought baskets, they rose simultaneously, and wrapping their black mantles about them, walked forth without saying another word. They were very uninteresting squaws.

A few days ago, I received a friendly visit from Mrs. Tom and little Moses, with half a score more squaws and papouses, and after most affectionately greeting me, and bartering some fine fish for flour and bread, they all expressed a desire for us to visit the wigwam, which was situated on Strawberry Island, the largest of the three islands in our lake. But a difficulty arose; they had only one birch canoe, and that was deeply laden, as you may suppose, when I tell you it had conveyed ashore Mrs. Tom, her really pretty sister, the widow, Nancy Boland, Mary Anne Fron, and Mrs. Muskrat, with two little Noggans, two little Bolands, and six Muskrats; you may imagine there could be little stowage for Jane and me, and little James; however, as the squaws had set their hearts on our company, they managed to overcome the apparent difficulty of the transport. An old leaky birch canoe lay on the shore; the lively widow set herself to work, and heating some gum, such as they use in stopping the seams and cracks of these frail vessels, she soon made it as safe as the other, and invited Jane and little James to take a seat at the bottom of it, while Mrs. Tom directed me to step in beside her among the papouses and the other squaws.[3] With that genuine politeness which is taught in nature's own school, the good creature gathered together some cedar boughs, which formed a smooth and fragrant matting at the bottom of the canoe; over these she cast her black cloth shawl, and then with a face radiant with benevolent smiles, that made ample display of a set of pearly teeth of unrivalled colour and shape, she beckoned to me to take my place. The sky was so exquisitely blue above, and the water so clear below, with all the richly wooded banks reflected in its depths, that I enjoyed my short voyage exceedingly, and could hear the rapturous shouts of my little boy from the other canoe, as it cut through the great beds of water-lilies, which were just rising to the surface and displaying their full fragrant silken cups and broad floating leaves, gemmed with the sparkling insects that rested on them. Hundreds of blue, purple, green, scarlet, and bronze dragon flies, just emerged from the pupa state, were to be seen at rest, or just fluttering their newly expanded wings; the neat deer-fly, that torment to cattle, and even to man, with its angular spotted wings and bright gilded green head, and many others; while the surface of the water, where it was quite glassy and smooth, was gay with the splendid blue shining water-beetle, and others of a brilliant scarlet, dancing their gleesome circles upon the watery mirror. Sometimes the eye was enlivened by the transient flash of the splendid scarlet tanager, or black-winged summer red bird, a living glory among the feathered tribes, which now and then was seen darting swiftly among the trees of the islands, while the ear was greeted with the full melody of the Canadian robin, or migratory thrush, and the sweet clear note of the little song-sparrow, flitting gaily from bush to bush, and pausing at intervals to cheer you with its pretty songs. These sounds were blended with the light dip of the paddle, and the hoarse rush of the rapids, as the waters gurgled and eddied round the fallen cedars and huge blocks of stone that obstructed their passage downwards.

A painter might have made a pretty sketch of the scene. The broad expanse of tranquil water, bounded on either side by the dense mass of forest, varying from the gigantic pine to the dwarf-silver-leaved willow that trembled beneath the swell of the mimic waves that undulated beneath them. The line of trees broken only by our clearing, with the little log-house and adjoining buildings, the green turf sloping down in emerald verdure to the brink of the lake. Higher up might be seen the islands with the rapids between them; at the head of one of these, on a little green platform above a steep bank, clothed with roses and other low flowering shrubs, might be seen the white canvass tents of the Indians; the thin blue smoke rising in light vapoury mist, and spreading among the young aspens and birch that crested the summit of the bank on either side; below, just rocking in the shallow water, lay two empty birch canoes; our own, freighted with the women and children, making for the island, completed the picture.

While I was dwelling with delighted eye on all before me, a temporary disturbance was caused by the rude behaviour of one of the papouses, an ugly ill-favoured imp, who persisted in leaning over the side of the canoe and snatching at the broad floating leaves of the water lilies, or paddling with his brown hands in the water, to the imminent peril of overturning the frail boat. Mrs. Tom, who was steering with her paddle, gently remonstrated against his wilful behaviour, but to no purpose; the urchin only raised a pair of broad shoulders with a significant grumble indicative of his determination to persist. The squaws expostulated with him by turns, but without raising an angry voice or menace. I do not remember ever hearing an Indian woman scold; the peculiar intonation of their voices rather sinks into a plaintive whine when they are displeased, and instead of speaking more rapidly, they seem to give force to their words by a slow and deliberate style of utterance.

At the first outbreak of the forward child the good-humoured mother only laughed, and seemed inclined to jest at the anger of the boy, till, losing all command of himself, he proceeded to acts of violence, and taking up handfuls of water dashed them in his mother's face. This undutiful conduct caused a burst of indignation from Mrs. Muskrat and Mary Anne Fron, while the now offended mother held up her finger and pointed upwards, as if warning the little fellow that God looked down upon his sinful conduct; but passion held the mastery over the rebellious child, and he became yet more ungovernable, and even struck his mother and flung more water in her face. Any one but an Indian mother would have boxed the delinquent's ear soundly, and poured forth a torrent of words; but she suited her punishment to the nature of the offence, by taking up in her turn large handfuls of water and pouring upon his thick black hair, patting it down as she did so, till he looked like a fierce drowned rat. He screamed with fury, and struggled in vain to escape from her grasp, but she gently laid him sprawling at our feet in the bottom of the canoe, foaming with impotent rage. I was not a little amused by the cool deliberate way in which the squaw conducted herself, and inwardly congratulated her on her command of temper, and the victory she had gained; but obstinate perseverance is a distinguishing trait of the Indian character, and no sooner was the refractory imp released from thraldom than he darted up and reseated himself, casting looks of defiance on his mother, whose heart had already begun to relent at her severity, for she gently drew forth a gay handkerchief and softly wiped his streaming hair and face, patting his head with soothing accents. The ungrateful child took advantage of his mother's advances towards reconciliation, but disdained her overtures, and, with an expression almost of malignant triumph, snatched the handkerchief from his head and flung it into the water. The squaw now seemed to think further opposition useless; the handkerchief was rescued at the end of the paddle, and the disobedient urchin continued to dabble in the water till the canoe touched the bank.

I must tell you that in the middle of the fray a nice brown girl, Anne Muskrat, fell asleep with her head on my lap; so the mother removed her gently to her own knee, and I took the opportunity of taking up the relinquished paddle, and made a pretty successful essay in the art of propelling the canoe up the rapids, to the great admiration of the whole party. For my own part, I enjoy the motion of a birch-bark canoe far more than a boat or a skiff; it is so gentle and gliding, no noise nor shocks from the effort used in rowing; the paddles are so slight and short, that a child may use them, and, provided the canoe be in good order and well balanced, and persons sit quiet in it, there is no danger. The chief care required is in shallow water to avoid sunken rocks and fallen trees. These last often fall along the edge of the water, projecting far into the stream and forming eddies, and are dangerous for such light craft unless shunned in time, for the branches are apt to injure the frail material of which they are formed.

Some of the old massy cedars that have lain for years in the water, become the depot for all sorts of loose floating matter; sticks, rushes, reeds, grass, and all sorts of water weeds, in tangled masses, find a lodging among the immersed branches; a variety of ferns, fungi, mosses, and small plants cover it with deceitful verdure, while the work of decay is rapidly proceeding beneath. You often see a flourishing growth of young pine, hemlocks, swamp elm, and other seedling trees on these trunks. Quietly, but surely, does Nature carry on her grand operations by the simplest and most insignificant agents. Corruption and decay become the foundation for life and renovation, and we wonder and admire the economy displayed in the works of an Almighty Creator as much as his wisdom and power, as if to set forth an example to his children. He is in no one thing wasteful or prodigal of the materials of the visible world, but has ordained that something should indeed "gather up all fragments, that nothing may be lost."

But while I am philosophizing I am wandering from my party. You must suppose us all safely landed, and, after a good scramble up the steep face of the bank just in front of the encampment, which consisted of two nice white canvass tents, the floor strewn with cedar boughs according to custom. The fragrance of this rural carpet, with the delicious odour of some bunches of the wampum grass, of which the Indians braid belts and necklaces and other ornaments, was sufficiently powerful to overcome the smell of the venison, that hung in an unsightly manner along the front of the tent, drying in the blaze of a July sun. A large piece of the same meat was roasting over a fire of brands outside; it was suspended by two cross sticks, much after the fashion the gipsies manage their roasts; three or four deer hounds lay stretched at their ease, lazily eyeing the meat, and snapping angrily at the flies that were buzzing about them.

The two men, Tom Noggan and Joe Muskrat, had been left at home to cook the dinner; but, from the black aspect of the viands, methought they had not been over faithful in the discharge of their office; indeed, when we arrived, the two men were fast asleep, covered up to their chins with great blankets, though the thermometer stood at eighty degrees in the shade. Muskrat did rouse himself, and taking out a well-thumbed Bible, began to read; but Tom, whose laziness is proverbial, just opened one sleepy eye, and, having examined the party with apathetic indifference, turned on his side, and only gave token of his being awake by sometimes pointing with a significant grunt to one of the children to bring him any thing he required.

The squaws soon disposed of the sleepy, weary children, and all were asleep in a few minutes, excepting one nice neat little gipsy-looking girl, Rachel Muskrat, who hung fondly about her father, caressing him with quiet tenderness; her black hair was all curiously woven, the ends into a braid with the sweet grass, and formed a sort of border, or cap, round her head; it looked neat enough, but must have cost great time and patience to have arranged it so cleverly. On her father expressing a desire for drink, the little dark-eyed maid snatched from the ground a square sheet of birch-bark, which she gathered up at the corners, and quickly returned, bearing a full draught of water from the lake in this novel and simple vessel. Surely here was a proof how few are the wants of man in a savage state, and how easily supplied. Here was a vessel capable of containing liquid, formed without toil or trouble. This valuable material supplies the want of all sorts of earthenware utensils; divided into thin sheets, it makes no contemptible substitute for writing-paper, and can be rendered as fine as the most delicate tinted note-paper. When cast into the fire, it curls and writhes like parchment, but quickly ignites, and then bursts into a most brilliant and gaseous looking flame, emitting a highly aromatic perfume, that I am sure might be made from it.

Whilst sitting under the tent I took notice of the perfumed grass, and the widow soon employed herself in weaving a chain of it, which she linked together very prettily with bands of coloured quills. When she had completed it she placed it about my neck, and said, with a most agreeable smile, "Present for you; wear it for me."

I was delighted with its fragrance, and ordered several more of the same kind to be made, for which I paid her some trifling articles; and send them to you, for they are far sweeter than lavender, to lay among your linen, for I know you, like myself, used to practice that sweet but now old-fashioned custom.

The squaws told me they got the sweet grass, or wampum, on an island in Stoney Lake, and that none of it grew anywhere hereabout; it is very long and rather harsh, but smells delightfully.

The only article I have been able to procure of their work for you, is a pair of bracelets, which I really think are very neat; the coloured quills, you may perceive, are cut as small as beads, and strung in a sort of antique pattern, some-thing like what we used to call the Grecian scroll,—these, with a little canoe and a knife-case, are all I could procure worth sending home. They make some things neatly enough, and others as carelessly. It is a mere chance your getting anything well made by them, and never if you order it. They invariably give me the same brief answer if I ask for anything pretty that I want to send home,—"Got-a-none," "Village," or "Go Mut-a-Lake" or "Stoney Lake," or some other place, and that old excuse of "By-and-by," or "To-morrow," which means some day or other.

〜

1   For other accounts of the Nogan, Boland, and Muskrat families, see Susanna Moodie's *Roughing It in the Bush* and Samuel Strickland's *Twenty-Seven Years in Canada West*. See also the "History of the Ojibwa of the Curve Lake Reserve and Surrounding Area, Vol. 1."

2   Mut-a-Lake or Mud Lake is now called Chemong Lake.

3   For further information about Jane see p. 70, note 2. James was born June 7, 1833. The events here likely took place in the summer of 1835 or 1836.

Ramblings by the River

In "Ramblings by the River," No. 6 in the "Forest Gleanings" series *Anglo-American Magazine* 2 (1853), 181–84, Traill offers the reader a more detailed account than *The Backwoods of Canada* provides of her activities during the first few weeks of her life in Upper Canada while she and her husband stayed with her brother, Samuel Strickland, and his wife, Mary (Reid), at their house on Lot 18, Concession 7 in Douro. She recalls vividly the backwoods conditions that nourished her curiosity and led her to become a "forest gleaner." The piece includes an interesting bit of inter-textuality in its comparison of English and Canadian rivers, a comparison also made by Susanna Moodie in the sketch concerning her family's removal to Douro Township, "A Journey to the Woods," in *Roughing It in the Bush*.

I remember being particularly struck during my first journey through the bush, by the deep, and to me, solemn silence that reigned unbroken, save by the tapping of a woodpecker, the sharp scolding note of the squirrel, or the falling of some little branch when stirred by the breeze which was heard moaning or sighing in the tops of the lofty pines above us, but was scarcely felt in these dense woods through which our road lay. For miles and miles, not a clearing was seen to break the lonely way, and let in a glimpse of light and air. Once my eye was gladdened by the bright and gorgeous flash of the summer red-bird, the tanager, as it darted across the path and disappeared among the shining beech trees. Accustomed only to the sober plumage of our British songsters, I marvelled at the glorious color of this lovely gem of the forest, and watched till my eyes were weary for another such beautiful vision, but watched in vain, for shy and solitary, these lovely birds seek the deep recesses of the forest and even there are not often seen. All day long we journeyed on through that deep, still, forest gloom, and night found us on the shore of the lake,* just where it narrows between two rounding shores and sweeps past the little headland with eddying swiftness, till it again for a brief space expands into a mimic lake, then hurrying on, passes two pretty wooded islands and dashes down steep, broken ledges of rocks, coiling and foaming in white crested breakers.

The hoarse, never-ceasing murmur, which for ages and ages has broken the silence of these solitudes unheard and unheeded, save by the Indian hunter, first met my ears at the termination of my first journey through the wilderness, at nightfall, as I sat watching the little bark canoe, with its pine torch dancing on the surface of the rapids, that my good brother was paddling across the lake to ferry us over to his forest home.

He had but just broken the bush in that location, and all was wild, and rough, and rude; but unbounded kindness went far to make the rough places smooth to the home-sick uninitiated emigrants.

---

* Katchawanook, one of the expansions of the Otonabee river.

How many things that then seemed new and strange, and incomprehensible in the economy of a Canadian settlers household have since become familiar and expedient. How many a time in after years did I recall to mind my dear good sister-in-law's oft repeated words—"Wait till you have been in Canada a few years, and then you will better understand the difficulties of a bush settler's life."

Perhaps, among the trials of the farmer there is none more trying to his patience, and often to his pocket, than receiving relations and friends from the Old Country into their houses. On the one side there is a great amount of disappointment, regret, and disgust to be overcome; and generally, this ill-humour is unjustly and ungraciously vented in the presence of the friends whose hospitality they are sharing. On the other hand, the mortified host and hostess are inclined to tax their guests with a selfish disregard of their feelings and convenience, and think while they eat of their hardly earned bread, and fill the limited space of their little dwelling, it is not grateful to repay them only with discontent and useless repining. Such things ought not so to be.

In a former number I pointed out the evil of such selfish conduct. Let no one take undue advantage of generous hospitality, but during an unavoidable sojourn with friends, let each strive to render every assistance in their power to lighten the burden. There is always needle-work that females can assist in teaching the young children, and many light household matters that may spare the weary wife or mother an extra hour of fatigue, while the men can help in the work that is going on in the clearing: it is not well to eat the bread of idleness.

During my sojourn at my brother's, after rendering any help that was required at my hands, and my labors I confess were very light, and probably not very efficient, I had still much leisure time at my command. Remote from any habitation—for with only one or two exceptions, his clearing formed the furthest line of settlement in the township—there was little opportunity for visiting. The mighty forest girded in the few acres of cleared ground on three sides, while in front it was bounded and divided from the opposite township by the waters of the larger and lesser Katchawanook: the Indian name signifying alternate rapid, and still waters.

With few inducements to walk, as regarded my social position in the neighbourhood, I was thrown upon the few resources that remained open to me, and these I eagerly sought for in the natural features of the soil. Whatever I beheld had the charm of novelty to recommend it to my attention; every plant however lowly, became an object of interest.

The season of flowers, with the exception of some few autumnal ones, was over; but while roaming over the new clearing, threading my way among stumps and unburned log-heaps, I sometimes found plants that were totally new to me, with bright and tempting berries that I forbore to taste till I had shewn them to my brother, and from him learned their name and quality. Among these were the bright crimson berries of the strawberry blite, or Indian strawberry, the leaves of which I afterwards boiled as a vegetable. That elegant little trailing plant *Mitchella repens*, sometimes called partridge-berry and also twin-berry, from the scarlet fruit having the appearance of being double. The delicate fragrant jessamine-shaped flower, that terminates the long flexile leafy branch, was not then in flower; the fruit has a mealy, spicy taste and is very pretty, resembling the light bright scarlet of the holly-berry in its color.

In damp mossy spots I found the gay berries of the dwarf cornel** the herbaceous species; there also was the trailing arbutus*** with its shining laurel-like leaves and scarlet fruit: and nearer to the lake on the low swampy shore grew the blue-berried**** and the white dogwood with wild grapes (frost grapes*****) that hung in tempting profusion

   ** Cornus Canadensis, low round, dwarf dogwood.

  *** Uva Ursi, bear-berry, Kinnikinnick.

 **** Cornus Sericen, red-rod.

***** Cornus alba.

high among the bushes, mixing its purple fruit with the transparent clusters of the high bush cranberry******, which, stewed with maple sugar, often formed an addition to our evening meal.

Into the dark angled recesses of the forest I dared not venture unattended, unless it were just a few yards beyond the edge of the clearing, for the sake of some new fern or flower that I coveted.

One of my walks was along the irregular and winding banks of a small creek that flowed within a few feet of the house; to trace its wanderings through the cedars that fringed its banks—to mark the shrubs and vegetables, the mosses and flowers that clothed its sides—to watch its eddies and tiny rapids—to listen to its murmurings and to drink its pure cold waters—was one of my amusements.

Another of my favorite rambles was along the river shore: the autumnal rains had not then fallen to swell its currents. The long dry ardent summer of 1832, had left the limestone bed of the Otonabee dry for many yards along its edge, so that I could walk on the smooth surface as on a pavement. This pavement was composed of numerous strata of limestone, each stratum about an inch or two in depth, every layer was distinctly marked. Between the fissures were seedling roses and vines, ferns and various small plants; the exuviae of water insects with shells and other matter, lay bleaching upon the surface of the stones. It was for want of other objects of interest that my attention was first drawn to the natural productions of my adopted country, books I had none to assist me, all I could do was to note facts, ask questions, and store up any information that I chanced to obtain. Thus did I early become a forest gleaner.

How many solitary hours have I passed upon the river bank, gazing with unwearied eyes upon its ever moving waters, hurrying along its dark bed, foaming, leaping, dashing downwards, now sweeping with resistless force against the stony walls that bounded it on the opposite side, now gliding

****** American guelder-rose, viburnam oxyvoccus.

for a space calm and slow, then with accelerated force hurling back its white spray, as if striving against the propelling force that urged its onward career.

Often did I repeat to myself Moore's lines written at the falls of the Mohawk River,

> "From rise of morn to set of sun
> I've seen the mighty Mohawk run,
> Rushing alike untired and wild
> 'Neath rocks that frowned and flowers that smil'd.
> And as I watched the woods of pine
> Along its surface darkling shine,
> Like tall and mystic forms that pass
> Before the wizard's magic glass
>
> * * * * * * * * * * * * * * * * * * *
>
> O! I have thought and thinking sighed
> How like to thee thou restless tide—
> May be the life, the lot of him
> Who roams along thy river's brim.
> How many a fair and loved retreat
> May rise to woo my weary feet,
> But restless as the doom that calls
> Thy waters to their destined falls.
> I feel the world's resistless force
> Hurry my heart's devoted course,
> From rock to rock till life be done;
> And the lost current cease to run.
> O may my fall be bright as thine,
> May Heav'n's forgiving rainbow shine,
> Upon the mist that circles me,
> As bright as now it falls on thee."[1]

The rapid onward flow of a river has been for ages past, taken by poets as a meet emblem of human life, an apt and natural simile—one that speaks to every heart—one of those natural witnesses that speak to the created of the wisdom and power of the Great Creator.

Contrasted with the quiet, slow flowing rivers of England, how different is the character of this wild picturesque Otonabee, running its course through the vast pine forests unfettered for miles and miles,—now widening into extensive lakes, diversified with wooded or rocky islands—now gathering its forces into a deep and narrow channel between rocky banks fringed with every variety of evergreens, from the gigantic pine, the monarch of the Canadian woods, to the light feathery hemlock and dark spruce and balsam, casting their funereal shadows athwart its waters or mirrored deep, deep down upon its glassy surface. Now gentle, like a sleeping child, anon impetuous as an impatient war steed, that smelleth the battle afar off, and pants to meet its shock.

The calm unruffled waters of England, designed as if by Nature to enrich and fertilize her soil, and contribute to the welfare and commerce of her people, are unlike the wild streams of Canada. The former may be compared to a highly civilized people, the latter to the rude, uncultivated Indians, and less refined settlers. Though less available for the purpose of transport; yet these inland waters possess a value in their immense power for working machinery, which is a source of incalculable wealth to the inhabitants of the country. Look at the inexhaustible pine forests, that clothe the banks of the lakes and streams. See the rafts of squared timbers that are borne down, year after year, on the bosom of those rapid flowing waters, and in due time find their way to the shores of the parent country. Might not a history of no mean interest, be written of one of these massive timbers, from its first dropping from the cone in its native soil, on the elevated ridge above some remote and nameless stream, to its voyage across the Atlantic and final destination in one of the British dock-yards. Shall we believe that no providential care was extended over that seed which was in the course of time to undergo so many changes, and which might even be connected with the fate of hundreds of human beings? We are taught by lips that spoke no guile, that the lilies of the field are arrayed in their glorious clothing by our Heavenly

Father, and that He careth for the fowls of the air, that in Him all things live and move, and have their being.

One word more, before I leave my favourite rivers. I was particularly struck by the extreme clearness and transparency of the water, in which every pebble and minute shell may be seen; every block of granite or lime-stone that obstructs its course, can be discerned at a considerable depth. Fragments of red, grey, and black and white granite, looking like bright and glittering gems, as the sun's rays penetrate the waters that cover them. Some future time I will give a description of Stoney Lake, which is a miniature of the Lake of the Thousand Islands; a spot so replete with beauty that none who have seen it can ever forget it. Those who wish to enjoy a treat, should visit this remarkable spot which possesses a thousand charms for the genuine lover of the beautiful and picturesque, for it is amid lone solitudes like these that the mind is naturally let to ponder upon the works of the Deity, and to worship him in spirit and in truth.

Oaklands, Rice Lake.

1   Thomas Moore (1779–1852), "Lines, Written at the Cohos, or Falls of the Mohawk River." Traill misquotes and misorders a number of the poem's lines.

FEMALE SERVANTS IN THE BUSH

This piece was first published in *Sharpe's London Journal* 15 (1852) 279–81; it appeared the following year as "Forest Gleanings" No. 10 in the *Anglo-American Magazine** 3 (1853), 83–85. The first third of the sketch is characterized by its practical advice to prospective or recent emigrants in the mid-nineteenth century about the quality and management of servants. Such content may seem to limit the relevance of "Female Servants" for the twentieth-century reader, but when it is read in conjunction with Traill's story "Barbara" (*The Literary Garland*, December 1841, 21–26), a fictionalized portrait of a Strickland family servant that illuminates the mutual closeness and loyalty of family-servant relations in England, it helps to clarify one of the most striking cultural changes that emigrants like Traill had to adjust to in moving to the New World. The emigration story that follows the opening advice is likely about one of the Payne (Pine) families who lived in Dummer Township, having emigrated from Wiltshire, England, in 1831. Mary Payne was in service to Traill in the mid-1830s. Several of the Paynes are referred to in chapters of Susanna Moodie's *Roughing It in the Bush*.

> "Let not ambition mock their useful toil,
> Their homely joys, their destiny obscure."

I have often heard families complain of the difficulty of obtaining and retaining good female servants, especially when they first come to this country, and dwell with much bitterness on the insolent freedom of manner they experience; that while the rate of wages is nearly doubled, they are worse served than by even indifferent servants at home.

In Canada, the demand for labor has hitherto exceeded the supply, and will do so for many years to come, excepting in places where a strong tide of emigrants has poured in on account of some tempting advantage offered them, such as the carrying on of public works on an extensive scale. The servant knows her own value, and is not unnaturally disposed to take advantage of the necessities of her employer. She is, in point of fact, less dependent on her mistress than her mistress on her.

Such being the state of things, it is impolitic to commence your acquaintance with your newly-hired servant by assuming an air of haughty superiority over her—or putting on an attitude of defence before attack is meditated.

In a new country like this, the same order of things does not prevail as in England, and something of dignity must inevitably be ceded, if you wish to live peaceably with all men. Even servants, fresh from the comforts and conveniences of good service at home, find much cause for discontent and unhappiness when they come to Canada. The change is not less felt by them than by ourselves; they also have to learn to conform to the ways of a strange country; they also feel the bitter pangs of expatriating themselves, though they have more to gain, and less ultimately to lose, by the exchange, than we have; but their regrets for a season are often as acute. Let us, then, think of these things; let us learn to treat them as human beings, as fellow-creatures subject to like feelings of joy and sorrow as ourselves, and let them see that we do so, not because it is our worldly interest, but because we are their Christian mistresses.

Begin, then, by treating them with kindness and consideration. Servitude is at best a hard position to bear; let us endeavor by judicious kindness to lighten the yoke of bondage. Take an interest in their happiness, their general welfare; lend a patient and not unwilling ear to their little histories; for they have all something to tell of their former trials that drove them to this country, their early wanderings and troubles in the first settlement they made, the hardships, sorrows, and sickness they have met with.

Believe me, that much interesting matter may be thus obtained, some useful knowledge acquired, some valuable lesson of patience learned, by which your own heart may be benefitted and improved, and, what is equally valuable, a feeling of confidence established between yourself and your household servants, who feel, by these little acts of sympathy, that you do not despise them.

Truly do I subscribe to the fine sentiments of the poet, whose truth must have been felt and experienced by every one capable of feeling aright:—

> Where is the heart of iron mould,
> Stern, inaccessible, and cold,
> That melts not, when its proud distress
> Is balmed by pity's gentleness?

Irish servants are more plentiful than English or Scotch, and you will find a marked difference between those that come from the Catholic, and those that come from the Protestant countries. The former are generally less neat in their persons and less perfect in their household work; but they are easily contented, more cheerful, good-humoured, and respectful, quick to take offence where their country or religion is sneered at, and, I might add, less trustworthy; in a word, they smile and joke, and yet have a latent feeling of jealousy in their hearts if you have offended them, which is only suffered to break forth when occasion suits.

The Irish Protestants are clean, active, full of expedients and energy, more truthful and upright in their dealings, approaching nearer to the Scotch in many of their characteristics, than to their Catholic brethren or to the English. Indeed, it is often hard to distinguish, but for their tongue, the emigrants from the north of Ireland and the west of Scotland; the complexion is often fair and ruddy, and the family names also assimilate. We have Gordons, Hamiltons, Dunbars, Campbells, Macdonalds, Drummonds, and a host more of Scoto-Irish names.

Though our best servants are from amongst this class, yet from the other classes faithful and active domestics are to be found.

I had a nice, good humoured, rosy Saxon-looking English girl in my house for some months, full of practical usefulness, but with a mixture of shrewdness and simplicity in her manners, that made me smile. I used to be amused by her remarks on this country, and often listened to her tales of humble life.

One day she told me the little history of the troubles that forced her father to leave his native country. He had been a blanket weaver at home, near Devizes, and when the trade became so bad that he could not live by his wages, he resumed his original occupation of laborer, and was one of the Marquis of Bath's numerous tenantry; but even here he found bread hard to earn, though Hannah, a lass of fourteen, and her mother still worked at the loom, or carded, or spun at home in the cottage, and the boys kept sheep in the commons for the farmers. Still things did not go on well, and at last they fell into arrears with the landlord, and the furniture, loom, and wheel, and all were sold for rent, by order of the steward; and so sorrow upon sorrow, and trial upon trial came, till their hearts were well-nigh broken. Just then wages were very low, and work hard to be procured, "and we could scarcely get food," said Hannah. "My father was suspected of snaring hares, and there were few that did not, near us; and the overseer was savage when we came for our weekly allowance, when father was sick and out of work. Uncle Henry had got a notion into his head sometime before, and had gone off to Canada, and he found plenty to do, and plenty to eat and drink, and good wages, and wrote to my father to come out. Well, this was not easy, for we had no money to pay his passage, and he went to the overseer, and he told him to go about his business and work, and not leave his family chargeable on the parish. Well, I cannot say how he picked up means to go, or who stood his friend, but go he did, unknown to the parish, who would not have let him off, and then came a hard time to us, for the parish folks were all angry when they found us all left on their hands, though mother and I did all we could, and so did the boys, and hard fare we had and hard times; and so a year wore over—a long, hard year it was to us. At last we got a word in a letter sent to Devizes, that father was well, and had got land and a bit of a shanty up, and we were to go to him as soon as we could find the means. Mother, she went off to the overseer, and told him how she was wanting money to get us all out to Canada; but though the parish had to allow us something weekly to keep us alive, not one penny would they give her, to get rid of us all, and he stormed, and blustered, and abused father; but then mother just let him know her mind, for her blood was up, and she said he was a fool, for the family would cost more in time than what she wanted for the passage money; but he only huffed the more, and called us all vagabonds and poachers.

"Well, mother comes home in great distress. At last, a neighbor came in, and when he heard what troubles we were in, says he, 'Why do you not go to my Lord Marquis's steward, or to the Marquis himself?' So mother gets up and tidies herself, and says, 'Then I'll go to his honor's ownself,' and so she went and takes us all with her, as clean as she could make us.

"Now the Marquis was at home, and he was so good as to speak to mother, and to hear all her story, and when he had heard it, he got quite savage like with the overseers; the Marquis said: —'Now, don't tell it to I,' because, he was riled like at them."

This speech, repeated with the most earnest simplicity, almost overcame my gravity, but the Marquis gave them an order on his steward for money to take them all out, and something for sea stores. Hannah's mother was a wise woman to tell her own tale and plead her own cause with the great man.

I forget now all the simple wondering that filled the minds of Hannah and her brothers and sisters at every thing they heard and saw in their voyage out, and up the great river St. Lawrence, and right glad were they when they met their father at Cobourg, for they had exhausted every morsel of provisions, and had begged a few turnips at some place, to keep them alive. And when they came up through the woods nearly fifty miles, they had to journey on foot. How strange it seemed to persons accustomed to the wide open treeless downs that form so striking a feature of that portion of England from whence they had emigrated.

"What a strange waste of wood and sticks and faggots, we thought it as we journeyed, and when we used to sit down to rest on our way, I used to gather up all the loose branches and pile them in little heaps on the path, and say,—'Oh mother, do'ee look here, we will come and fetch these to make fires with one day.' And then father would laugh at me, and say,—'why hunny, I have burnt more wood in one day, than we ever burnt in all our lives at home.' And how we did stare at the great log heaps that fall, and still I would think what a pity to destroy what thousands of poor creatures would go miles to fetch, to warm themselves with in England, and dare not pick a stick to light their fires out of the hedges or woods." Hedges, indeed there are few or none, for the enclosures are all of stone, not like the bowery hawthorn fences of Norfolk, Suffolk and Essex.

The old man had settled among some of his own country folks, and so they were soon visited by old familiar friends, and a short time reconciled them to the change of country, and though they had their privations and hardships, at first, they labored in hope and are now surrounded by many comforts. My little maid is at this time a careful, busy, thrifty wife, well to do in the township, with cows, and pigs, and fowls, and flocks and herds around her homestead, and three or four rosy, fat, well-clothed children, as good tempered and English as their mother. I wish the Marquess of Bath could see them.

C.P.T.
Oaklands, Rice Lake.

HUMOURS OF HOLY EVE

This sketch is No. 9 in the series of "Forest Gleanings"; it
appeared in the *Anglo-American Magazine* in 1853, 82–83.
Although apparently written in the early 1850s while Traill
lived at Oaklands, the family farm above Rice Lake, like
several other items in the series it offers fond recollections
of her early days in Douro Township (1832–39). Frances
Stewart was likely the friend whom she accompanied to the
Holy Eve or New Year's Eve party near Court-house hill
in Peterborough where Traill was introduced to the
celebrations of Scots and Irish settlers in the area.

Among the few old customs that have been introduced into our colony by the Irish and Scotch settlers, Holy Eve is one that is still kept up, not only among the lower class of emigrants, but also among those who occupy a higher order in society, more especially among the Irish, whose genuine love of fun and frolic has always distinguished them from their more sober-minded and less excitable neighbors of England. Christmas is the Englishman's national holiday, from the peasant's cot to the earl's castle, but Holy Eve and Yule or New Year's Eve are the great days observed by the Irish and Scotch; these are days that enliven the young and cheer the hearts of the old, bringing back again to them joys long since past—kindling former smiles again

"In faded eyes that long had wept."

Reason may laugh and ascetics frown, and yet I question if any one is the worse for such meetings and relaxations from the cares and sorrows of life; even Solomon says there is a time to laugh as well as a time to weep and mourn.

The humours of Holy Eve were quite new to me before I came to Canada, for, living in an easterly angle of the isle of Great Britain, I had mingled with neither the Irish nor Scotch, and only knew of the Holy Eve through reading Burns' humorous poem. It was during the first visit that I paid to the town of P[eterborough], then in its infancy, that I first became initiated in the merry mysteries of Holy Eve.

Arriving unexpectedly at the house of a married friend, I found her dressed with more than usual smartness, she was evidently preparing for an evening party—going out to tea, I hinted that I feared my visit was *mal à propos*.

"Cannot you take Mrs. T[raill] with you, my dear," asked her husband, "Mrs. M—— will be delighted with such an addition to her party; she will meet some of her friends there—we can take such liberties in Canada, and it is Holy Eve."

I had no objection; I was sure to be well received, but I had a baby, a weaned baby of only a few months old,—it would be troubled some.

"Never mind; I have a good nurse who will mind it, and it will sleep well, never fear!"

Cloaks and hoods were brought, and though so early in the season the snow was falling fast, and we had to cross the high bleak hills near the bank of the river, among lofty pines and oaks that then grew on Court-house hill. I was young and full of spirits in those days, for it is nineteen years—nearly twenty years ago, and I heeded not the stormy wind nor the snow-drift which beat it in our faces, and by the time we reached the hospitable door of our Irish friend's house we were wrapped in a mantle of snow.

A hearty voice, whose cheerful much-loved tone, alas! I shall hear now no more, bade us a kindly welcome, and ushered us into the large parlor, bright with the cheerful blaze of a log fire, and gay with smiling faces of young and old, who were ranged on benches round the room for the better accommodation of so numerous a party as were there assembled. Our coming was greeted with infinite satisfaction by many a kind face, and I was soon comfortably seated among a little knot of lively laughter-loving girls, whose merry glances inspired mirth in the very gravest of the papas and mamas.

A plentiful supply of tea and coffee, cakes and preserves, were carried round by the young men, who officiated as waiters on the occasion. There must have been some thirty-five or forty guests, consisting of young men and maidens, girls and boys, with a respectable scattering of matrons and their partners. There was indeed, as the boys hinted, lots of nice girls and plenty of fun.

As soon as the tea was over a game of family coach was started, which set every one laughing and scampering for places,—forfeits were gathered in a pile in the lap of one of the elder ladies.[1] Blindman's-buff followed, and Wilkie might have caught a few ideas had he seen the sly tricks of some of the demurest-looking of the young girls.

Then there was fishing for a wedding-ring in a bowl of porridge—it should have been sillibub, but milk or cream were rare articles in those days in our backwoods.[2] Then there was bobbing for apples in a dish of clean water; this was of course confined to the gentlemen,—and sometimes a mischievous girl urged on by one of the older sisters would dart forward and give a sly push to the candidate for the apple and souse his head into the pan of water to the infinite enjoyment of his comrade. The one who caught the apple was, according to the augury of the wise ones, to be married before his fellows. Then came jumping for apples with hands tied behind the back of the party, the apples hung by strings from the frame of a reel such as spinners use to wind off the yarn from the wheel; between the apples lighted candles of an inch or two in length were stuck, and the chance was as much in favor of catching a candle as an apple, as the machine swung lightly round from the ceiling to which it was suspended by a nail and a string.

One trick caused great mirth to the lookers-on, but I ween not to the luckless wight who was the subject of the joke. A forfeit was called, and a tall lad of six feet in height was doomed to walk blindfolded three times round the room, and then sit down on a joint-stool before the kitchen fire till one of the young ladies should come to release him, and lead him back to the parlor. Three times the poor dupe was paraded between two of his friends round the kitchen to the great admiration of the giggling maid-servants, and then led to the seat, but it proved a stool of repentance; a tub of cold water covered treacherously with a bit of board so short as to give way instantly it was touched, precipitating the young man into the icy fluid; being very tall he found it no easy matter to regain his balance, and uttering execrations on the villains who had played the trick, he rose from his seat by no means a convert to the cold-water cure. One of the *humane society* present, petitioned for a dry suit and a warm blanket-coat, but it took some time to reconcile the shivering victim to the expediency of the practical joke—but it was Holy Eve and all sorts of pranks were allowable, if no one was hurt no one cared, and a fiddle and a cleared floor, and Scotch reels and Irish jigs, with country dances, put all things right. The dancing in those days and in those remote places, did not then include waltzes, polkas, and quadrilles—now, even in the backwoods, these dances are alone practised by the young folks, though the reel and country dances still remains in favor with the old, who look on the familiar whirl of the waltz with an evil eye. When tired with dancing, songs were sung with skill and feeling, and eyes that before were brimful of mirth now overflowed to the touching melodies of "Savourneen Deelish," "Mary Le Moor," and that wild old ballad so full of mournful pathos, "Mary Queen of Scots' Lament," beginning—

"From the walls of my prison I see
The birds how they wander in air,
My heart how it pants to be free,
My looks they are wild with despair."

And there were cheeks that kindled as the lays of Auld Langsyne were chorused that night by old and young, and thoughts of days gone by, and friends of early youth, came over many a heart I ween right sair that night,—then *viva la compagnie* was improvised by all present, and so ended Holy Eve, 1833.

⌒

1   Family Coach or General Post was a popular parlour and party game. Participants held roles as parts of a coach such as the step, whip, or dashboard while one player told a story of the coach's journey from one town to another, in the process mentioning the coach's various parts. When a player's part was mentioned, that player had to get up, turn around and try to resume his seat before the storyteller took it. Occasionally the storyteller would call a "general post," at which point everybody had to rise and scramble for a new seat; the player left over became the new storyteller.

2   Sillibub is cream or milk mixed with wine to form a soft curd.

Bush Wedding and Wooing

Like several of Traill's sketches, this one was published first in *Sharpe's London Journal* 13 (1851), 90–93, and later in the *Anglo-American Magazine** 3 (1853), 276–78. A variation of it also appeared in E. S. Caswell's 1929 edition of *The Backwoods of Canada*. In these entertaining anecdotes of pioneer social life her usual preference for English decorum gives way to a relish for the comic elements of backwoods gossip and the exuberance of her Irish neighbours. Clearly, Traill had the literary skills to exploit such subjects. In her Upper Canadian version of Sir Walter Scott's "Lochinvar," her descriptions of character and action convey her admiration of the spirit and independence of the young Irish girl. But when the topic becomes the folly of "Irish pride," she shrewdly shifts from her own didactic voice to those of the Irish clergyman and his scheming debtor, although she does return as moralizer at the end. While Traill was reasonably adept at creating Irish dialect, she was not committed to satirizing Irish behaviour. In her four-part story "The Settler's Settled; or, Pat Connor and His Two Masters," which was published in *Sharpe's London Journal* 10 (1849), such satire as she employs is directed to English reserve and impracticality, while Pat's energy, practical wisdom, and good humour are celebrated.

Wedding and wooing in Canada are not always conducted in the sober, matter of fact way, that they usually are in the old country among the lower order, especially where the parties are among the excitable sons and daughters of the Emerald Isle, who often contrive to give a good deal of éclat to affairs of this kind. From a number of curious facts that I have been made acquainted with, I will select a few for the entertainment of my reader. First on the list stands a bridal with something of romance in it. In short, an Irish Lochinvar.[1] It is nearly twenty years ago since the event of the story I am about to tell, took place in the township of ———. An avaricious old settler whom I shall call Mat Doolan, had a pretty smart daughter named Ellen, who was attached to a young man, the son of a neighbouring farmer, and as long as no better suitor offered, old Mat suffered the young couple to keep company as lovers, but as ill luck would have it, the wife of an old man in the neighbourhood died, leaving her spouse, a cross grained, miserly old creature, at liberty to take to himself a third, for I believe that the old wretch had starved to death with scanty fare and hard work two honest wives.

Now old Jim Delany had a log house, sheep and cows, oxen and horse, a barn full of wheat and stacks of hay, the produce of a good lot of bush land. The father of the dear Ellen thought this a famous chance not to be overlooked. The widower was at a loss what to do with his cows and poultry and the wool of his sheep, now the old wife was gone. Mat was invited to the wake, and before the funeral was well over, the widower and the crafty old fox had made a bargain for the fair Ellen's hand; as to the small matter of the heart, that was of no consequence, and as a matter of course would be won when she was endowed with all old Jim Delany's worldly goods.

Great was the consternation of the affianced, when her father with the greatest coolness told her that she was to be married in the short space of a month from that date. She was very indignant, as well she might be, that the matter should have been settled without her consent, but her father gave her to understand that it was useless to rebel and that the best thing she could do would be to put a good face on the occasion. As to her former lover, he would soon get another sweetheart, as to marrying for love that was all stuff.

When Ellen found that it was useless to remonstrate, she dried her tears and said that if it must be so, it must, but told her father that she must have money to buy wedding clothes, as she was in want of every article of wearing apparel and should not like to come to the old man directly for money to buy clothes. The father was so well satisfied with her dutiful acquiescence in his scheme, that he gave her an order on one of the stores in the town to buy anything she required, not limiting her as to the exact outlay, but recommending economy in her purchases.

Ellen got all the things she wanted, and contrived to make out a very handsome outfit.

The important day at length arrived, the guests arrived from all quarters—old men and young ones, wives, widows, and maidens—a goodly party. The season was early spring, the roads were in a bad state—half mud, half ice—too bad for a sleigh; so the wedding party arranged to go, some on horseback, and others in lumber waggons and ox-carts.

The breakfast was plentiful; the bride showed no reluctance, but appeared in excellent spirits, bore all the jokes and compliments with a good grace, and finally set off at the head of the equestrians, declaring she would have a race to the church with one of the bridesmaids. Just as they reached the concession line near which the old sweetheart lived, who should ride out of the clearing ahead of the cavalcade, but the gentleman himself, dressed in a new suit, as smart as could be! It had all been arranged beforehand. The bride, at a signal from her lover, gave the reins and a slashing cut to her pony, which dashed forward in good style, leaving the bridal cortège far in the rear. Away they went, stopping for no obstacle—clearing root, stone, and stream; nothing checked them. "They'll have fleet steeds that follow," quoth young Lochinvar.

The wild shouts and yells of the bride's astonished companions only seemed to give greater spirit to the race. Gallantly the young man led the way, and fearlessly his fair partner kept her seat. At the church they were joined by some chosen friends of the bridegroom—the parson was ready—the license, duly attested, was forthcoming—and the discomforted father of the bride and the mortified husband, that was to have been, had the vexation of meeting the happy couple coming out of the church gates as they went in! The laugh went against the two old men, who had been fairly outwitted by a young girl of seventeen. The young folks declared it was fine fun, and the old ones said Ellen was a lass of spirit and deserved a young husband; and one old farmer was so well pleased that he invited the young couple to eat their wedding dinner at his house, and so ended the runaway wedding.

Of all pride, there is no pride like Irish pride, and an Irishman will bring all his native shrewdness and talent to bear him out in the support of his darling principle, trying to convince you that he is richer, and grander, and a better man than he really is. The Irishman calls it pride; but, in fact it is nothing but vanity carried to an absurd excess. As an instance, I will relate as nearly as I am able, an amusing story told with singular humor by an Irish clergyman, who greatly enjoyed the joke, though he was the sufferer by it in the end. It was Diamond cut Diamond, and no mistake. So now for the story of

HOW THE PARSON OUTWITTED THE BRIDEGROOM AND HOW THE BRIDEGROOM OUTWITTED THE PARSON.

A young fellow, whom I shall call Rody Calaghan, contrived to get in my debt to the amount of some eight dollars. The rogue wheedled me into lending him the money when I happened to be in an unfortunately good humor, and from that time never a copper could I get from him in payment. In despair, I gave the eight dollars up in my own mind as one of my bad debts, of which I had more than enough, and I ceased to think at all about Master Rody; when one day, who should ride up to me as I was going to church but Rody Calaghan! Surely, thinks I, but the rogue is going to pay me that which he owes me. His errand, however, was on a matter matrimonial. He was going to be married on the following day, and his call was simply to ask if it would be convenient for me to go out into the country to the bride's father's house to marry him and his betrothed— the license was all ready, and no impediment to his happiness. I was in a hurry, and said, "Yes, yes." I would be there at the hour named. I was punctual to the time, as I always like to be on such occasions; but just as I was preparing to enter the room where all the bride's family and friends were assembled together, Rody drew me on one side, and said,

"Och, Parson, but ye're the kind man ye are, and I'll be thinkin' it's yerself will do me the good turn just at this partickler time."

Thinks I to myself, it's to borrow money of me, Master Rody, that you are coming the blarney over me so strongly. But no, as if guessing my thoughts, he let me see a handful of dollar notes as if by accident, which he had cajoled some friend out of, I suppose.

"Ye see, yer Riverence, what it is. I don't want to look small potatoes before *them*," and he pointed significantly to the party within the room, "and so I shall just put down six dollars on the book as a wedding fee to yourself."

"Oh, very well," says I, "I understand—that's all right Rody, and I am glad to see you so honestly inclined."

"But Parson, dear," says he, again in a great hurry, "you know its only a make-believe, jist to make them think that I am as well off as she is, and cut a bit of a shine before them all for pride's sake, and so you'll be so good as to give me back the dollars when no one is looking on—sly like."

"And so that's it, is it Rody Calaghan," says I, "and what's to become of my dues and the money you owe me?"

"Sure thin your Riverence won't be thinking of the dirty rags jist at this saison," he added in a coaxing tone, laying his hand on my sleeve, "yer honor knows that you would not do the thing shabby and they looking on all the while." I laughed to myself, and thought I would play the knave a trick for his blarney and roguery.

The ceremony was over, and the bride and the brides-maid all kissed round as a finale, when out steps Rody from the throng and comes forward with a most self-important air, and lugging out a large leathern purse, took from it notes to the amount of six dollars, counting them out one by one with great exactness, holding them up separately to the light as if to ascertain that they were good ones, and bidding me count them twice over that there might be no mistake. I thought of Gil Blas[2] and the six reals that he so ostentatiously dropped into the mendicant's hat one by one, but I entered into the humour of the thing, and paid some compliments to the bride, saying that my friend Rody seemed to value her very highly if one might judge by the price he had paid for her, while Rody affected to think on the contrary that he had been very shabby in paying so little for so great a prize, throwing a peculiar expression of intelligence into his cunning grey eyes which he expected me to understand, as in fact I most perfectly did. I carefully pocketed the whole of the six dollars, taking no notice of the agonized look with which Rody watched my proceedings. At last he could endure the suspense no longer, and beckoning me aside said, "Now your Riverence will you be pleased jist to hand over them six dollars again as we agreed?"

"*As you proposed*," I said, very coolly; "I shall lend myself to no such rogue's trick, you owe me two dollars and the marriage fee yet, so there is an end of the matter." Rody looked confounded, but said not a word. Just before I left the house, he came up with his bride and several of his own folks and said, "Yer Riverence must do us the favor of giving us your company to a hot supper at our own house this evening." I demurred, but, however, curiosity got the better, and I promised to look in at eight o'clock, and rode home.

A famous feast there was; roast, boiled, and fried; pies, cakes, and tarts of all imaginable sorts and sizes, and at the head of the table a most uncommon fine roast goose swimming in gravy. I had the fellow of it fattening in a pen in my own yard, or I thought I had. I had bought it of Rody's own mother.

"Sure and it's no wonder the craythur should be like its own brother," said Rody, as he heaped my plate and wished me a good appetite.

The first news that I heard in the morning was that my fat goose had disappeared. I need hardly say that I had supped off him at the wedding feast. If it had not been so well cooked, I would have sent the rogue to the penitentiary for three months.

This last speech of course was only said for fun, but the truth was that the parson was too kind hearted to distress the newly wedded bride and her family, by a public exposure of Rody's delinquency.

1   Lochinvar, the hero of a ballad by Walter Scott, rescues his Ellen from an unhappy marriage by claiming a dance with her at the wedding feast and then riding off with her.

2   "The Adventures of Gil Blas of Santillane," a picaresque romance by Le Sage (q.v.), was published in the 1700s and set in Spain. It was translated into English, reputedly by Smollett, in 1749 and was very highly regarded by Pitt, among others.

THE OLD DOCTOR.
A BACKWOODS SKETCH

"The Old Doctor" is a sketch that languished in Traill's papers in the National Archives of Canada until it was edited and published as a pamphlet by Jean Murray Cole in 1985 for the Hutchison House Museum in Peterborough, Ontario. The narrative is both a study and a celebration of Dr. John Hutchison (1797–1847), a Kirkcaldy native who came to Upper Canada to practise medicine in the 1820s and arrived in Peterborough in 1830. There in the mid-1830s the citizens of the town helped Hutchison to build the stone house, which now is his memorial. He died of typhus in 1847 when, after having suffered a stroke, he continued to help local citizens—many of them poor Irish—stricken during the epidemic.

The sketch presents Hutchison as a strong-minded, active practitioner, "a great utilitarian" who was outspoken in his condemnation of folly, be it domestic or personal. Yet, as Traill makes clear, his bluster masked a genuine benevolence and compassion. Doubtless, in serving a largely rural community in its early stages of settlement, he saw much to tax his patience. Hutchison was Traill's doctor and delivered five of her children from 1836 to 1844. He was also a close friend of Thomas Traill and Thomas A. Stewart. Stewart's family, here depicted as the Gradewells of Brae-head,[1] where "old Canadian comfort" was always to be found, were, for both Hutchison and Catharine, "patterns to the country." Three of Stewart's daughters, Ellen (here Ellen Eastwood), Bessie, and Anna, serve to represent that pattern, as does Edward [Brown], an orphan adopted by the Stewarts, whose fiddle provided a regular source of entertainment for the family despite the rigours of pioneer life.

"This is comfort Sir—old Canadian comfort such as I rarely meet with now, even in the backwoods," said the old doctor as he extended his half frozen hands to the cheerful blaze of the log fire that roared and crackled in the ample stone chimney at "Braehead."

"This fire, my dear Sir, is worth all the fine grim-crack stoves that ever came out of a foundry—lung-destroying, life-destroying, house-destroying, stoves."

"You are eloquent Doctor. What has moved your wrath against iron today?"

"The misery of my fellow creatures and their stupidity moreover," said the old man, rapidly divesting himself of sundry woollen mufflers that were wrapped around his throat and chin, of a thick homespun greatcoat and spencer of super-fine cloth, that old-fashioned sort of overjacket that used to be worn fifty years ago by elderly gentlemen, especially medical men.

The doctor was a model of strength, both mental and physical, of middle height and half as much above it but not fat; his hair silvered, but not white, still curled in thick masses above a high broad brow. The form of the head indicated mental power, firmness and decision; the height from ear to the crown showed a little too much destructiveness but the fine arch over the upper region of the forehead displayed benevolence in a still greater degree. The keen blue fiery eye, mouth slightly sarcastic, indicated to those who were skilled in reading the human mind from the human face the decisive character of the man.

The old doctor was a Radical in his way, but it was against abuses and follies, all, as he said, for the good of his species. He ran atilt at idleness and vice, knocking down all opponents with the power of his keen sarcasm and down-right bluster. However, when real sympathy was required to the sick and unfortunate he was tender and generous and loving as a father. But while he shewed benevolence to such as were suffering from the visitation of God or incidental causes, he gave no comfort to the idler who was content to fold his arms and sit down in hopeless apathy lamenting over a hard fate that might have been averted by energy of body or prudent forethought. "Up and be doing," "Set your shoulder to the wheel," "God helps those who help themselves," and many other such pithy maxims were among his household words. Such was the old doctor who now stood on the wide grey hearthstone of the log house at "Braehead."

One of his great antipathies was a parlour stove. "Let the women use a cooking stove in the kitchen, though I do not even like that, but give me the soul-cheering, heart-warming ruddy blaze of a good large log fire with a backlog that needs a stout arm to bring in. Hurl into the chimney back split maple, birch or oak, a few chips judiciously placed to keep up the draft and a kindling of cedar or pine below. There, Sir, is a fire such as our ancestors used to sit beside of a Christmas eve or a cool fall night."

"The stoves give more warmth," timidly interposed a delicate young girl who sat in the chimney corner.

The old man turned and eyed her for a minute, "How is your cough Miss Ellen? Did the burgundy pitch plaister ease your chest?"

"Not much, Doctor."

"No Madam, and it never will while you continue to breathe that stifling over-heated atmosphere of your father's house—thermometer rising daily from 85 to 100 degrees; no ventilation by means of a good wide chimney like this; air rushes in at an open door in a current and you may yourself be sitting in the direct line between it and the hot stove. No wonder you are a sick child."

"I am never too hot Doctor when you come to see us and make such a fuss . . ."

"You were going to say—about the heated room," the old man interrupted.

"Well, I am often quite chilly."

"No wonder Madam. Flesh and blood cannot stand it. Why, man is not a salamander to live in the fire. You would have been a good subject for that tyrannical old King of Babylon to have exercised his authority over. I think you would have stood the fiery furnace as well as Shadrach, Meshach and Abednego."

The invalid laughed, though she felt a pang of conscience in doing so.

"Then at night you have a fire lighted in your bedroom and sleep under a weight of blankets and coverlets and the room is again heated to a degree that is quite inimical to health. Fever, restless nights and languor is the consequence."

"I am perished when I awake if the stove is out Sir."

"There it is. You are roasted or stewed half the night and literally frozen the other half. You feel the cold twice as much as you would do if you went to bed in a moderately cold room and covered yourself up warmly. I do not object to an open fireplace, or a hall stove if there must be a stove at all to take off the keen edge of the frosty air, but no bedroom stove at all. I never sleep in a hot room—neither allow one for my children and look at them—cheeks like roses, eyes bright and lively as kittens—do you think those English cheeks would bloom so brightly in a hot house? Half the sickness that prevails in this naturally fine climate arises from the folly of those who make iron ovens of their houses and then think to breathe like the hardy children of the soil. Why they might as well expect fish to live out of their own element. What makes all our women fade and their cheeks lose their colour and turn yellow? The hot stove. It puts one in a rage to think of it!"

"You think the stove heat hurts the lungs Doctor?" asked his nervous patient.

"Yes I do. The air is completely changed by the heated iron. I could explain it from chemical causes, only you would be none the wiser if I did."

"I have read 'Conversations on Chemistry'."

"Pooh, poor child. Stuff. Girls never do understand these things from reading books. Learn the practical chemistry of the kitchen. That is the thing for them. The rapid change that the delicate respiratory organs undergo passing from a heated room into the open air when the mercury is below zero must be very trying to them. You girls will coddle yourselves up in one of these hot rooms and then think nothing of going out for a sleigh drive by moonlight, into the air perhaps ten or fifteen degrees below zero, or dance away till morning at your picnics and enjoy a good mouthful of cold in the coldest part of the twenty-four hours just before sunrise and yet are surprised that you are delicate and are subject to influenza and coughs and chest disease."

"It is singular, the prevalence of colds and coughs, influenza and consumption, that we hear of in late years," said Mr. Gradewell, who had been listening attentively to the pronouncements of his guest.

"It is not at all singular, Sir. It is just what was to be expected from the insane folly of the settlers."

"The dearness of wood in the towns is one of the reasons for the adoption of stove heat," said Mr. Gradewell.

"The government ought to have restricted settlers from cutting down too much wood. A forest reserve might have been made and the right of cutting it paid for at a moderate price. The people would have grumbled a little at first but would have found the blessing of it after a time. They should be prevented in their deeds from clearing up all the timber land on their lots. People are fools and should be curbed in their folly and ruled for their own good."

This was a pet refrain of the old doctor's, who also believed in preserving a portion of pleasantly wooded land in the vicinity of large towns for public walks and parks. It roused his furious indignation when he beheld the natural beauties of a place disfigured, and spots that seemed by nature fitted for man's recreation despoiled of trees and turf and crowded with buildings. He considered it a great oversight that a portion of such land was not reserved by the government for the use of the people.

Ellen Eastwood was the daughter of a gentleman residing in the neighbouring town whose delicate consumptive habit had alarmed her friends. Yielding to the doctor's advice she was on a visit to her uncle, Mr. Gradewell, who lived on a cleared farm five or six miles out of the town.

In summer, in spite of the distance, the hale active old man used to walk to visit his patients with no other help than the twisted thorn staff that he had cut on one of his botanizing rambles through the woods. In winter he drove himself in a stout dark-painted cutter, the woodwork made by his own hands, for the doctor was no mean mechanic. So active was he that he considered it one of the seven deadly sins to be idle. If he was not working with his hands, he was with his head. The first question that he put when he heard of a fresh arrival in the township was: "Are they sober? Can they use their hands?" He believed "Mere bookworms will starve in Canada. Idle hands make no head. If the young men can only drink and shoot let them get back from whence they came. They are not the right sort for a colony." The first thing in his estimation was to know how to use tools and with this idea he constantly advised any young men who came from the old country to learn a little of the craft of the carpenter, the blacksmith, and even the mason, before they settled on a farm. It was one of his maxims that no man should emigrate as a farmer to a Colony till he could help to build his own house. He had been settled many years in the Province and had seen a great deal of the ups and downs of life in Canada.

The hardships and toils of a Backwoodsman's life he knew from his constant acquaintance with settlers of all sorts and conditions. He would predict from his experience who would drive and thrive and who would sink utterly or drag on in a more shifting sort of life, ever in need, and who would go down and perish. The doctor was a great utilitarian. He valued most those who did most, but it must be for others as well as themselves. He was not selfish and did not love those who were.

The doctor was always a favoured visitor at "Braehead" and its cheerful log fire always put him in good humour—that is as soon as he had had his grumble out, for he was sure to have seen in the exercise of his vocation something that had roused his anger at deeds done or deeds undone that ought to have been done.

He was always pleased to see the girls usefully occupied in a household and took pleasure in praising the bread or puddings, pies or preserves if he knew they had been prepared by the hands of any of the ladies of the family. He loved to see a girl spinning at the large wheel. The hum of it, he said, was more pleasing to his ear than the sound of a piano, though he loved music too. He viewed with satisfaction the busy fingers plying the knitting needles and always commended any of the young folks whose hands were thus employed.

One of his lady friends reproached the doctor for his leveling system.

"Nay Madam," he replied curtly, "it is that you would level your family by managing idleness among them. The diligent hand maketh rich and the sluggard shall starve in harvest."

His friend Gradewell's family he regarded as patterns to the country. "They will be happy and respected," he used to say, "when others have gone down in the world, merely because they have wisely conformed to the lot in life to which Providence has called them. There is Bessy, now. See how bright and neat and cheerful she looks. I hear her voice singing by sunrise as she trips to her dairy. She is not ashamed to help milk the cows and make the butter and cheese. She never seems idle, for the knitting needles are going if she sits down by the fire. She loses no time lolling on a couch reading a novel. No, she is up and doing. And there is Anna. See how steadily she attends to all her employments. She is a pattern for girls of her age."

"These girls are complete household drudges," observed the lady to whom the remark was made, with a shrug. "The poor girls are worked like slaves. What time can they have for enjoyment? I wonder what their mother and father think is to become of them."

The doctor almost glared at the speaker. "I will tell you Madam. They will become good wives and sensible mothers and will be blessings to their husbands and children. They will flourish when others fail. If there were thousands more brought up like the girls and boys in that house the Province would in time be the wonder and glory of all lands."

"They can have no time for recreation of any sort. It is always the same—work, work, work."

"You are quite mistaken there. I know of no family that enjoys more pleasure than the Gradewells. Not a day in the winter, if the horses can be spared, that my friend or one of the boys does not take out a load of them, young and old, and merry enough they are—singing and enjoying themselves with all their hearts. Then at night they dance to Edward's fiddle and make a great circle round the fire and chat and sing and talk till bedtime."

"How do they get time for all this enjoyment?"

"By order Madam, which, like economy, makes a little go a long way. They have time for everything, for work and also for play."

The lady sighed wearily and went away, but did not profit by the Doctor's exhortations. He complained that very few did.

&

1   Braehead—The Stewarts' Douro home was called Auburn; they were Anglo-Irish, not Scottish. The Stewarts in fact provided the Traills with a home for brief periods in 1832 and 1839.

On the Rice Lake Plains

THE RICE LAKE PLAINS

Although many of Traill's "Forest Gleanings" and other fugitive pieces were based on her experience in the backwoods of Douro Township, where she lived for seven years, the series was sent to the *Anglo-American Magazine* from Oaklands, the Traills' home above the south shore of Rice Lake. The family lived there for nearly a decade, and it is given a prominent place among her literary landscapes. The most notable representation of it is in the novel *Canadian Crusoes* (1852). There and in her Rice Lake sketches, she tends to associate the Plains with the desire of the pioneer to transform the wilderness into a "fruitful garden," and in so doing to create the image of a picturesque landscape. Nevertheless, as will be noted in this sketch (it was published as "Forest Gleanings" No. 2, 1 [1852], 353–54), an element of doubt about that transformation is given expression in the poem, "Hurrah for the Forest," because the transformation necessitates the loss of a different glory, the dense wilderness.

Twenty years ago, I passed over the Rice Lake Plains, by the rich but uncertain light of an August twilight. We had just emerged from the long, dark forest of pines through which in those bygone days the rough, hilly, and deeply channelled road lay, forming the only line of direct communication between Cobourg and Sully and thence to the town of Peterboro', at that date containing about 300 inhabitants. It was the second day after my arrival from Montreal, and a thousand vivid recollections of the country of my birth—my own beloved and beautiful England, were freshly painted as it were upon my heart. Nevertheless I was charmed with the beauties that even a partial glance of the fair lake and her islands revealed to my admiring eyes. Weary and worn as I was with recent illness (I had gone through the ordeal of the cholera at Montreal, and was still weak from the effects of that direful disease), I wandered out into the moonlight, and climbing the rough snake fence that encircled the orchard ground, I stood on the steep hill above the old log tavern, and gazed abroad with delight upon the scene before me. There lay the lake, a sheet of moon-lit crystal reflecting in her quiet depths the wood-crowned islands; while beyond stretched the dark mysterious forest, unbroken, save by the Indian village, and Captain Anderson's clearing, which looked like a little oasis in the wilderness, that girded it in on three sides.[1] I thought of my own future home, and said to myself "will it be like this?" How busy was fancy—how cheering was hope that night. Beneath me lay the rude tavern, and its still ruder offices; and the foreground of the picture was filled up with a group of poor Irish immigrants—picturesque even in their dirt and wretchedness, which happily the distance concealed from my eyes. Their blazing log fires, around which they reposed or moved, gave broad light and shadow to the scene, and would have rejoiced the heart of a painter. Our little steamer (she was thought a wonderful affair in those days) lying at the rude wharf, ready to receive her motley cargo of live and dead stock, by early morning's light, completed the picture.

At the period of which I write, there were not more than five or six settlers on the Rice Lake plains. Few emigrants of the better class had been found with taste enough to appreciate the beauties of the scenery, and judgment sufficient to form a correct estimate of the capabilities of the soil. By most people it was regarded as utterly unfitted for cultivation. The light loam that forms the upper stratum which on first turning the soil, is of a yellow color, but which darkens by exposure to the air, was at first sight declared to be sand, and not worth the labour of clearing. Land on the plains was a drug in the land market, and so continued till within the last six years, and the few who in defiance of public prejudice, bought, builded, and cultivated farms on the plains, were regarded as visionaries, who were amusing themselves with hopes that would empty their pockets, but, not fill their barns. Among the very few who chose to think for himself on this matter, was that highly respectable, and intelligent gentleman, William Falkner, for many years a District Judge in this portion of the colony, who may with justice be termed the "Patriarch of the Plains," after many, many years of solitude, he has lived to see his hopes realized, and his judgment confirmed.[2] The plains are now settled in every direction, the despised, sandy desert, has become a fruitful garden, "the land is at rest and breaks forth into singing." It is now found to be highly productive for every sort of grain and green crop, and for gardens it is unequalled.

For years that lovely lake haunted my memory, and I longed to return again to it; and fondly cherished the hope, that one day I might find a home among its hills and vales. The day dream has been realized; and from the "Oaklands," I now look towards the distant bay beyond the hills where I spent my first night on the Rice Lake Plains, and can say, as I then said "truly it is a fair and lovely spot."

I know of no place more suitable for the residence of an English gentleman's family. There is hardly a lot of land that might not be converted into a park. The noble oaks and majestic pines, (not here as in the forest, subject to certain destruction and overthrow) form an enduring ornament, to be cut down or left to grace the clearings, at the taste of the owner, an advantage which is not to be looked for in the woods, or on old long cleared lands, where few have been planted, and none left. Here, too, the diversity of hill and valley, wood and water, afford such delightful building sites, that you can hardly choose amiss. The excellence of the roads, and facility of water transport, are great advantages, and, what many persons will regard as a still greater inducement is the society, which is principally English and Scotch, with a few Irish settlers of the higher class. Mills are in operation on the lake shore; a village in progress, with stores and taverns, steamers plying upon the lake, and a railroad is being surveyed which is to cross the lake, and form a rapid communication between Cobourg and the far back country. Such are the changes that a few brief years have effected on these despised Rice Lake Plains.

HURRAH FOR THE FOREST.
A SONG FOR THE WOOD.

Hurrah for the forest, the old pinewood forest,
The sleighbells are jingling with musical chime,
   The still woods are ringing,
   As gaily we're singing,
O merry it is in the cold winter time.

Hurrah for the forest, the dark pinewood forest,
With the moon stealing down on the cold frozen snow,
   When with hearts beating lightly,
   And eyes beaming brightly,
Through the wild forest by moonlight we go.

Hurrah for the forest, the dark waving forest,
Where silence and stillness for ages have been
   We'll rouse the grim bear
   And the wolf from his lair
And the deer shall start up from his dark leafy screen.

O wail for the forest, the proud stately forest,
No more its dark depths shall the hunter explore,
  For the bright golden main
  Shall wave free o'er the plain,
O wail for the forest, its glories are o'er.

C.P.T.

∽

1   Major Charles Anderson (1786–1844) of the 1st
Regiment, Frontenac Militia, operated a trading post at the
mouth of the Otonabee on Rice Lake, the clearing referred
to here. He was married to a Mississauga woman and led
a party of Natives during the Mackenzie rebellion. See
Norma Martin et al., *Gore's Landing and the Rice Lake Plains*
(Heritage Gore's Landing, 1986).

2   William Falkner (1782–1854) was appointed judge of
the Newcastle District in 1828. He established Oaklands,
Lot 11, Concession 8 that same year and the Traills bought
the farm from him in 1849. Falkner also built the first
sawmill on the Lake shore, Lot 14, Concession 9, in 1833.
See Martin, *Gore's Landing*, for accounts of the development
of the village.

Rice Lake Plains—The Wolf Tower

The Traills first had an opportunity to move to the "Wolf Tower" in the late winter or spring of 1839. It was offered to them when its owner, the Reverend George Wilson Bridges (1787–1863), whose story is partially told in this sketch, had decided to return to England to facilitate his son's education. Bridges had arrived in Upper Canada and had the tower built in 1837 after having read *The Backwoods of Canada*. He returned to England in 1841. The Traill family occupied the tower, located on Lot 25, Concession 8 of Hamilton Township, for about a year from the spring of 1846, this time taking up Bridges' offer of free accommodation. The geographical and botanical inventory begun at that time found expression both in this sketch and in the novel *Canadian Crusoes*. The Mr. Gedley referred to in a footnote is in fact John Robert Godley, whose *Letters from America* was published in London in two volumes in 1844. The passage on Bridges that Traill protests reads as follows:

> One day he suddenly departed as mysteriously as he had come, with the view, it is said, of spending the rest of his life in the East; and his tower remains untenanted and unclaimed, as a memorial of his strange eventful history. He seems to have been quite a realization of the character of Basil Mertoun in Scott's "Pirate."

Bridges was a well-travelled man and authored several books pertaining to Jamaica and the legitimacy of slavery prior to his arrival in Upper Canada. (See *The Annals of Jamaica*, 2 vols. [London: John Murray, 1828].) His strange octagonal house seems to anticipate the fictional garrison structure described in Marian Engel's *Bear* (1976). "Rice Lake Plains—The Wolf Tower" first appeared as "Forest Gleanings" No. 3, *Anglo-American Magazine* 1 (1852), 417–20.

S trangers visiting the Rice Lake, will be led by curiosity to see the "Wolf Tower," an octagonal building that occupies a beautiful grassy mound, near the shores of the crescent-shaped bay, formed by Pine-Tree Point and the bold promontory near the head waters of the Lake, formerly known as Bank's Bluff.

The Tower itself has lately undergone some changes: it is no longer what it was, and it is unnecessary to describe it, but some slight sketch of its original owner may not prove altogether uninteresting among the local features of the Rice Lake and her shores.

∽

It is now many years ago,—long before the Plains had attained to their present popularity,—when they lay in solitary loneliness, uncared for, excepting by the deer-hunter and those few settlers, who, like my friend, Judge Falkner, had taste to enjoy their beauties and appreciate their real value,—that a stranger, of gentlemanly appearance and highly polished manners, came to the tavern at Sully, and sought there a temporary shelter for himself, his little son, and a female domestic, who had been the child's nurse. This gentleman had been the Rector of St. Anne's, in Jamaica.

After some time, he purchased a picturesque lot of land, about three miles below the head of the Lake—a lonely and lovely spot. There on an isolated mound, at the foot of a range of lofty hills, which form the sides of one of those singular ravines that diversify the Plains,—he caused the Wolf Tower to be built, greatly to the admiration of the workmen, and the few scattered settlers thereabouts; and much they marvelled that the strange gentleman should content himself in the rude log shanty that he caused to be put up, while the more important building was in progress.

The rooms were all of an octagon form, and were fitted up with ornamental mouldings of red cedar, brought from the adjacent islands, and sawn into boards: tables, chairs, shelves, were all of the same brittle, but odoriferous wood,—and these were the work and amusement of the recluse in his lonely retirement.

To strangers, the deep melancholy that at times pervaded his features, his solitary habits, and love of retirement, were matters of speculation,—but to those who were acquainted with the sad history of his domestic afflictions, it was no matter of surprise that he should seek, in seclusion from the world, healing for a wounded and almost broken heart. With the suffering prophet of the Hebrews, he might have been led to exclaim:—"Surely there is no sorrow like my sorrow." At one stroke, it had pleased the Almighty to deprive him of the light of his eyes and the joy of his heart,—in one brief moment the unhappy father beheld the treacherous waves of a calm and unruffled sea, close over his four lovely and interesting daughters, and their faithful attendant (the sister of his little boy's nurse). Thus suddenly was his home left unto him desolate.*

Surely the ways of the Lord are mysterious and his counsels past our human ken. Yet does he often lead the bruised and broken spirit to confess—"It is good for me to have been afflicted; before I was troubled I went astray." And well, indeed, is it with those who can look upwards and say—"In the multitude of the sorrows that I had in my heart, thy comforts, O Lord, have refreshed my soul."

Such was the cause of this gentleman's estrangement from the world; and in the various occupations that he found, within and without doors, (for he was never idle), in the education of his little boy, and literary pursuits, he in a great measure regained that tranquility of mind which this sad bereavement of his beloved children had deprived him of.

A strong desire to see an aged parent in England, joined with the necessity of giving his son the advantages of

---

* The sad circumstances connected with the oversetting of the pleasure-barge, with the loss of the Rector of St. Anne's four lovely daughters, the female servant, and two young married ladies, with some others of the party, were well known to the inhabitants of St. Anne's.

a classical education and the improvement of his health by travelling in the warmer parts of Europe, at last decided him on the propriety of forsaking his beloved solitude, and he disposed of the Tower and his Canadian property, and returned to England. "The Wolf Tower" has passed into the hands of strangers, and for some months afforded a temporary residence for my family and myself.**

When I came to reside at the "Wolf Tower," in the spring of 1846, I was in weak health, scarcely recovered from the effects of a dangerous fit of illness, but so renovating did I find the free healthy air of the hills about the Tower, that in a very short space of time, I was strong and able to ramble about with the children among the wild ravines, and over the steep wood-crowned heights around this romantic spot, revelling, with almost child-like delight, in this rare flower-garden of nature's own planting.

For some time, the rich scenery around the Tower formed the limits of our rambles. My children were never weary of climbing the lofty sides of the hills that shut in the deep-winding ravine which opened out upon the green pasture at the foot of the mound on which the Tower is built. To this beautiful spot they gave the name of the "Valley of the Big Stone," from a huge boulder of red granite that occupies the centre of it. And here, of a Sunday evening, we used to hold our little church, seated upon the disjointed fragments that were scattered about it, and sheltered by the lofty banks, clothed with oak, birch, and a

---

** Perhaps I have dwelt more particularly on the Tower and its former proprietor, from having read a very erroneous statement respecting this gentleman, by a Mr. Gedley, in a work written in the form of letters from Canada, where he speaks of the *mysterious disappearance* of the eccentric owner of the Tower, adding that the place has lain tenantless ever since, with other observations equally opposed to facts. Now, it happened that the sale of the Tower and adjacent lands, with the furniture, stock, &c., was effected without the least mystery, and the departure of the former owner was a matter well known throughout the neighbourhood, and conducted quite openly.

flowery undergrowth of roses and cornel, and other sweet-scented shrubs,—and here we often took our little treat of milk and bread, and ripe-red strawberries, gathered on the heights above by the children's busy hands. We gave names to all of the remarkable spurs and promontories of the valley. There was the "Wolf Crag," the "Raven's Crag," the "Hill of the Pine," the "Birken Shaw," and the "Brae Head," with many others,—while nearer home were the "Tower Hill," and "Traitor's Gate."

Soon we began to extend our walks, rambling on from one hill to another, till we had explored, westward, the deep defiles and rounded hills that form that remarkable hill-pass, leading to Sackville Mill,[1] and the high promontory which commands the whole extent of the lake and its islands, to Gore's Landing, where a pretty neat cottage has been erected by a Devonshire gentleman,[2] and which forms a pleasing object from the lake, nestled among groups of pine, oak, birch, and poplar, that surround it.

Eastward of the Tower, and running up inland from Pine-Tree Point, there is a deep valley, commonly known as Thilvert's Ravine, a lonely spot, once inhabited, but now nothing but a few charred logs, half overgrown with moss and weeds; a spring with its moss-grown stones and slippery plank, scarcely visible from the turf that covers it,—are all that remain to mark where a dwelling has been. At the head of the valley, just above the spot where the house once stood, there is a rocky pasture-field surrounded by a dilapidated fence half filled in with briars and scrubby oaks and bushes of various kinds; large girdled oaks, long since dead, stretch their bare leafless arms against the sky, giving an air of sadness and desolation to the scene. Just where the path turns round the corner of the fence, there is a small enclosure, not many yards in extent: it contains the grave of a lady, the wife of the former possessor of the soil. I remember the first time I visited the Tower, our road lay along the hill-side, near that very spot. It was winter, and the snow lay thick upon the ground, yet I noticed the fresh-raised mound by the road-side; there still stood the pick-axe and shovel that had been used in breaking the frost-bound earth; and now I never pass the grave, over-grown by a rank luxuriance of herbs, wild-flowers, and shrubs, without a feeling akin to sadness. The little dwelling levelled by fire to the dust, her husband and children distant,—silence and the stillness of desolation seem to brood over the spot where she sleeps, unconscious that a sympathizing stranger's step often lingers on the path that leads to her last lone resting-place.

A still finer and deeper ravine is that which lies at the side of the high table-land, which terminates in a cliff-like descent towards the lake, and to the westward. From the precipitous hill-path above, you look down upon a mass of waving foliage, and the jutting spurs of the valley, clothed with flowers and wild roses and shrubs, extend to a considerable distance, and add much to the wild beauty of the scenery. The high land above this glen is known by the name of Mount Ararat. It was a lovely evening that I first descended Mount Ararat: the sun was setting behind the dark pines that clothe the higher ground towards the westward, or head waters of the lake, and a flood of golden light was on the waters. The islands lay almost at our feet, some in deep shade, and others just catching the last radiant glance of the retiring sunbeams. A deep indigo tint was on the distant shore, and all looked so lovely, that I could have lingered there as long as a ray of twilight remained to lighten the landscape.

These ravines form some of the most interesting natural features of the Plains, and give a singular and furrowed aspect to the shore, when seen from the water. They are evidently the channels through which, in ages past, poured down vast sweeping torrents, when the higher table-lands emerged from the state of chaos, caused by some mighty natural convulsion, and these deep gorges formed drains by which the waters found an outlet to the lake below. What a scene of wild and fearful desolation must these hills and valleys then have presented! Now how changed! The rushing tumultuous waters have ceased to flow. The rocky fragments that they bore down with them in their headlong course have found a resting-place. The sides of the valley are clothed with herbs and flowers, and the waving foliage of graceful trees; the evening air is scented with the perfume of roses and other odorous shrubs—

"The land is at rest and breaks forth into song."

The partridge leads her young brood forth to feed upon the soft luscious fruits of the huckleberry and squaw-berry. The lone cry of the Whip-poor-will is heard in the still evening air. A thousand birds find nourishment and rear their broods in their deep valleys, while the solitary lord of these solitudes rears its young on some stately pine, upon the highest hills above the lake.

He who would wish to see the Plains in their fullness of beauty, should visit them in the latter end of May and the flowery months of June, July, and August, and his eye will be gratified by an assemblage of lovely blossoms; he may also revel in abundance of sweet summer berries, among which the strawberry, huckleberry, and filberry, may be named with many others of less note, while grapes, of no mean size or flavour, abound on the lake shore, and even give name to one of the smaller islands. I have tasted excellent grape-wine, made by our friend of the Tower, from the fruit gathered on Grape Island—the genuine juice of the grape, as he termed it.

I scarcely know a more delicate and attractive little shrub, than the common huckleberry of the Plains, with its slender branches of pale green leaves and waxen heath-shaped bells—sometimes tinted with a soft blush-colour or greenish-white; these are quickly followed by a succession of ripe blue-berries, sweet and pleasant, and very wholesome, though wanting a slight flavour to make them agreeable to some palates: as a mixture with red currants they are excellent either as a preserve or in pastry. This humble fruit forms, during its continuance one of the great attractions of the Plains. Large parties come from the distant towns of Cobourg, Port Hope, and Grafton, to gather berries and pass a day of rural enjoyment among the fruits and flowers of the Rice Lake Plains.

In rambling over the hills and valleys, the eye is attracted by the vast beds of azure lupines, which give a soft tint to the ground, especially on the more sandy spots, where they mostly delight to grow. Seen on its native soil, and blooming beneath its own warm summer skies, this flower is seen to far greater advantage than the cold and somewhat coarse-looking flower that we cultivate in our gardens at home. The spikes of richly laden blossoms present every variety of shade, from the pale pearly blue to the deep velvetty purple. The seeds are small and of ivory whiteness, and from their abundance, no doubt form no inconsiderable addition to the food of the smaller quadrupeds and birds, that have their haunts and homes among the oak glades of the Plains.

Springing up among these azure lupines, we see the splendid Enchroma or Painted Cup, in brilliancy of colour not inferior to the most vivid scarlet geranium, yet it is a wild and hardy plant, nurtured in a dry and gravelly soil, adorning sunny wastes and barren spots. This remarkable flower derives its splendour from the calyx and involucrum that surrounds it. These are divided and subdivided in many segments, the points of which appear as if they had been dipped in a dye of brightest vermillion. The blossom itself is ringed of a pale yellow or straw-colour, and is scarcely discernible from the folds of the bright fringe that envelopes it. And hardly less attractive, from its large snowy blossom, is the stately trillium,—seen by the moonlight, the hills seem studded with bright stars so pure and dazzling in their whiteness,—I often wonder that this exceedingly lovely flower so widely spread as it is all over this continent has never found a place in our English gardens.

The large lilac crane's-bill or wild geraneum, of no ordinary gracefulness and beauty, here displays its elegant blossoms. The curious yellow mocassin flower, Cyprepedium arietinum, tosses its golden balls to the wind, a canopied couch where Titania might hide herself and her elves from "jealous Oberon." There are abundant varieties of lilies, the pale erythionum or dog's-tooth violet, with its single drooping flower and curiously variegated leaf. The gay orange martagon, with every variety of the convollaria, from the many flowered gigantic Solomon's seal, to the lowly C. bifolia, with its pretty starry flower and ruby-spotted fruit. Not less attractive are the various low shrubby evergreens, pyrolas and dwarf arbutus; some of these with their myrtle-shaped leaves of glassy green, and bright scarlet fruit, are an enduring ornament, and appear to beautify even the most barren spots. There, too, is the pentagala, by some called milkwort and satin flower, a gem worthy of a place in any lady's green-house; twined among the tall stalks of the deer-grass, asking support from every slender twig, we find vetches of all the most delicate hues; the pencilled, the white, the blue, the flesh; all charming in their way. These are a few among the thousand floral beauties that one short month brings forth; but how shall I describe all that the succeeding months reveal, of fruits and flowers, mosses and ferns—and then what store of roses the month of June unfolds; on clearings, on hilly banks, in shady glens, and open levels, they spring up bright and beautiful. In old clearings it is delightful to walk out at dew-fall to smell the roses and that light feathery shrub, so widely diffused among the underwood, the ceanothus, or New Jersey tea, the scent of which resembles the meadowsweet: Canadians and Yankies use an infusion of the leaves as tea. Among our odoriferous flowers the monarda, a gigantic mint with pale lilac flowers bears a prominent place; the sweet gale or shrubby fern, smells like nutmeg, this also is in great repute among the old Canadians as a substitute for tea—many of the pyrolas, or many flowered wintergreens, give out a delicious odour, and that lowly but charming creeping evergreen, the mitchella ripens, or partridge berry reminds one of the white jessamine in the delicacy of its smell,—the scarlet twinberry it is called by some, and I am told the fruit is pleasant to eat. These flowers like many others of our Canadian plants are united at the germ so as to give a double berry. The stately milkweed (asclepias) are very fragrant, and one pretty shrubby plant with corymbs of pale pink striped bells, (apocynum, dogbane,) gives out its odour only after sunset. Our low grounds along the lake shore present a vast variety of shrubs—the snow berry, the large mezereon, the high bush cranberry, or single American Gueldres rose, wild cherries of various kinds, and plums, with vines, and various climbers are here to be found. The bittersweet, a solanum of great beauty flinging its slender branches over the saplings wreathing them with its dark green foliage and scarlet fruit; this plant is in high esteem with the Indians who use both root and berry in various ways as medicine—and outward applications, as an ingredient in a salve for burns and scalds, it is very efficacious. I must not in my floral notice of the plains, forget to mention one of its brightest ornaments, the deep blue larger blossom gentian, and the elegant gentiana ciliata or fungus gentian; these are Fall flowers, and are chiefly found on rather dry open levels, such as the ground of those remarkable spots known by the settlers on the plains as the upper and lower race-course, from the dead level surface they present, which strange as it may sound are almost the only level grounds upon the plains—the common term *plainsland* seems in Canada rather to mean open partially cleared ground, and is in most instances composed of an endless variety of hill and dale. A volume might be compiled on the floral productions of the plains, which would be no inconsiderable addition to the very scanty library of botanical works that have yet been written on the plants indigenous and peculiar to Canada.

Though a great proportion of our natural plants are widely diffused all over the country, there are others that are confined to certain spots, favourable to their peculiar habits—every township affords some plants peculiar to certain localities.

One growth of plants is confined to the shores of certain lakes and still waters—the rapid waters again where the banks are mostly rocky and elevated, present others. The rich alluvial flats, composed of decayed vegetable matter, give plants of rank and luxuriant quality. The deep recesses of the forest where the beams of the noon day sun scarcely find leave to pierce, grow plants and flowers that are foreign to the open sunny wastes and dry pastures. The spongy mossy soil of the cedar swamps, or the dry pine barrens afford others of the most opposite characters, while a lovely aquatic garden floats upon the bosom of the still waters, rivalling in beauty their terrestrial sisters.

There are rare and evanescent flowers that no hortus siccus can preserve, the produce of the rank soil of the deep wood whose beauties have never been given to the world.

The time is not far distant when many of these sweet children of the wilderness will be sought for in vain, those more especially that love the cool and shady recesses of the forest; that have their haunt by mossy stone and bubbling rill; as the axe and the fire level the woods where they flourished, they disappear. Like the wild Indian, they fade away before the influence of civilization, and the place that knew them once shall know them no more.

Man has altered the face of nature. The forest and its dependents will soon be among the things that were. The stately plantations of Indian corn, the waving fields of golden grain, have usurped the places of the giant pine, the oak, the beech, and the maple. A new race springs up, suited to the nature of the soil, and the wants of man and his dependents, but—

"But the flowers of the forest are a'wede away."

BY THE AUTHORESS OF THE "BACKWOODS."
Oaklands, Rice Lake.

⌒

1   The Sackville Mill was on Cold Creek, near the western end of Rice Lake.

2   The Devonshire gentleman was George Ley (1820–93), an Oxford graduate who moved to Canada West about 1845 and purchased Lot 28 in the 8th Concession of Hamilton Township. He later married a niece of Judge Falkner. See Martin et al., *Gore's Landing*.

A Walk to Railway Point

"Forest Gleanings," No. 12, *Anglo-American Magazine* 3 (1853), 401–4, accentuates Traill's ambivalent feelings about the pioneers' transformation of the wilderness. On the one hand she gives voice to the economic benefits that will be derived from a railroad to the back country, but on the other she manifests her delight in the unmarred forest. While she makes it clear that the railroad is no source of aesthetic pleasure for her, the essay is also informed by her realization that, had communications been better during the time that she and her husband lived in Douro Township, their farming might have been more successful and their lives much different. Ironically, the railroad bridge that was built across Rice Lake proved unsafe after a few years and was abandoned in 1861. All that remains today are a few footings that extend out from the point near Harwood on Rice Lake's south shore.

Thirty years ago, the emigrant who desired to settle himself and family in the townships, north of Rice Lake, on reaching its southern shore, after a weary day's journey through roads deeply cut by ruts and water-worn gullies, could obtain no better mode of conveyance across its waters than what was afforded by a small skiff or canoe, unless he committed himself and his worldly goods to the safer keeping of a huge, flat-bottomed ark, called a scow, which usually took two whole days to perform its toilsome voyage up the long-winding Otonabee; the navigation of which in these days, and indeed for many a long year after that time, was considerably obstructed by rapids, on the spot now occupied by the fine, substantial locks, which afford an easy entrance to the little lake; and may be called the key to Peterboro'.

Ten years passed on, and the wants of the traveller who was wending his way northward, were met by a small steamer which plyed on Rice Lake, and took passengers and goods part of the way, being met by the scow when the water was low in the river some miles below the town. At a certain part marked by a tall pine, called the *Yankee Bonnet*, from its top bearing a resemblance to that article. Scanty as were the accommodations on board, the advent of this boat was hailed with infinite satisfaction, and great praise was bestowed on the spirited proprietors, gentlemen and merchants of Cobourg, who had thus met the requirements of the public, and doubtlessly greatly facilitated the settlement of Peterboro' and her back country.

By degrees a better class of steamers were launched on Rice Lake. At this date, no less than four are cleaving its waters, and enlivening the lonely shores of the Otonabee River. And here it is but just to remark, that where a public benefit is to be conferred, the men of Cobourg, whatever may be their politics or private opinions, are ready to come forward heart and hand to promote the work.

Roads have been constructed to enable the traveller after crossing the winter flooring of Rice Lake to reach Peterboro' and the surrounding country by the shortest possible route, but ice is but a treacherous foundation to trust to, and moreover, there are intervals in early winter before its safety has been tested, and in early spring, when the sun is exerting its power over the ice-locked streams, that a total stop is put to journeys, either business or pleasure, unless by a circuitous route through the worst of roads by the head of the lake.

To meet the wants of the fast increasing population, and to enable Peterboro' to send forth her abundant stores of lumber, grain, wool, and dairy produce, to a ready market, something more was required,—and lo! ere the blessing was asked, it was as it were cast into her lap. No sacrifice of labour, time or money, was demanded. Let us hope that the townsmen of Peterboro' will unite in gratitude towards the enterprizing men of Cobourg, the spirited movers of this great work, and national benefit—a RAILROAD AND BRIDGE ACROSS THE RICE LAKE. A work which when completed will enrich even the poorest of her backwoodsmen, and be the means of opening out a wide extent of unreclaimed forest; a field for the future labours of the industrious farmer, and skilful mechanic. Will not a work like this ultimately prove more beneficial to the Colborne District than the discovery of mines of silver and gold in her vicinity?

As a lover of the picturesque, I must confess that I have a great dislike to railroads. I cannot help turning with regret from the bare idea of scenes of rich rural beauty being cut up and disfigured by these intersecting veins of wrought iron, spanning the beautiful old romantic hills and rivers of my native land; but here, in this new country, there is no such objection to be made, there are no feelings connected with early associations, to be rudely violated; no scenes that time has hallowed to be destroyed. Here, the railroads run through dense forests, where the footsteps of man have never been impressed, across swamps and morasses on which the rays of the sun have scarcely ever shone, over lonely rivers and wide-spread lakes, that have never echoed to the dash of the oar, or reflected aught on their bosoms but the varied foliage of the overhanging woods.

216　　　　　　　　　　　　　ON THE RICE LAKE PLAINS

If little can be said in behalf of the picturesque beauty of a railway, it may be observed on the other hand that it is quite as pleasing a sight to the eye of most persons as a chaotic map of fallen pines, and decaying cedars stretching across each other in wild confusion; that a rail-car is at least as sightly as an ox-cart, or lumber-waggon. If its presence does not embellish, neither can it mar a country where it interferes with none of our natural beauties, or ancient works of art. Nay, in future years will it not be looked upon with veneration and admiration, as were many of the public roads and viaducts of ancient Rome?

Here we have scope and verge enough to act upon, without offending the eye of taste, or intruding upon any man's prejudice or taste. If the old settler be in the neighborhood of a railroad, he can remove elsewhere, and dispose of his lands to great advantage: the new comer need not purchase in its vicinity, if he does not value the advantages that it offers. The benefit to a new country, so deficient in really good roads, must be great; therefore, I say, let the work go on, and prosper—let it stretch from East to West; from the shores of the Atlantic, even to the Georgian Bay.

Twenty years ago, the most sanguine speculator would have smiled sceptically at the suggestion of a bridge spanning the wide extent of the waters of Rice Lake,—five years ago, he would have laughed at such an idea. Nay, within the last twelve months, the scheme was regarded as an impossibility, and, behold, it is now half completed. The difficulties have vanished before the enterprise and skill of engineers and mechanical operatives, incited by the assurance of certain remuneration from the Shareholders.

Quietly and steadily has the work progressed; the neighbourhood has not been disturbed by scenes of riot or drunkenness; there has been no bloodshed nor disorder among the hands; no man's property has been pillaged, and no one has suffered wrong; strict order has been observed, greatly to the credit of the overseers, whose respectability of conduct deserves all praise.

In a few weeks longer, and the great work of pile-driving will be completed, and the shores of the Township of Hamilton and Otonabee will be linked together by an enduring monument, greatly to the credit of American ingenuity, and Canadian enterprise. Were I as well skilled in the science of political economy, as Miss Martineau,[1] I might have enlarged on all the advantages to be derived from the railroad, but I must leave it to wiser heads than mine, to discuss such matters.

It was on a bright summer afternoon, in the early part of July, that accompanied by my eldest daughter and some young friends with whom we were spending the day, I set out to visit the works at Railway Point, for as yet I know no other more significant name for the site of the Railway station and future village on this side the lake. We thankfully accepted of the escort of the master of the house, who graciously gave up some important out-of-door work to accompany us, a sacrifice of time for which I hope we were all sufficiently thankful.

The sun was so hot that we were glad more than once to rest under the shade of some noble butternut trees, which spread their most refreshing branches across the narrow sandy rood, and as I looked up among the broad-spreading leaf boughs, I marvelled at the size of the trees which had been only saplings when first I passed along that very road some twenty-one years before. Near the spot where formerly stood the old inn at the landing place, known as Sully, the path turned abruptly in a direction parallel to the lake eastward, and we crossed a crazy log bridge over a small creek and a wilderness of the blue iris and rushes, thistles and wild camomile, and entered on a newly-cut road which had been opened by the Railway men for a more ready communication with the Sully road.

Through an old bit of marshy clearing, thick covered with rushy grass and small bushes of dwarf willow and alder, lay our path: the black sphagnous soil, owing to the long draught was fortunately for us dry, but an hour's rain would have made our footing far from agreeable. Through this meadow ran a bright stream which was unbridged, save by sundry blocks of granite and fragments of limestone which afforded a stopping place to our feet; from this point our way lay through a regular growth of forest trees, lofty pines, maple, bass and oak, the dense thicket of leafy under-wood shutting out the lake from our sight. You might have imagined yourself in the very heart of the forest; many rare and beautiful flowers we gathered, flourishing in the rank soil among the decaying trunks and branches that strewed the leafy ground. There, among others, was that gem of beauty, the chimaphila or shining-leafed wintergreen; rheumatism weed, as some of the natives call it, its dark glossy leaves of holly-green, and corymba of peach-coloured flowers, its amethyst-coloured anthers set round the emerald green, turban-shaped pistil, forming a contrast of the most perfect beauty. This elegant flower might well be called by way of distinction, the "Gem of the Forest." There were pink milk weeds as fragrant as beautiful, white piroles, and the dark rich crimson blossoms of the red flowering raspberry, with many others with which we quickly filled our hands; nevertheless, we were not sorry when we emerged from the close sultry forest path, and felt the delicious breeze from the lake blowing fresh upon us. There lay the bright waters glittering in the sunlight full before us. The ground in front sloped gently down to the shore, forming a little peninsula; on one side a deep cove wooded on its banks to the water's edge, in front the long line of piles stretching towards a small island on which a station-house is to be erected for the keeper of the gates, which are to admit of the egress and regress of boats and rafts.

Far to the eastward, the shores rose, rounded with dark forest trees, forming bold capes and headlands, with bays and inlets. Full in the opposite shore, lay the extensive clearing of the Indian village, with the green slopes of Anderson's Point,[2] once the memorable scene of an exterminating slaughter between the Mohawks and the Ojibbewa Indians; their bones and weapons of war, axes, arrow-heads and scalping knives, are still to be found on turning up the now peaceful soil, where the descendants of the war-chiefs now reap a harvest of golden grain, and bow the knee at the bloodless altar beneath the roof of that humble village church which silently points upward to that gracious Saviour who said to his disciples:

"My peace I give unto you, not as the world giveth it."

Many there are who can recall the time when the very men who inhabit that village knew not the Lord, but wandered in the darkness of heathenism, whose hand was against every man, and every man's hand against them, but who now worship their God in spirit and in truth.

It is somewhere eastward of the church that the bridge will strike the shore, and so stretch on through the low lands, which we may call the vale of the Otonabee, towards Peterboro'. Further on, westward of the Indian village, are the two mouths of the river, divided by a low swampy island; and there, on the Monaghan shore, far up towards the head of the lake, are sunny clearings and pleasant farms, looking bright and cheerful in the warm beams of the afternoon sun.

Our own southern shore is the most picturesque; but to obtain a sight of it we must go out upon the water; but just now we are glad to rest on the broad bench beneath a clump of bowery basswood trees, which have been most judiciously left on the cleared space to afford a shady seat for the workmen at noon-time; and here we can sit beneath the thick foliage which shuts out the sultry summer sun, and look at the busy scene before us. The shore is all alive with workmen. From that long low shed rings the clank of the blacksmith's hammer; that column of blue smoke rising among the graceful group of silver birches and poplars, points to the forge. There is a boat building at the edge of the water; there is a scow, and a small steam-engine is being fixed to move the hammer of that pile-driver; it will be the third or fourth in operation; boats, skiffs, and scows are moving to and fro, each guided by some hand who has his appointed labor in the bee-hive. On that little eminence stands a young man, whose figure and bearing mark his situation to be one superior to the common mechanic. The sun's rays fall with dazzling effect upon some brass instrument that rests on a high stand. He courteously returns the greeting of one of our party, and informs us "He is taking an observation of the level of the bridge."

Those three principal buildings are, a boarding-house for the workmen, and two stores, where all the necessaries of life may be purchased in the shape of groceries, provisions, and ready-made clothing. You see no women in this temporary village: but there peeps out a sweet baby-boy, with fat-dimpled shoulders and bright curls; his gay red frock sets off the whiteness of his skin, and you are sure a mother's gentle hand has brushed those sunny locks from his broad white brow, and made those hands so clean, though she herself is not visible.

The eye follows that line of posts, four abreast, which stretches its leviathan length far far across the rippling waters of the lake. There, at the utmost limits, is the mighty machine that looks in the distance like a tall gibbet, against which a huge ladder is leaning, but that dark figure midway on the scaffold is no miserable felon, but a good, honest, hard-working Yankee, who directs the movements of the ton weight of iron that now slowly ascends between the sliding grooves in the tall frame; and now, at the magic word, "All right!" descends with lightning swiftness upon the head of the pile that has just been conducted to its site. It is curious to see the log of timber, some twenty-five or thirty feet in length, emerge from the depth of the lake; you do not see the rope that is fastened to it, which that man in the skiff tows it along by—it seems to come up like a huge monster of the deep, and rearing itself by degrees, climbs up the side of the frame like a living thing; then for a second swing to and fro, till steadied by the least apparent exertion on the part of the guide on the scaffold. Now it is quite upright, plumb—I suppose the carpenter would say—then at the signal, clack, clack, clack, goes the little engine on the scow: slowly aloft mounts the great weight, down, down,

down, it comes—the first blow fixing the timber in its destined place—and sends a shower of bark flying from the pile; when the weight comes down on to the head of the pile the jerk disengages a sort of claw that is attached to it; this ascends and again comes down, seizing the ring of the weight in its own grasp, and bearing it again triumphantly upwards—again to descend upon the pile with unerring aim—lower it sinks, and every fresh blow comes with accelerated force, till it is brought to the level of the others. From a quarter of an hour to twenty minutes is the time employed in sinking each of these posts—that is, if the lake is calm; but when much swell is on the water the work is carried on much slower, or the pile-driving is delayed after for some days.

To obtain a near view of the process, a boat was procured, and we were rowed within a few feet of the machine; and there, as we lay gently rocking to and fro, we could see the whole of the process, and enjoy the delightful scenery of the southern shore, the green-wooded island, the bold hills, with sunny slopes where the grain was beginning to acquire a golden hue, the graceful trees relieving the open clearing, with their refreshing verdure; even the new sheds and buildings on the little point seen among the embowering trees, had a pleasing effect—so truly does "distance lend enchantment to the view," and harmonize in nature all objects to one pleasing whole.

But the bang of the last hammer has ceased to vibrate on our ears, the little skiff is turned towards the shore, and, fearing that my unartist-like description will convey but a faint idea of this great work, I will leave it to abler pens than mine, and only close my article with wishing success to Canadian enterprize and American ingenuity, and may they ever work in brotherly unity, and be a mutual support to each other.

NOTE.—I was assured by the contractor, that the bridge, when completed, would be a greater achievement as a work of engineering skill than the bridge over Lake Champlain, on account of the superior depth of the water. The distance from shore to shore of the Rice Lake at this point is about three miles; the average depth as far as they had hitherto sunk the piles did not exceed fifteen feet; but the deepest part was supposed to be north of Tick Island.

～

1   Harriet Martineau (1802–76) was a Norwich-born writer of great repute at this time. A journalist, novelist, and social commentator, she was an ardent advocate of social reform and used her stories and sketches to popularize economic and reform-oriented subjects. Her *Illustrations of Political Economy* (1834) was among her most popular works.

2.   See page 201, note 1.

FLORAL SKETCHES
AND ESSAYS

FLORAL SKETCHES NO. 1.
THE VIOLET

In Letter XIV of *The Backwoods of Canada* Catharine Parr Traill wishes she had available the guidance of her eldest sister, Elizabeth Strickland, in her "rambles among the clearings" in search of floral treasures. She also regrets her own inability to "make faithful representations of the flowers of [her] adopted country" or to understand, as Eliza immediately would, "their botanical arrangement." Nevertheless, she proceeds in that letter to offer an impressive botanical inventory of her neighbourhood. Botany was to be a subject of inexhaustible value and interest to Traill, equal in importance to the heroic activity of the pioneer as a subject for literature. The major expression of her interest was *Studies of Plant Life in Canada; or, Gleanings from Forest, Lake and Plain* (1885), the result of many years of searching and gathering. In the early years of her life in Canada, however, Traill continued to write in the sphere of her sister's influence. Three essays that she contributed to the *Literary Garland* in 1843 show that influence: "Love of Flowers" (January, 41–42), "Floral Sketches No. 1. The Violet" (February, 87–90), and "No. 2. The Rose" (March, 129–31). Indeed, they rely heavily on Eliza's "Biography of Flowers"— a series of eleven essays that was published in *The Lady's Magazine* in England during the 1830s—for information on such subjects as the traditional association of women with botanical study, the cultivation of plants, medicinal uses, informative anecdotes, and poetic fragments. Catharine in her turn became a kind of advisor in North America. In September 1852 she wrote a letter to the editor of the *Genesee Farmer* (Rochester) advocating that the women of North America leave the greenhouse and search the woods for the indigenous flora so rapidly disappearing "before the destructive agency of the chopper's axe." She set an example both in her "Forest Gleanings" and in her botanical essays that were published in two Rochester, New York, publications, the *Horticulturalist* in 1853 and *Vick's Magazine* in the 1880s. "Floral Sketches No. 1. The Violet" reflects the rich traditional association of women and botanical study out of which Traill's commitment to the study of Canadian flora developed. It is here printed in abridged form—several paragraphs consisting mostly of literary quotations about violets have been omitted.

Here's flowers for you;
Hot lavender, mints, savory, marjoram;
The marigold, that goes to bed with the sun,
And with him rises weeping: these are flowers
Of middle summer.

Winter's Tale.

In former times, before Botany had become a regular and scientific study, every lady who held a distinguished place in the neighbourhood in which she resided, was a herbalist; and, though possibly, not so minutely acquainted with the botanical structure of flowers as her descendants, she was better skilled in the knowledge of their medicinal qualities, and culture. One of the apartments on the first suite of rooms was devoted to the purposes of a dispensary, and was fitted up with stills, alembics, a small furnace, presses, shelves, &c.; it was called the *still-room*, and even to this day one of the housekeeper's attendants in great houses, bears the quaint appellation of the Still-room Maid. The office of this damsel was to attend the housekeeper, or, more generally, her mistress, when occupied in the simple chemical process of distillation, to supply the furnace, mingle the ingredients of the medicines to be dispensed, assist in the important business of preparing conserves, jellies, decoctions, &c.

Very delicate were the perfumes prepared by these maidens, and excellent the simple waters, whether for the toilet or as stomachies, that were concocted in the still-room; most healing were the precious ointments, and soothing the fomentations supplied by the Ladies Bountiful of those days, for the relief of the suffering poor. What cool and refreshing wines, drawn from the fragrant balm, the honeyed cowslip, or the luscious elderberry, supplied the place of our modern fiery compounds; these even the very fairies might have sipped from their acorn cups, without fear of inebriety—so delicate, so pure, and perfumed was their quality.

While bending over the silken flowers which they traced with their needles, the young females of those days could discuss the various healing or aromatic virtues for which the original flower was famous; could tell you its time of blossoming, the soil it loved best, and of what country it was a native; illustrating their subject by quotations from Milton or Shakespeare, or the still earlier and quainter poets of former times. Perhaps, though knowledge has increased with such rapid strides in these our enlightened days, our modern belles, if more scientifically, were not more happily employed than those who roamed the woodland dale or heathy moorland, in search of the fairest and earliest blossoms, from which to extract the healing balm that was fondly intended to alleviate the suffering of their fellow creatures.

But while science unfolds to us her lifted page, the simpler branches of knowledge need not be disregarded. Merely to load our memories with the learned names of trees, and plants, and flowers, is after all but a barren and unsatisfactory acquisition; which, while it adds little in reality to our store of practical knowledge, is apt to make us pedantic. How many youthful pupils turn away from the study of botany with disgust, pronouncing it a dull, dry science, equally uninteresting as unprofitable; yet, what can unfold to the female mind sources of purer, more intellectual, yet simple enjoyment than the floral world?

Every flower artist, if she wishes to excel in her art, ought also to make herself acquainted with the growth, culture, and structure of the flowers she essays to portray: an intimate acquaintance with the natural history of her favourites, will add a far greater interest to the subject she selects for her pencil: from the delicate tinted rose to the modest violet, or humbler daisy, she will find something to repay her for her attention, and to call forth her admiration; something that will add fire, and life, and spirit to her labours.

The following sketches were written with the view of affording both information and amusement to the female reader, and, by uniting the lighter labours of the florist with the graver studies of the botanist, render both pursuits more interesting and agreeable:

VIOLA.

We begin with the violet, the sweet spring violet of England, as our favourite of all the vernal flowers. *Viola Odorata*, the sweet violet, is the most distinguished member of a numerous family of plants designated by the Latin word Viola;—the first part of its name may properly be considered as its family name, the last (*odorata*) as expressing its peculiar quality.

Viola Odorata is often called in English the March violet. Although you may occasionally, in warm seasons, gather its blossoms, in sheltered situations, through March, yet it is not till April, that month of wild flowers, that its blossoming time becomes general.

The whole plant, plucked from the ground, is from the root to the blossom, singularly elegant, and worthy of attention, more particularly as a study for the pencil. It is observed in the greatest perfection, when growing in a light, vegetable, or sandy soil, duly shaded, for it loves to hide its beauties in deep dells and forest glades. The root runs along the ground, extending itself by light fibres, from which it throws up a thick general stalk—from the heart of this stalk arise groups of leaves and flowers. The leaves are of perfect heart shape, scolloped round with great regularity, fringed with minute silver hair, and veined with a delicate net work, which may better be observed by holding up the reverse of the leaf to the light.

The blossom may be considered as approaching to that termed by botanists, papilionaceous, butterfly or winged form of flower, of which the pea bean, lupin, vetch, acacia, broom, trefoil, and mimosa, will serve as illustrations.

The outward appearance of the violet is familiar to every one, yet among its many admirers, possibly there are but few that have examined the structure of its blossom with the minute attention it deserves. Let me now recommend it to the young botanist, with the assurance that it will well repay his or her trouble.

The stalk, with its delicate floral leaves and calyx, is of a fine olive tint; it is united to the calyx with a graceful bend, and the latter is beautifully adapted to the irregularity of the blossom. The flower consists of a pair of upper petals, a pair of side ones, and one broad curved petal below. The upper pair are of the deepest tint and purple, the side pair and lower one, are somewhat paler, and veined with many exquisite pencillings of a redder shade, which may be observed by placing the flower in such a point of view that the rays of light may fall upon it.

The two side petals are finished with two velvety knobs, of a fine orange or deep yellow colour; in these knobs the odour of the violet is supposed to reside, though I am disposed to think the perfume is dispersed through the whole blossom, as is the case in the damask rose, and many other flowers, a single petal of which will convey the delicious fragrance of the flower. In some plants the odoriferous qualities exist in the leaves, in others the fork or rind, while in many it is confined to the flower alone.

The nectarium, or receptacle for the honey, terminates in a curled horn behind, which forms a peculiar feature of this elegant flower, though it is not confined to this tribe alone, being common to many others, larkspur, monkhood, fumitory, &c. According to the Linnæan classification, the violet belongs to the class Pentandria; five anthers meeting in the centre of the flower, forming a small orange coloured cone over one pistil, which marks the order to be that of Monogynia.

The only violets which belong to that called Odorata, are the deep purple spring, or March violet, the pure white, the reddish purple, and the double garden purple, all of which retain the exquisite odour of their sweet original.

The inodorous varieties of the violet are numerous and beautiful. Among these we enumerate the large blue wood violet; this delights in mossy woodlands, and under shady trees on light sandy banks, in close lanes and hollows; it grows low to the ground, on rather a short footstalk sometimes slightly clustered; the outer side of the flower is all but white, next to this comes the pale blue dog violet, the red-veined, and the white-veined with blue; these last are chiefly summer flowers.

Canada presents us with several sorts of scentless violets during the spring, and till late in the fall may be gathered different shades of pale, and bright blue, small white flowering violets, the lower petal marked with deep purple veinings, the leaves very small and growing close to the ground; the capsules of this latter sort, are spotted irregularly with purple, and instead of drooping, stand upright above the foliage; besides these there abound several varieties of yellow violets, some of a pale yellow, others of a deep brimstone, also pale green. The flowers of the yellow varieties for the most part spring from joints in the stalk, accompanied by buds and leafits—the capsules or seed vessels of these plants, are covered with a hoary soft down, that looks like some white bud rather than a seed pod—the brimstone is the tallest I have seen, growing from six to eight inches from the ground; in rich mould, it blossoms freely from May, or June, till September. The leaves of this violet are larger, of a bright green, and less decidedly the heart shape than any of the British violets.

The heart's-ease, with all its different shades of colour and form, belongs to the tribe Viola. The heart's-ease has one advantage over the violet, that its blossoms seldom quit us; even beneath the snows of winter it flourishes. I have seen a plant of the small deep blue heart's-ease bloom thus for eighteen months; during that period I never sought the plant without finding a blossom to reward me.

The culture of the heart's-ease is simple; it may be propagated by roots, or slips, or seed; but to have fine and perfect flowers, the soil should be very rich light mould, and the plants of different varieties, set far apart, or the colours will be mixed, the blue and yellow forming streaky shades, very derogatory to the beauty of the original.

. . . .

We shall close this by a little poem lately published, seeming written after the manner of the older poets:

TO EARLY VIOLETS.

Children of sweetest birth,
Why do ye bend to earth,
Eyes in whose softened blue
Lies evening's pearly dew?
Has not the early ray
Yet kissed those tears away,
That fell with closing day?

Say, do ye fear to meet
The hail and driving sheet,
That gloomy winter stern
Flings from his snow-wreathed urn?
Or do ye fear the breeze,
So sadly sighing 'midst the trees,
Will chill your fragrant flowers,
Ere April's silvery showers
Have visited your bowers?

Why come ye, till the cuckoo's voice
Bids hill and vale rejoice?
Till Philomel, with tender tone,
Wakening the echoes lone,
Bids woodland glades prolong
Her sweetly tuneful song?
Till skylark blithe and linnet grey,
From fallow brown and meadow gay,
Pour forth their jocund roundelay?
'Till cowslips wan and daisies pride
'Broider the hillock's side,
And opening hawthorn buds are seen
Decking each hedgerow screen?

What though the primrose, drest
In her pure paly vest,
Came rashly forth
To brave the biting north;
Did'st thou not see her fall
Straight 'neath his snowy pall?
And heard ye not the west wind sigh
Her requiem as he hurried by?
Go, hide ye, then, till groves are green,
And April's clouded bow is seen,
And suns are bright and skies are clear,
And every thing that does appear,
Proclaims the birth-day of the year.

Westover [sic], Douro, C.W.

THE FOREST MONARCH AND HIS DEPENDANTS.

A FABLE

Traill began her association with Robert Lay's *The Maple Leaf*, a juvenile monthly magazine, with its first issue in July 1852; it was to be an important though brief association. It allowed Traill to further her desire to be an important writer for children, an ambition partially realized with the publication of her novel, *Canadian Crusoes*, in England earlier that same year. She was a major contributor to *The Maple Leaf* throughout its short history, which ended with the December 1854 issue. "The Forest Monarch and His Dependants" was her second contribution, appearing in November 1852, 152–53. Late in that year she wrote to its editor, Robert Lay, proposing to write "an article every month, illustrative of the Natural History and Botony [sic] of Canada, expressly adapted to the capacity of the younger branches of the families who take the 'Maple Leaf.'" Lay included the letter in his editorial for January and in that same issue published the first of twelve installments of "The Governor's Daughter: or, Rambles in the Canadian Forests." It was later published as a book in England under the title *Lady Mary and Her Nurse* (1856). The characteristics of fable recognized in "The Forest Monarch and His Dependants" are continued in "The History of the Squirrel Family," a narrative sequence that forms a significant portion of "The Governor's Daughter." Moral lessons are interwoven with observations concerning natural history. Hence in "The Forest Monarch" the importance of gratitude is mingled with Traill's informed sense of the interdependence of everything in an ecological system. It is not an exaggeration to say that she was ahead of her time in articulating such a theme.

On a green extensive plain, grew a lofty oak, of noble stature; its wide-spreading arms affording a refreshing shade from the scorching sunbeams. Thither the cattle came every day, to repose upon the velvet turf, and rest beneath its graceful shelter. The breeze played among its shining leaves; the birds sang joyfully amid the boughs; there they built their nests, and securely hatched their young brood. Myriads of insects dwelt there; the leaves, the bark, the wood affording them food and shelter. At its roots sprung the greenest grass, among which grew deep blue violets, that scented the air with their odor, and gladdened the eye with their half-concealed beauty—and the violets grew and spread on every side, protected by the Forest King.

Spring came and went, and still the birds sang on, and built new nests, and hatched new broods; and the oak rejoiced in their prosperity, and asked them not why they came, or whither they went. The squirrel gambolled freely among the topmost branches, and gathered there his store of winter food; the gay-winged insects fluttered their little day of pleasure among the glossy leaves; the violets blossomed sweetly at its roots; and the cattle found shelter and comfort in the cool shade. None had cause to complain of their patron; he extended his blessings alike to all his dependants. Ignorance begets envy. A stranger came and rested himself on the green sward beneath the Oak, and he looked upward, and admired its grandeur and its beauty, its mossy trunk, and its wide-spreading arms, its glossy foliage, and shining fruit; but he gave no heed to the birds, or the insects, or the blue violets, and went on his way. Then there was a murmur of discontent. The birds were indignant that their songs had been unheeded; the insects, that their bright wings had not been noticed; and, most of all, did the violets complain, that their beauty and perfume had been disregarded. Envy and hatred filled their jealous hearts, and they lifted up their voices with one accord, to reproach the mighty monarch of the wood, and clamorously desired that the woodsman would come with his axe, and level the oak with the ground. Then the oak was moved with anger at the injustice and malice of his ungrateful dependants, and said, "Have I not sheltered you and your children from the summer's scorching heat—from the gales of autumn, and the bitter frosts of winter? The thunderbolt that would have smitten you, has fallen upon my head—my arms were spread over you—my leaves nourished and sheltered you—from my own vitals have I fed you—O! ungrateful children!" and the sighing breeze that swept sadly through the branches seemed to lament the rebellion among the dependants of the mighty Forest King. But the birds, and the insects, and the violets still sighed for the destruction of the oak, that they might rise into public notice. That day, the stranger returned, and with him, many woodsmen, with axes and hatchets. "Let us cut down this glorious old tree," they said, "that he may help to build a mighty ship to navigate the seas." And the axe was laid to the root of the tree. The turf, torn and bruised, no longer hid the violets from the iron heels of the choppers, who trode them beneath their feet, and crushed their slender stems. The oak fell, and, in its fall, buried the envious flowers, never again to rise. The birds no longer sang among its branches—the cradles of their unfledged younglings were broken, and scattered to the winds of heaven—the squirrels saw their magazine of food destroyed, and, with the mighty monarch, perished the happiness and prosperity of his dependants.

A GLANCE WITHIN THE FOREST

This piece, which was published in the *Canadian Monthly and National Review* 6 (1874), 48–53, ends with a repetition of the lament, sounded by Traill in "Rice Lake Plains—The Wolf Tower" and in other essays, that the rich diversity of the forest flora must disappear with "the removal of the sheltering woods." In this case the lament is preceded by Traill's guidance of the reader/traveller through the dense "old-growth" Canadian forest. Her principal purpose is to direct attention not to the mature trees, but to the processes of decay and the emergence of new plant life along the forest floor. While many of Traill's earlier works present her as a collector of flowers, this essay is distinguished by her fascination with the mosses, lichens, fungi, and moulds. From the early 1850s through the rest of her life whenever she went to the woods she searched for such unspectacular growth. It was her hobby to collect and press grasses, mosses, and lichens, identify them, and mount them for submission to agricultural exhibitions, or to create albums for sale or as gifts for acquaintances or friends. As this essay indicates, Traill found spiritual nourishment in manifestations of the economy of the forest world "under the Great Director." The importance to her of such subjects is extensively affirmed in *Pearls and Pebbles; or, Notes of an Old Naturalist* (1894). The last nine chapters of that book (about a third of the whole), including such titles as "Some Varieties of Pollen" and "Indian Grass," constitute the basis for the faith to which she gives poignant expression in its concluding section, "Something Gathers Up the Fragments."

"If thou art worn and hard beset
With sorrows thou wouldst fain forget;
If thou would'st read a lesson that will keep
Thy heart from fainting and thy soul from sleep,
Go to the woods—no pale-faced fears
Dim the sweet face that nature wears."

Longfellow

On entering a thickly-clad tract of woodland, the first impression made on the traveller is not so much surprise at the height and bulk of the trees as at the dense and crowded mass of vegetation that everywhere meets the eye, mingled with the confused trunks of fallen trees, broken branches, and every sort of decaying *débris*.

He looks upward and around for the ancient monarchs of the wood, with hoary rifted trunks, wide-spread arms bleached by centuries of wintry snows, and scathed by the tempests that have passed over their heads—such trees as were familiar to him among the ancient oaks and beeches of England, and which he had imaged to himself as existing on a grander scale in the primeval forests of the new world. These he does not see in the Canadian woods. The impression is conveyed that rapid growth tends to rapid development and swift decay.

The younger growth screens the few that have withstood the effects of time; the oldest lie prostrate at his feet, hidden by rank herbage, or covered by a thick coating of variegated mosses. It seems indeed marvellous how mother earth can support so vast an amount of vegetation, since all her numerous vegetable family alike demand nourishment and a suitable space within her bosom. Ample as we know her resources to be, at first glance they would seem unequal to the demand, so great is the drain upon them; yet in nothing is the wise economy of the Great Creator more manifestly shown than in the consumption and renewal of the soil, and the supplies for the support of plant-life. But let us continue our survey of the forest, simply as such. Here we behold trees in every stage of progress, from the tiny seedling of a few leaves, just pushing forth its tender head from the sheltering bed of moss or decaying foliage, to the aspiring sapling which seems in haste to rival its loftier companions in the race of life; while others, further advanced to maturity, have gained the higher regions, and, lifting their leafy heads above their fellows, are revelling in light and air. Straight upward and onward has been their growth. The few sparsely-scattered lateral branches that had been developed during their early career have fallen away, and even the scars where they had been are scarcely discernible on the smooth trunk of the oldest trees. It is not till they gain space and a full exposure to the effects of the sunlight and atmospheric influences, that they make a full and leafy head. It is this which gives the forest trees that straight, pillar-like trunk which is their grand characteristic. The young trees are drawn up like seedlings in a hotbed. These saplings remind one of the overtasked children in a factory, toiling on in heat and steam and dust, the vigour of their frames, like the young operatives, destroyed and weakened through lack of free circulation of air and sunshine.

Beneath the living lie the prostrate dead in every stage of decay—a mass of vegetable matter returning to its original elements, and slowly giving back to the soil what it had gathered during the long period of its existence, in the form of fertilizing gases and organic matter, again to act their parts in nourishing a new and rising generation. In this great chemical laboratory the work of decomposition is ever going forward,—unseen, silent influences are ever at work; no idlers are here.

Let us for a few minutes pause to consider some of the labourers that God has appointed to reduce those mighty fallen trunks that encumber the ground. There lies one—it has been a giant in its day; but look upon it now. Its round, pillar-like form is all that is left to tell us of its former fair proportions, and this is merely a crumbling shell. Touch that deep velvet clothing of verdure that covers the surface, and the foot or the hand sinks into the decaying mass—the fabric falls into ruin beneath the pressure. What has destroyed that hard vegetable tissue that, when in health and vigor, required the sharp axe and nervous arm of the chopper, or the rending teeth of the saw to separate its parts. Those soft plumy masses and grey coating lichens, and, more powerful than either, those large hoof-like fungi of the genus *Polyporus*, have been the unresisting forces—the wedges that have divided the woody fibre; those myriads of tiny insects that have found a home and nursery below the forest of mosses—the axes and saws that, in conjunction with the rain and snows of heaven, have effected the work of destruction.

Take now a little of the soil that lies below the roots of the mosses in your hand, and you will find rich black mould, fit for your most delicate green-house plants to grow in. Years pass on; return again and seek for the tree-trunk and its destroyers. Where are they? A few spadefuls of fine fertilizing mould, over which rank herbage now grows, is all that marks the spot. The woody fibre is changed, the mosses having done their part, and no longer find occupation. The insect tribes, no longer sheltered, also are gone. The Master's work has been accomplished; and it is marvellous in our eyes—that is, if we will reflect upon the work, the labourers employed, and the consequences, as we ought to do. These obedient labourers of the forest-world, under the Great Director, have been preparing a field and soil for man's use countless ages before the ships of Cabot or Columbus had furrowed the waters that girdle the forest-clad shores of the western hemisphere. Should we not "Praise the Lord for his goodness, and for the wonders which he doeth for the children of men."

Beside the mosses and fungi that take possession of the fallen trees, as soon as a little soil has been prepared for their reception, a variety of seedlings spring up—a tiny forest nursery, ready to supply the waste of their predecessors.

Here you may see a seedling pine not exceeding two inches in stature, a miniature resemblance of yonder lofty tree, the top of which reaches nearly fifty feet above the heads of the tallest oak, maple, or elm; and there are some of these last that will give a straight trunk, free of the branches, of fifty feet from the root upwards.

That tiny seedling, with its few delicate thready leaves and soft green stem, and that majestic, pillar-like trunk, with deeply rifted bark, and twisted, cable-like roots, whose top is hidden by the lower growth of hardwood trees—are they not both vegetable wonders, proclaiming the glory and power of their Creator, who formed the things that be out of nothing? Do they not equally bear witness to His care for man, to whom He has given power alike over the parent tree and the little seedling—to save or to destroy, as may seem best to him—to plant or to root up, as he may choose?

On a first journey through the forest, the traveller is impressed by the deep unbroken silence that reigns around him, and also of the absence of animal life, if we except the insect world, but even these (with the exception of the mosquitos and other winged tribes) are seen only in the Spring and Summer months; the rest, working in secret, or among the leafy tree-tops, are not perceived. During the winter this stillness is most remarkable; it is a silence that may be felt—if I may so express the profound stillness— where the sound of your own steps or the monotonous creaking of some tree, loosened at the root, swaying to and fro, alone breaks the almost unearthly repose of the scene.

The deer lie mostly concealed in the tangled covert of the most lonely parts of the forest, in thick cedar swamps along the margins of lake and stream; and, as civilization increases, these wild denizens of the woods and wilds retreat further from man and his improvements.

Towards the early spring, a solitary chipmunk may be seen on warm sunny days sporting on the mossy logs, or you may hear the saucy, chattering note of the red squirrel, as he hurries up the rugged bark of a forked pine to his nest. Or, during a long day's journey, you may sometimes, even in mid-winter, be cheered by the whispering note of the little chickadee (the small blue titmouse) greeting you from among the hemlock boughs, or the rapping of the little midland (downy woodpecker) may be heard at long intervals awakening the echoes of the vast unpeopled solitude, but even these sounds are of rare occurrence.

There is a solemn grandeur in those old pine woods that insensibly inclines the mind to musings inspiring the soul with high and holy thoughts of Him whose wisdom and mighty power originated and sustains those noble vegetable pillars that support the leafy roof of the forest aisles above your head, where the wind, sweeping among a thousand aerial harp-strings, makes music that seems more of heaven than earth.

The soul needs such moments of tranquillity to recover from the toil, the wear and tear of busy life, with all its daily vexations and disappointments. It is repose to the careworn spirit to withdraw itself from man and live a brief space among the trees, the flowers, the ferns, and lowly mosses, and to consider the lilies of the field, how they grow, cared for by Him who clothes the grass of the field, and weaves His rays of gorgeous light into their glorious tissues, giving them a stamp of grace and loveliness whereby to gladden and refresh the overburdened hearts of the children of men.

In the contemplation of these things all worldly care and strife is forgotten, and peace, and joy, and love, with holy reverence, steal into the heart, and there light up upon its altar a pure flame of spiritual adoration and thanksgiving to God, and of peace and good-will to his fellow-creatures, and to all that the Creator has called into being.

Surely it is well if in the lonely churchless wilderness the poor settler, oppressed with many cares, can look around him through the leafy aisles of those huge forest trees that wall in his path, and can find in them something to interest and enlighten his mind. Such teachings have ere now been drawn from this source, proving a consolation and pleasure to the lonely sojourner in the woods, and who shall say that they have been without profit to his soul?

Beside the living trees, bushes, and rank herbage that meets the eye in the thick uncleared forest, there is a mass of fallen timber, broken limbs, and decaying branches heaped across each other in wild confusion, through which young saplings are thrusting up their plumy heads, while many a graceful wood-fern and flower is flourishing, all green and bright, beneath surrounding decay.

The confusion is still more remarkable if it be the precincts of a cedar swamp—here indeed it would puzzle the most adventurous hunter to explore the tangled desolation. Trunks of great size lean one above the other, the intervening trees forming a wall of support so strong that the falling are upheld; we thus see the living and dead mingle together in an impenetrable mass; if a spark should by chance fall within that thicket, how great a matter would it kindle, and this accident often happens. What volumes of smoke during the daylight! what magnificent jets of flame shoot up at night, casting a red glare upon the murky veil of smoke-cloud above! Now behold the fire quickened by the rising wind which accompanies fire, springing from heap to heap of the fallen brushwood, darting up the shreddy bark to the very tops of the tallest trees, sending abroad fiery showers of sparks, which, seizing on the dry twigs and long waving moss of other trees, continue to spread the work of destruction. Sometimes such conflagrations have been known to rage for many weeks together during the prevalence of a long, dry, hot season.

Such was the dry summer of 1826, in which an extensive district in New Brunswick was made desolate. Whole villages were reduced to ashes, rivers and streams were dried up, and thousands of settlers in Miramichi were rendered homeless and childless. During that awful conflagration a cry of despair went up from the miserable inhabitants that the day of fiery wrath had begun, and that the vials of God's anger were being poured out upon the earth—beginning with the people of New Brunswick.

A modern writer—Burton on Emigration[1]—gives the following fearful picture of this terrible catastrophe: "The clearing unfortunately formed only a strip about half a mile wide along the banks of the Miramichi, and the great amphitheatre of flame spreading over the surface of several thousand square miles, filled it with a fiery air which ignited the wooden houses of the settlers.

"Anything more frightful than the devastation caused by this fire has never been known save in the earthquakes of Portugal and Southern America. The towns or villages, of which Newcastle was one, (containing 1,000 inhabitants,) were almost entirely reduced to ashes. The burned bodies lay putrifying in the ruined streets, mingled with those of the wild beasts which had been driven among the haunts of men by the progress of the devouring flames. So intense was the heat of the air, that those miserable wretches who sought for safety and refuge in open boats and rafts on the river and its tributary streams, died from suffocation. In many places the streams were dried up, or the sparks communicated by the high wind brought the very danger to them from which they were fleeing. Famine, too, followed in the wake of the fire. The harvest was destroyed, the cattle perished, and the land became for a time a howling wilderness, on which had settled the blackness of desolation."

Nor is man benefitted by these impromptu fires running through the forest. The land becomes very much more difficult to clear. The charred pines and hemlocks especially, become almost indestructible, and encumber the ground for a long succession of years.

It is indeed a grand and exciting thing to watch the progress of a forest on fire, but when it ceases to burn we look with regret upon the scene; instead of the bright, refreshing verdure that once delighted the eye, there remain blackened trunks, withered foliage, reddened and blasted by the fire, and a blot for years to come upon the face of the land, till nature once more renovates the scorched ground with a new race of herbs, and shrubs, and forest trees, which in course of years shut out the charred trunks that strew the earth; but more than a quarter of a century must pass before the scene of ruin assumes its former cheerful aspect. The tall burnt spars often remain for a much longer period, while the stumps of the larger pines will continue uninjured by time for nearly a century. It is long before the usual process

FLORAL SKETCHES AND ESSAYS

of decomposition by means of the mosses and fungi can have any effect upon them; even the moisture of the atmosphere is scarcely felt, the charred surface resists the water, and offers no nourishment for the roots of the succulent parasites. Instead of mosses, grey lichens in the course of time effect a lodgment within the crevices of the slowly crumbling charcoal, but the process of decay goes on for years almost imperceptibly.

Among the new race of vegetables that spring upon the burned soil, the first and most luxuriant in growth is the fireweed (*Erechthites hieracifolia*) a tall rank weed with the aspect of the common sowthistle. This plant seems to delight in the newly burned soil; like many other Canadian weeds, it comes, we know not from whence; and disappears, we know not wherefore. It must, as we suppose, be borne upon the wings of the wind to seize upon its inheritance; it comes up, flourishes luxuriantly—a thick crop as if sown by some careful hand; it blossoms, perfects its silken winged fruit, is cut down by the earliest autumnal frosts, goes hence, and is seen no more. No second crop appears the ensuing year. We can only form the conjecture that the soil has been exhausted of the principle that fed the parent plant, and no suitable nourishment is left for the young crop that should now succeed to it. It is a mystery, nevertheless, that the soil prepared by accidental cause, should receive so bountifully seed hitherto foreign to it—that the winds (if the winds be the agent employed) should waft the seed, and drop it upon this particular soil. What has become of the newly perfected seed—has it gone forth to reappear in some distant locality under circumstances more suitable to its growth?

But, while we note the disorderly appearance of the forest, the unsightly decay of its fallen timbers, and the desolation exhibited after the fire has scathed it, we must not omit to take a glance at it in its wintry aspect.

Snow, like Christian charity, covers a multitude of defects. Go forth into the dense forest after a heavy snow storm, and behold how marvellously beautiful has every object there become, touched as by the wand of an enchanter; the trees are gleaming as with diamonds and pearls. A glistening mantle, unrivalled by any other object in Nature, is upon everything that meets our sight. The eye is no longer offended with the aspect of ruin and decay. All now is fresh, pure, and unsullied. No earthly stain has yet dimmed its lustre; like the robe of its Creator when He was beheld by the chosen disciples upon the Mount, it is white and glistening as no fuller on earth could white it.

Of these unseemly heaps of dry withering branches, every twig is now laden with spotless snow. Those slender, attenuated saplings that looked so weak, and drawn upward, are now bent down and converted into bowers of beauty bending in graceful arches over the paths, and, if the keen breath of frost have touched them, changing them to crystal till they glitter like gems of price: even the stumps, those unsightly objects, are now capped with turbans in whiteness surpassing the far-famed muslins of Dacca.

The young evergreens, the spruces, hemlocks, and cedars, have caught, and sustain the snowflakes on their fan-like branches, till they look as if they were laden with flowers of shining whiteness; even the rugged trunks of the forest trees have been whitened by the new-fallen snow, and for a brief space look like columns of purest marble.

Where the swamp is the thickest, and the confusion of fallen trees the greatest, there the effect is the more striking, from the fantastic forms produced by the lodgment of the masses of snow among the branches. When the full moon is shining down among these snowy glades, the coldest and most apathetic of men must acknowledge that there are beauties in a Canadian forest scene, even if he have failed to perceive it during the leafy months of spring and summer.

Of such a scene, may we not say with the homely poet Bloomfield, "A glorious sight—if glory dwells below, where Heaven's magnificence makes all the show."[2] Although the snow lingers longer within the forest than on the open clearings to which sunbeams have more ready access, yet vegetation is more rapid within the boundaries of the former. No cold biting winds or searching frost penetrates the woods to nip and chill the early buds as on the more open exposures; within all is quiet and warmth, when without the air is cold and blustering.

It is among the low bushes and sapling trees that we find the first green tints of early spring. It is in the forest that the hungry cattle hasten to browse on the tender shoots and swelling buds of the sugar maple and basswood, or search out the oily succulent blades of the wild garlic.

Go to the woods as soon as the snow has melted, and you will see the seedlings of many plants springing up from beneath the thick carpeting of dead leaves that strew the earth. There is the wood ruffe (*Galium stellata*) and the creeping veronica, matting the ground bright and verdant; the winter greens, (*Pyrola eliptica* and *Pyrola rotundifolia*) fresh and green as when the feathery snow first hid them from our view. The graceful fronds of the wood-fern, (*Aspidium spinulosum*) though lying prostrate upon the soil, are fresh and bright, no withering frost having blighted them. The shining parsley-like leaves of the Sweet Cicely (*Osmorhiza ciliata*) are there too, looking so fresh and tempting that you wish it were, what it greatly resembles, English parsley.

While the garden shrubs and border flowers are hardly visible in the warm shelter of the moist woods, we find already bursting forth the leaf-buds of the Bush Honey-suckle (*Zyloxteum ciliata*). The swamp gooseberry and currants of many species are putting forth their leaves, while the brown, downy buds of the Leather-wood or Moose-wood (*Dirca palustre*) are ready to open, and shew the pale yellow, funnel-shaped blossoms that they had so carefully sheltered on the grey leafless branches, and here are trailing garlands of nature's own weaving. The elegant *Linnæ Borealis*, the sweet flower so dear to the great father of botany whose names it bears; and there, covering that little mound of forest mould, is the dark-leaved, graceful *Mitchella repens*, the twin-berry of the Squaw—a lovely, fragrant flower it is, loving deep shade, and shrinking from the withering glance of the hot sunbeams. There are evergreen wood-ferns of rare grace of leafage and of verdure, and club mosses like miniature forest trees, all evergreens. A kindly nursing mother is the forest to these her lowly offspring; the earth their cradle, the snow their coverlet—warm, soft and light.

To those who love the forest and its productions, the continual destruction of the native trees will ever be a source of regret, even while acknowledging its necessity, for with the removal of the sheltering woods must also disappear most of the rare plants, indigenous to the soil, that derive their nurture from them, some indeed so entirely dependent on the decaying vegetation of the trees beneath which they grow that they perish directly they are deprived of it. Exposed to the effects of drying winds and hot sunshine they wither away and are seen no more. Soon may we say, in the words of the old Scotch song—

"The flowers of the forest are a' wede away."

⌒

1   Traill refers to John Hill Burton (1809–81) and his work *The Emigrant's Manual: Australia, New Zealand, America, and South Africa* (Edinburgh: William and Robert Chambers, 1851). She misquotes a passage from pages 41–42.

2   Robert Bloomfield (1766–1823) was a Suffolk poet whose work *The Farmer's Boy* (1800) and several other volumes on rural subjects was well known to the Strickland sisters.

The Canadian Short Story Library, Series 2

The revitalized Canadian Short Story Library undertakes to publish fiction of importance to a fuller appreciation of Canadian literary history and the developing Canadian tradition. Work by major writers that has fallen into obscurity will be restored to canonical significance, and short stories by writers of lapsed renown will be gathered in collections or appropriate anthologies.

John Moss
General Editor

The Canadian Short Story Library

SERIES 1

Selected Stories of Duncan Campbell Scott
Edited by Glenn Clever

Selected Stories of Raymond Knister
Edited by Michael Gnarowski

Selected Stories of E.W. Thomson
Edited by Lorraine McMullen

Waken, Lords and Ladies Gay: Selected Stories of
Desmond Pacey
Edited by Frank M. Tierney

Selected Stories of Isabella Valancy Crawford
Edited by Penny Petrone

Many Mansions: Selected Stories of Douglas O. Spettigue
Edited by Leo Simpson

The Lady and the Travelling Salesman:
Stories by Leo Simpson
Edited by Henry Imbleau

Selected Stories of Robert Barr
Edited by John Parr

Selected Stories of Ernest Thompson Seton
Edited by Patricia Morley

Selected Stories of Mazo de la Roche
Edited by Douglas Daymond

Short Stories by Thomas Murtha
Edited by William Murtha

The Race and Other Stories by Sinclair Ross
Edited by Lorraine McMullen

Selected Stories of Norman Duncan
Edited by John Coldwell Adams

SERIES 2

New Women: Short Stories by Canadian Women,
1900–1920
Edited by Sandra Campbell and Lorraine McMullen

Voyages: Short Narratives of Susanna Moodie
Edited by John Thurston

Aspiring Women: Short Stories by Canadian Women,
1880–1900
Edited by Lorraine McMullen and Sandra Campbell

Pioneering Women: Short Stories by Canadian Women,
Beginnings to 1880
Edited by Lorraine McMullen and Sandra Campbell

Forest and Other Gleanings: The Fugitive Writings of
Catharine Parr Traill
Edited by Michael A. Peterman and Carl Ballstadt